The Renegade Merchant

A Gareth and Gwen Medieval Mystery

THE
RENEGADE
MERCHANT

by

SARAH WOODBURY

To my mom

Cast of Characters

Owain Gwynedd – King of Gwynedd (North Wales)
Cadwaladr – Owain's younger brother, former Lord of Ceredigion

Hywel – Prince of Gwynedd (illegitimate)
Cynan – Prince of Gwynedd (illegitimate)
Madoc – Prince of Gwynedd (illegitimate)
Cadifor—Hywel's foster father
Madog—King of Powys
Susanna—Queen of Powys, sister to Owain Gwynedd
Llywelyn—Prince of Powys

Gwen – Gareth's wife, a spy for Hywel
Gareth – Gwen's husband, Captain of Hywel's guard
Tangwen – daughter of Gareth and Gwen
Meilyr – Gwen's father
Gwalchmai – Gwen's brother

Evan – Gareth's friend
Gruffydd – Rhun's captain
John Fletcher—Deputy Sheriff of Shrewsbury
Abbot Radulfus—of the Abbey of St. Peter & St. Paul

1

March 1147

Gareth

"**G**areth knelt by the dark liquid, careful not to come close enough to stain his breeches. The morning sun shone brightly down and glimmered off the film that had formed on the surface of the little pool.

This particular road was narrower than most Gareth had seen so far in Shrewsbury, more of an alley than an actual street, though it was still wide enough for a single cart to pass. The ground was so smoothed by the passage of years and many feet that the hard-packed earth had been worn nearly to the bedrock. Thus the liquid was taking its time to sink into the soil.

He hesitated briefly before dabbing the tip of one finger into the liquid. It was lukewarm to the touch, a second indication that it hadn't been there very long. Holding his finger to his nose, he sniffed it before touching his tongue. The taste made Gareth's heart sink. A half-hour ago, when John Fletcher, the newly appointed Deputy Sheriff of Shrewsbury, had requested that he come to the alley, Gareth had assented. But even as he'd agreed, inside he'd been thinking *please God, don't let this be a murder.*

"Blood," Gareth said. "It's still warm, too."

"How long could it have been here?" Beside Gareth, John bent forward with his hands on his knees.

Gareth lifted one shoulder, not really sure how to calculate such a thing, but he gave it his best guess anyway. "An hour or two before dawn."

"You can see why I requested your assistance, Sir Gareth." John spoke more formally than he might have four months ago when he was only an inexperienced undersheriff. Given the sheriff's absence, John was temporarily *the* law in Shrewsbury, so Gareth didn't begrudge him his pomposity. "I was hoping you could help me discover whose blood this is."

"Perhaps it isn't human blood at all."

Gareth looked up at the man who'd spoken. His name was Luke, and he was one of John's underlings, a watchman nearing fifty, with a graying beard that hid most of his face.

"You are perfectly correct to wonder that," Gareth said, "and I would like nothing more than for you to be right. While it is my experience that human blood tastes different from pig blood, one can never be sure without a body. Still, I would say this is human."

"But you could be wrong." Luke spoke with a snide tone that Gareth couldn't help thinking was due to Gareth's Welshness.

Calling upon his very limited well of patience for such behavior, Gareth decided to look upon Luke with amusement rather than irritation. "Indeed. Though, sadly, I think we can all agree that it would be surprising to learn that a pig had been butchered in this alley."

John wasn't nearly as forgiving of Luke as Gareth. "He isn't wrong, and you know it. Get back to your post, Luke." John pointed with his chin to a few curious onlookers who'd gathered near the eastern entrance to the alley. "We don't want any of them to disturb the scene."

"Yes, sir." But as Luke turned away, Gareth saw the sneer cross Luke's face again, directed this time at John.

When John had given Luke the order, Gareth had grimaced inwardly. As John was a good twenty years younger than Luke, the older man had to be wondering why he hadn't been appointed Deputy Sheriff instead of John. Having eaten a late meal with John last evening, Gareth could have told him why: while younger than Gareth by half a decade, John Fletcher came from a good family. He was the stepson of the castellan of Bridgnorth Castle, located on the Severn River some ten miles as the crow flies to the southeast of Shrewsbury.

John wasn't a Norman, not with a last name like Fletcher and a Welsh mother, but he was born to be more than a guard, which was all Luke would ever be. In addition, John was passionate about wanting the job—and not solely for use as a stepping stone to better things. To Gareth's mind, the sheriff could have done far worse than pick John as his second.

"Luke may have a point, you know—not about the pig but about whether or not someone is dead," John said, once Luke was out of earshot. "I admit it's a terrible amount of blood, but the person whose blood this is could be merely injured."

"I would be overjoyed if that were true." Gareth rose to his feet and contemplated the pool, tired to the point of despair at the way death had become his life no matter where he went. "But to have bled so much might mean he's dead by now anyway." He glanced at John. "I didn't come to Shrewsbury to deal in death."

John ducked his head in acknowledgement of that truth. "I know why you came here, my lord. But with the sheriff called to war, along with most of the garrison, I'm alone with these remaining men. I need you."

The blatant appeal softened Gareth's heart, as it was meant to. "I will help in any way I can as long as I am here, but—"

John cut him off, speaking more fervently than ever. "Anything you can do would be helpful." He bobbed his head again at Gareth in an after-the-fact apology, his sincere brown eyes shining brightly from underneath his mop of unwashed brown hair.

Gareth narrowed his eyes at the younger man. "John." His voice held warning, because John's behavior indicated that his request was the result of more than simple need or because John felt momentarily out of his depth.

John flushed, giving himself away as he always seemed to—not only in Gareth's presence but in everyone's. John would need to learn to control his expressions if he was going to ultimately earn the respect of men like Luke. "The sheriff ordered me not to pursue any investigation while he was gone beyond what was absolutely necessary. I need to be able to show him that everything I do in his absence was well-thought out and purposeful."

"What would make the sheriff say such a thing?"

John made a rueful face. "He didn't explain specifically, but I know what he was thinking: he fears that in his absence I will act impulsively and accuse a worthy of the town of wrongdoing or do something else in my ignorance that will embarrass the office of the sheriff. He doesn't want to have to clean up after me when he comes home."

"Surely you're being overly hard on yourself." Gareth laughed under his breath. "I've found that trying to impress one's superiors is the surest way to disappoint them."

Like all men in his position, the sheriff served at the pleasure of the king, so when the king called his army to him, the sheriff went, along with most of the men in the castle garrison. Gareth understood completely, for his life was similarly ruled by the demands of his lord.

Understandably also, the sheriff had taken his best and most able-bodied men with him, which left him with the dilemma as to who to leave in charge of Shrewsbury's garrison and the watch. All of the watchmen Gareth had encountered so far were either not yet twenty or well past forty. It could be true that the sheriff hadn't brought John Fletcher on the march because he was young and inexperienced—in war as in everything else. By the same token, he hadn't made an older man deputy sheriff either.

"Still, I can see that if you do a good job here, if you discover what this pool of blood is all about, the sheriff will be favorably disposed towards you." Gareth hoped he was right, and he felt it was important to be encouraging, especially when men like Luke appeared to be constantly trying to undermine John's authority. He looked John in the eye. "Your sheriff wouldn't have left Shrewsbury in your hands if he didn't think you could do the job."

"You comfort me, but I fear you're wrong. He left me in charge because he was making the best of a bad situation." John's eyes skated away, and he spoke in an undertone, making sure his voice didn't carry to the other men a few yards away who were waiting for his instruction. "More than anything, I need the incident with Cole Turner to be forgotten."

Cole Turner had been a brigand whom Prince Cadwaladr had recruited for the purpose of deceiving the Earl of Chester into helping him overthrow King Owain for the throne of Gwynedd. After the failure of the plot and the death of Prince Rhun in the process, Cadwaladr had fled Wales for England and, as far as Prince Hywel had been able to discover, hadn't been seen or heard from since. It was too much to hope for that Cadwaladr was dead, so that meant he was out in the world somewhere. Prince Hywel was fierce in his determination to find out where that was.

Thus, upon arriving in Shrewsbury yesterday afternoon, Gareth had put in an appearance at the castle. He'd assumed he would be meeting with Shrewsbury's sheriff. Instead, it had been John who'd greeted him with the news that the sheriff and most of the garrison had been called away in service of King Stephen. And, unfortunately, John had no news of Cadwaladr to give him.

Discovering Cadwaladr's whereabouts couldn't bring Rhun back, but it might do something to ease the grief that had consumed Gwynedd in the months following the prince's death. King Owain's lamentations were ongoing, such that Hywel had effectively taken over the running of the kingdom. Here it was, nearly three months past the Christmas feast, and the king had hardly stirred from his bed at Aber, unwilling to face life without his eldest son.

Gareth's absence from Gwynedd had required him to leave the planning for the assault on Mold Castle in others' hands. It was a small price to pay for the opportunity to spend several weeks in the company of his wife and daughter, and Gareth had been thankful to leave Aber.

Thus, as Gareth stared down at the pool of blood at his feet, it came to him that if he was to quickly discover what this whole matter was about, the next and most important step in the investigation had to be to send for Gwen.

2

Gwen

"Why are we worrying about a murder when we don't even know that someone is dead? Fletcher clearly doesn't know what he's doing, and this Welshman—" Luke, one of the men at the east entrance to the alley, made a dismissive gesture with one hand to indicate Gareth, "—how could he possibly help?"

"I hear he serves Prince Hywel of Gwynedd." This was put forth by a second, gray-haired man named Alfred. They, and men like them, guarded each gate to the city and worked alongside the castle's garrison to patrol the streets and discourage crime in the town.

Except for a quick glance in Luke's direction, Gwen kept her attention determinedly on the ground, forcing her shoulders to relax and resigning herself to the inevitable curious looks and whispered conferences that were going on around her.

Gwen's spoken English marked her as Welsh from the moment she opened her mouth, but from the years her father had traveled throughout Wales and the March, she understood much more English than she spoke. While she didn't assume Alfred and Luke were involved in whatever had happened to the poor person who'd bled in the alley, understanding the undercurrents among the English who surrounded her could only help her discover who was.

In truth, Gwen should have been grateful that neither man was gossiping about *her*. Maybe they had sense enough not to do so while she was in close proximity. Certainly, a better question they could be asking would be how *she* might be helpful to the investigation. Gwen had enough experience with men and their expectations to understand how unusual she might seem to them. As always, however, she wasn't going to let other people's opinions stop her from doing what needed to be done.

Turning away from the two useless watchmen, she swallowed hard, refusing to allow her stomach to revolt at what lay before her. The blood itself wasn't vile or terrible smelling—it was the stench of the whole town that had her holding her breath from the moment she set foot inside the walls. Thankfully, a brisk wind had come with the dawn, and if she faced into it, she could momentarily banish the odors that threatened to upend her hard-won serenity.

More importantly, she didn't want Gareth to regret her presence. As she was newly pregnant with their second child, he would have been well within his rights to use her pregnancy as an excuse to exclude her. Instead, he had sent for her specifically. She loved working with him. She loved being with him, even when it meant standing over a pool of blood in a stinking alley in Shrewsbury.

Debris of all sorts lined the street on both sides. Earlier, sunlight had been shining directly into the alley, but as the sun had risen farther in the sky, one wall now cast a shadow across most of the alley's width. Gwen kicked at the detritus that had accumulated in the darkness against the south wall. Then, as she moved within a few feet of the pool of blood, she saw something that didn't belong there lying beneath scattered leaves and sticks of splintered wood.

Bending, Gwen picked up a stick and used it to move leaves aside to reveal what they were covering: a string of wooden rosary beads with a simple wooden cross, strung on a slender leather thong.

"Has John returned yet?" Gwen spoke in Welsh, so that only Gareth, who was looking at something on the ground on the other side of the pool, could understand her.

He rose to his feet and came towards her before answering. "No. He's still questioning the residents of the adjacent streets. Did you find something?"

Gwen craned her neck to look past her husband to the spot he'd been standing over. "You first."

Gareth gestured past the pool. "Can you make out the wheel tracks from here? Someone rolled through the blood as he drove through the alley."

"Oh good. Maybe they came upon the person bleeding on the ground and helped him." Gwen drew Gareth's attention to the rosary. "A good Samaritan might wear this."

Gareth grunted his approval as he crouched beside her. "I was starting to feel guilty about taking you away from Tangwen."

"She's fine," Gwen said. "Gwalchmai is teaching her to sing scales."

"A worthy endeavor." Gareth smiled and made a motion as if to touch Gwen's belly, though he withdrew his hand at the last moment, since there were so many people around. "I look forward to the day that Tangwen can do the same for this child. Perhaps he will be a great bard like his uncle and grandfather."

"That will be a great day," Gwen said—and meant it, even as her stomach twisted a bit at the thought.

Until their departure to Shrewsbury, she'd lit a candle every day that this time she would give Gareth a son. Gareth swore it mattered to him not at all, but she knew what having a son meant to him and to every man. Hywel already had two. King Owain had a dozen, effectively ensuring his legacy into the next generation. She and Gareth had two foster sons, Llelo and Dai, both of whom were serving in Prince Cynan's retinue, but the boys had come to them at ten and twelve. It would be a different matter entirely for Gareth to hold his infant son in his arms and name him for his own.

Gareth didn't note her sudden silence and said, "Trust you to be the one to find something useful. If those fools weren't moderately helpful blocking onlookers from coming into the alley, we'd be better off without them."

Gwen didn't disagree, and she didn't tell her husband that Luke's and Alfred's opinion of him was equally low. Instead, she pointed to the two ends of the rosary. "See how the ties came undone rather than breaking? This wasn't pulled off in a fight—or if it was, it was loose to begin with."

Because the thong was knotted at the ends before the two ends had been tied together, the beads hadn't come off the string. It was the normal way to make a rosary. Gwen owned one very much like it, as did Gareth.

"If the rosary and the blood belong to the same person, he wasn't wealthy—or at least he didn't show his wealth with expensive beads," Gareth said.

"A rosary and a pool of blood should never go hand-in-hand," Gwen said.

"More likely, the rosary has nothing to do with the blood at all because it belongs to one of the monks at the abbey." Gareth was referring to the Abbey of St. Peter and St. Paul, located to the east of Shrewsbury, outside the city walls. It also happened to be the place where they were staying, in the abbey guesthouse.

"We can show it to the hospitaller and the abbot." Gareth leaned in to pick up the rosary, his expression thoughtful, and he let the beads run through his fingers, as if he was saying his morning prayers.

Gwen shook her head slightly, still somewhat bemused that they were here in Shrewsbury at all, much less embroiled in an investigation within a day of their arrival. Ten days ago they'd been enduring the gloom at Aber when Meilyr, Gwen's father, suddenly took it upon himself to wring permission from the king to travel to England on the trail of his as yet unacknowledged daughter, Adeline. She'd died alongside Cole Turner last autumn in the run up to the initial attempt to take Mold Castle.

Permission had been granted, if reluctantly, and they'd taken the ride from Aber to Shrewsbury slowly, enjoying fully the leave from their duties they'd been given. The fine weather had meant that Gwalchmai, despite being fifteen and a man, had spent much of the journey scampering about, Tangwen either running after him or on his shoulders as they explored the terrain on either side of the road. Gareth and Gwen had enjoyed long bouts of uninterrupted time to talk, and her father had been in full spate, composing songs while on horseback and regaling them with the results of his labors in the evening.

In fact, it had been the first time in nearly four years—since that fateful day when Gwen, Gwalchmai, and Meilyr had traveled north at the invitation of King Owain—that they'd been anywhere together as a family.

Gwen could remember, as clearly as if it were yesterday, the moment when she realized it was Gareth crouched over the body of King Anarawd. She often thought back to that day— recalling the way, between one breath and the next, her life had been transformed. For King Anarawd—and possibly for this poor person who'd shed his lifeblood on the ground—change had meant death. But for the living, it was important to remember that change wasn't always bad.

"If anyone was going to act like the good Samaritan and help the victim, it would have been a monk," Gwen said. "As far as I know, however, few ever leave the abbey proper—at least, that's what one of the guests told me last night at dinner. And surely we would have heard if one of the monks had brought a man who was bleeding to death into the abbey."

Gareth shrugged. "If the rosary has no connection to the victim, then at least we can do *our* good deed for the day by returning   it."

3

Gwen

Gareth held out his hand to Gwen to help her rise to her feet. "Before I send you back to the monastery, let me show you the tracks."

Gwen went willingly, not because she didn't want to be with her daughter, but because she'd barely sunk her teeth into this investigation, and she wanted to continue at Gareth's side.

Two of John's men were sifting through more debris that had accumulated on the ground on the other side of the pool. Recognizing one of them as Oswin, the young man who'd come to fetch her from the monastery, Gwen spared them a glance and a smile and then turned her attention to the tracks. They looked nothing unusual to her. "What are you seeing that I'm not?"

"To begin, these weren't made by a handbarrow, of which I've seen many in the day we've been here. The distance between the wheels is too wide for that. The cart was pulled by a horse. You can see hoof prints in between the tracks all along the road, since the horse got its hooves bloody too."

"That means the owner is either a farmer who brought hay or food into Shrewsbury to sell, or a wealthier resident of the town," Gwen said.

"Or from the abbey. They have horses and carts."

"Or from the abbey," Gwen amended. "You're right about the handbarrows. I have seen far more of them than horse-drawn carts. They're easier to maneuver along these narrow streets."

"And," Gareth continued, "like any wheel that's been in use for a while, each of the four has a distinctive rotation."

Back before she'd started working for Hywel and had married Gareth, the idea that a wheel track was worth paying attention to would have seemed a preposterous notion. Now, as Gareth traced what he'd observed with one finger, she acknowledged how much they could discern from common things. She'd learned, over the years, that solving a crime sometimes meant looking at the everyday and seeing what others didn't.

"One of the wheels is missing its metal rim," she said.

Gareth shot her a grin. "It looks that way to me too."

"And one of the wheels is narrower than the other three—not by much, but enough to notice when you look at them side-by-side. Maybe at some point the owner had to replace the original."

"I don't know how John will feel about inspecting every cart in Shrewsbury," Gareth said, "but if we find the right one, and it one of the wheels has blood on it, we've found our cart."

"I must point out that we don't know if the owner of the cart had anything to do with this person's death," Gwen said. "It would be helpful if the tracks were left by the person who took away the body, but they could easily have been made by a passer-by, who drove his cart through the alley without knowing what had taken place in it not long before. In the darkness before dawn, he could have mistaken the blood for a water puddle and rolled through it without even seeing it—or thinking anything of it if he did see it."

"That may be, but even if the owner of the cart is a complete innocent, he might have seen something or someone that could lead us to the victim." Gareth looked around him. "I'm not used to towns, and I have no idea how many people might have been out and about at that hour."

"By the time John interviews the people who live near this street he should know," Gwen said, "or at least have come a ways towards finding out."

"My lord, we may have something." Oswin lifted a hand to gain their attention. He was hardly older than Gwalchmai, with beardless chin and blue eyes.

Gwen and Gareth moved towards him, and he shifted to one side to show them what he and his companion had found: a dozen broken slats from a now-worthless crate. A few of the slats were still attached to one another, and several were stained red with blood.

Oswin pointed to one in particular, which had been splintered along its whole length and the sharp end of which bore a strong resemblance to the point of a sword. "If one man stabbed another with that, it would be no surprise that he bled out."

"The assailant could have injured himself in the process," said the second watchman, whose name Gwen didn't know. He was young too, not even into his twenties, with blond hair and a scruff of beard on his chin and upper lip. "Good job gripping it without finding your hand full of splinters."

"Perhaps that means the wounded person wasn't actually the victim here," Gwen said.

"What do you mean by that?" Oswin said.

"If one man was attacking another, the person under assault could have defended himself with the slat," Gwen said. "It isn't a weapon to bring to a fight."

Gareth let out a low, quick laugh, since it seemed Gwen had thought of something he hadn't. "At the very least, the confrontation would have been spur of the moment."

A rattling sound came from above them, and Gwen looked up to see a woman poke her head out of an upper floor window. She held a basin in her hand and looked as if she was about to dump it on their heads. Oswin saw her too, stood, and pointed a finger at her. The woman didn't need Oswin to speak to know what he was telling her. She made a face and pulled back inside. Gwen told herself that the basin had contained dirty water, but that was probably a false hope.

Gwen had lived in castles most of her life, but none had ever provided shelter to more than a hundred residents. Two thousand people in one place was difficult to get her head around. When they'd ridden to Chester last year, Gwen had thought it was a busy town, but Shrewsbury was twice as large. Its houses were packed in close to one another and surrounded by a river and a wall, which prevented the town from expanding outward—and made appropriate and convenient disposal of waste a problem.

Prosperity—in Chester under Earl Ranulf or in Shrewsbury under its town council—meant either packing more people and buildings into the narrow spaces between current houses and businesses or building upwards. Gwen could see the join in the wall of the woman's house where two stories had become three.

"My apologies, ma'am," Oswin said to Gwen. "This is a rough part of town."

"It does seem that the neighborhood uses this street for their refuse pile," Gwen said. "That might explain the presence of the crate."

Oswin dropped one of the unbloodied slats onto the pile he'd created. "It's surprising that anyone would discard a crate like this one. It's of no use anymore for carrying anything, but it would make good kindling." He glanced upwards again at the now-empty window. "It's unlikely it lay here long, because someone who lives around here would have scavenged it."

"There must have been a great deal going on in this alley this morning in a very narrow window of time," Gwen said.

Gareth nodded at the two watchmen. "Good work. I'm sure John will want to see what you've found when he gets back."

Oswin nodded. "Yes, sir. Thank you, sir."

Leaving the men to continue their work, Gareth took Gwen's arm and walked her back towards the eastern entrance to the alley, past the pool of blood, which was finally sinking into the soil.

The audience had mostly dispersed, which wasn't surprising given how little there was to see. The only onlookers remaining were a young woman, two boys, and an elderly gentleman who appeared to have stopped to rest on his walk up the hill rather than specifically to find out what was happening in the alley. Luke and Alfred had abandoned all pretense of searching for clues and were now chatting with the young woman.

As Gwen edged past Luke and out into the main street, she heard him say, "—not even sure it's human blood."

Gareth heard him too and grunted in disgust, though not loud enough for Luke to hear. Maybe it would have been good for Luke if he had. Gwen dearly wished they were back in Wales where Gareth would have been assured of the respect and loyalty of his underlings.

Once they were out of earshot, she said as much to Gareth.

"They're English. A Welshman has to be twice as good as any Englishman at what he does if he's going to win their respect. If I'd sworn it was pig's blood, Luke would have insisted it was human."

Gwen wrinkled her nose. "At the very least, I wish they would stop undermining John's authority."

In the distance, church bells rang, the sound blending with the call of an oxcart driver urging his charges along the street below theirs. Gareth halted across from the entrance to the alley, near the front door to a tavern. The tavern had a green door and a whitewashed front, in keeping with its neighbors on either side. Most of the homes and business in Shrewsbury were well taken care of, at least on the street side. The refuse was left in the alleys.

At this hour, nobody was going in or out of the tavern, but Gareth made sure they weren't directly underneath an upper story window. He looked down at her and spoke in an undertone, though there wasn't anybody close enough to overhear.

"Don't worry about him. What John's men think of him is of no concern. The sheriff appointed him, and whether or not John feels confident in his authority, I am comfortable with John and his men handling the official investigation, which I truly don't want any part of. I can provide support if he needs me. As it is, Hywel will have my head for calling as much attention to myself as I already have."

"You haven't done anything!" Gwen said. "This isn't your fault at all. You could hardly let a pool of blood go uninvestigated, and King Owain wouldn't thank you for refusing to help the Deputy Sheriff of Shrewsbury when he asks. King Owain's alliance with Earl Robert has been long established, but Shrewsbury belongs to King Stephen, and his relationship with Gwynedd is new. What we do here could go a long way towards engendering real good will."

Gareth made a *maybe* motion with his head. "I can't see how this rises to the importance of saving the life of Prince Henry, as we did in Newcastle-under-Lyme, but you're not wrong— especially since Gwynedd has all but failed to keep up its end of the bargain in regards to the Earl of Chester."

"With Rhun's death—"

Gareth made a dismissive motion with one hand. "You don't have to defend Prince Hywel to me. The treaty with Chester was the right thing to do at the time, just as renewing hostilities against Mold Castle is the right thing to do now. King Stephen might even thank us for attacking Mold, given that Ranulf decided to march his men to Lincoln while the king is otherwise occupied. Prince Hywel wouldn't object to any of that."

"Then what will he object to?"

"If Cadwaladr is in the area, and I involve myself in this investigation to the point of asking questions among the people of Shrewsbury, and Cadwaladr hears of it, he's going to think I'm here for him. It may have been mere courtesy that prompted me to introduce myself to the sheriff in the first place, and as the captain of Prince Hywel's *teulu*, it would have been rude of me not to make myself known to him upon my arrival, but unfortunately, it also means that Hywel's hope that no rumor of my presence would reach Cadwaladr's ears died the moment I had set foot inside the town."

Gwen sighed, nodding her understanding. King Owain had specifically ordered that they not pursue Cadwaladr, which is what it now looked like they were in Shrewsbury to do.

To say that King Owain had been capricious in the last few months was a gross understatement. One of his most puzzling decrees involved the pursuit—or lack thereof—of his brother. Hywel and Cynan had successfully ejected Cadwaladr's retinue from Meirionnydd, but instead of sending Cadwaladr's people to

England—to wherever it was that Cadwaladr had gone to ground—King Owain had sent them to Aberffraw, which had been the lesser of Cadwaladr's two seats. Thus, through the administration of Cadwaladr's wife, Alice, for all intents and purposes, Cadwaladr retained his lands in Anglesey.

Hywel couldn't understand it. Nobody could understand it. King Owain had been consumed by Rhun's death to such a degree that he had no thought for anything else, not even revenge, retribution—or justice. In desperation, Hywel had resolved to shore up his own position on the chance that his father lost his mind completely and chose to reject him as his heir or asked Cadwaladr to return to his side.

Consequently, Hywel had brought his next three oldest brothers, Cynan, Madoc, and Cadell, into his inner circle. He'd also sent word to his foster father, Cadifor, that he was needed. Cadifor had come at Hywel's call, bringing with him two of his sons. A third, Ithel, was already at Aber, having been named captain of the king's guard. The position had been briefly held by Cynan, Hywel's next oldest brother, until Rhun's death had given him new obligations.

Gareth and Gwen liked these newcomers well enough, and Gwen was glad that Hywel was forming a reliable cohort of companions to protect him, but their presence did make Gareth himself feel like he wasn't needed and should be doing other things.

Which, as it turned out, was exactly what Hywel had intended. King Owain's permission for Gwen's father to ride to

Shrewsbury had then become an excuse to send Gareth (along with Gwen and Meilyr) into England on a quest to ascertain Prince Cadwaladr's whereabouts without the king becoming suspicious.

"Worse, this could make Cadwaladr target you again," Gwen said. "He tried to murder you, remember. Just because he misfired and killed Prince Rhun doesn't change how much he still hates you."

Gareth looked down at his wife and spoke softly. "I haven't forgotten."

"I know. I just—"

"You worry, and I don't blame you for that."

Gwen took in a breath before speaking again. "So, what do we do now?"

"We ask the questions we came to Shrewsbury to ask, and if that takes us along a path similar to the one we would have followed at John's behest, so be it."

Gwen looked at him curiously. "You mean about Adeline? Surely questioning townspeople about her is going to bring us close to Cadwaladr."

"Ah, but King Owain gave us permission to pursue that line of inquiry, didn't he?"

"He gave my father permission."

"Yes, and since I'm his son-in-law, that's as good as giving it to me."

Gwen shook her head, but she was smiling. "It's happened. You're splitting hairs. Hywel's way of doing things has finally rubbed off on you."

"Hywel doesn't split hairs; he doesn't even accept their existence." But Gareth smiled too. "It's only fair, since it may be that some of my way of doing things has rubbed off on him too."

Gwen moved closer to her husband and put her forehead briefly into his upper arm, as the only sign of affection she could allow herself in so public a place. "You've been a rock for him. We all know it."

"As have you."

Gwen pulled a long face not unlike the one the woman from the upper floor of the building had made when she discovered she couldn't dump the contents of her basin into the alley. "I can't see how I'm going to be much use to you among the people here. I don't know what I was thinking. It wasn't as if I expected the inhabitants of Shrewsbury to speak Welsh, but what's clear is that my English just isn't good enough to enable me talk to them."

"We've been staying at the abbey, which has few Welsh monks," Gareth said. "I think you'll find that more people than you might expect speak Welsh. Shrewsbury is only seven miles from the border with Wales after all. And besides, with you by my side, just by your very presence, people are more likely to talk to me."

"Why would that be?" Gwen said.

Gareth rolled his eyes, but he was smiling. "Gwen, didn't you notice the way the watchmen looked at you as you came in?"

Gwen's brow furrowed. "I suppose." Quite honestly, her eyes had been only for Gareth, and a scruffy, bearded Englishman held no interest for her beyond her anger that they were deriding Gareth.

"You forget that you look like Adeline, who grew up here," Gareth said. "As long as you are with me—or with your father when he starts asking questions about her—we aren't going to have any difficulty getting people to talk to us."

Gwen hadn't forgotten that she looked like Adeline. She and her father had decided it would be better if she didn't go with him to visit Tom Weaver because they hadn't wanted to scare him by having Adeline—or Gwen looking like Adeline—suddenly appear on his doorstep. It was just that the pool of blood had temporarily driven that knowledge from her mind. "What about you? Has anyone accused you of being Cole?"

"While the story of Cole's and Adeline's deaths has spread far and wide," Gareth said, "he never did look much like me. John attacked me when he saw me for the first time only because Cole was at the forefront of his mind. With my hair shorn and without a beard, I am a different person."

Gwen's expression turned thoughtful. "I had wondered why everyone has been so kind to me. Now I know why. It would be nice to know if she really was my sister."

Gwen hadn't ever met Adeline herself—she'd only seen her body—but the reminder of why they had come to Shrewsbury in the first place had her wondering how her father was getting on. He'd been cheerful last night, if a little tipsy from the good wine the abbey stocked, but she'd hadn't had a chance to speak to him more than briefly this morning.

And now that she thought about it, one benefit to whatever gossip was flying around Shrewsbury about Gwen and Gareth was that Tom Weaver, Adeline's father, and Roger Carter, Adeline's betrothed, would know in advance that Gwen's father was here too—and that sooner or later he would be coming to visit them.

"It could simply be that your father and hers are long-lost cousins," Gareth said.

"True, but even if Father clears the path, I don't relish the idea of walking up to Adeline's father's house with this face and reminding him of his dead daughter." Gwen's laugh was mocking. "Imagine what my father is saying right now: *I might have fathered your daughter* can't be the most welcome opening."

"Had Meilyr left before I sent word to you?" Gareth said.

"Yes," Gwen said. "I saw him off into Shrewsbury shortly before you summoned me to the alley."

Gareth checked the sky. "Then he would have reached Tom Weaver's shop long since. Whatever Meilyr ended up saying to Adeline's father, it has been said." Gareth took Gwen's elbow again, to begin walking down the street as it sloped towards the river.

Gwen had taken only one step, however, when the sound of running feet echoed from the alley. She exchanged a glance with Gareth, who shrugged, and together they headed back to the entrance. They reached it in time to watch the messenger—a tall, thin, young man with a shock of short blond hair—leap what remained of the pool of blood in an easy stride and then come to a halt in front of Luke.

The young man spoke urgently to the watchman, words Gwen couldn't catch because they went by too quickly, but Gareth must have understood something of them because he hastened forward.

Although the elderly man and the young woman had moved on, the two boys stopped their game of throwing stones against a wall to listen. Gareth stepped between them and the messenger, who turned to him with a relieved expression on his face. Luke wore a cynical frown, as if whatever the messenger had just told him couldn't possibly be true, but he didn't openly discredit it.

"Start again, Cedric." It seemed Gareth had met the young man already, although he wasn't among those to whom Gwen had been introduced.

"My lord." Cedric took in a huge breath to steady himself after the running he'd done. "I'm glad to see you here, but I was looking for John Fletcher."

"I don't know where he is at the moment," Gareth said. "He went to find a witness who could tell him what might have transpired here."

At a movement from Gwen, Cedric's eyes tracked to her, and he did a double-take. Gwen gave him a gentle smile, acknowledging the widening of his eyes without mentioning it. In a way, it was gratifying to see, now that she was paying attention, that they hadn't been mad to think Adeline and she looked alike.

Cedric put one hand to his chest and bowed at the waist. "My lady." He straightened and looked again to Gareth. "Then perhaps you can help me, my lord. We've found another body."

4

Gareth

"The error would be in the use of the word 'another',"
Gareth said as he and Gwen hustled after Cedric,
who, while slightly shorter than Gareth, had even
longer legs. Cedric's rapid pace had Gareth regretting his winter
cloak, which he'd put on before leaving the monastery, but now at
nearly noon was causing him to sweat. They were past St. Dafydd's
Day, and the sun gave more warmth and rose higher into the sky
with every day that passed. After an unusually cold winter, Gareth
had feared that spring would come late. But during the journey
here from Aber, spring had moved into full bloom, with green
fields, flowers, and rich pastures for the sheep. "We haven't found
the first body yet—if there even is one."

"This man was strangled, if that helps." Cedric spoke from
just ahead of Gareth, having apparently overheard his comment
since Gareth had been speaking English to Gwen out of politeness.
Speaking Welsh would have been easier, but he'd traveled enough
and had been on the receiving end of others resorting to their
native language in his presence as a way to exclude him, that he

wasn't going to do the same to Cedric without real cause. "There is no blood on him."

They'd left the alley and followed the street that ran all around the town along the inside of the palisade. Shrewsbury was canted at a northeasterly angle and surrounded on three sides by the Severn River, which made it resemble the shape of a flagon with a wide base and a narrow top. The castle was located in the neck and guarded the entire city behind it as it sat to the southwest in the protective curve of the river. While the city was well over a half-mile wide from bank to bank at its widest point, the land between the bends in the Severn at its narrowest, where the castle sat, was only three hundred yards wide.

Stone gatehouses, made of the same red sandstone used to build Shrewsbury Castle and Abbey, guarded bridges across the Severn in case an enemy tried to cross the river in force. Gareth could count on one hand the number of stone fortresses that had been built by Welsh kings, but the English were replacing more and more of their formerly wooden forts with stone ones. From what he understood, however, Shrewsbury Castle had been built in stone from the start—and had been one of the first stone castles in England.

For visitors, the city could be entered and exited by three gates: the Welsh gate, which faced northwest across the Severn and connected with a road that led west into Wales; the English gate, which lay on the opposite side of the town and also guarded a bridge across the Severn; and the northeastern gate by the castle, which was the only access to the town by land.

Residents of Shrewsbury could also enter and leave the town by a southern gate, which opened onto the fields that lay between the town and the curve of the river. Additionally, many homes and establishments that abutted the city's protective palisade had private gates in them, which gave their owners immediate access to the river. Although these created giant holes in the town's defenses, none of these exits allowed access to any land beyond the river, unless someone chose to boat or swim across it.

"You have seen the body yourself, Cedric?" Gareth said.

Cedric nodded, even as he loped along at an even faster pace. "His neck is purpled, but it doesn't look to me as if a man's hands did it. I couldn't see any bruising from fingerprints. If I had to guess, I'd say the killer used rope or a fishing line to do his work."

Gareth pressed his lips together, hiding a smile. Cedric was very earnest in his manner, and the words had spilled out of him in a rush, as if he'd been waiting for Gareth to ask him about the condition of the body. If John Fletcher wasn't careful, he would find himself usurped by the younger man. Unlike Luke, however, who was struggling with John's authority, resulting in an overbearing attitude, Cedric appeared to want to please and to be helpful. Gareth could use the help, especially in a strange city where he wasn't quite welcome.

The pool of blood had been found in an alley off the river street, in the northwestern quadrant of the town. Following Cedric, they crossed the town to the south of the castle and ended up in the southeast quadrant, in the exact opposite quarter of Shrewsbury from where they'd started. As they approached this area of the town, however, Gwen's steps slowed. The wind had shifted slightly and the vile smell of tanning leather, which was emanating from some of the buildings ahead of them, wafted strongly in their direction.

In England and Wales, the wind tended to come from the west or southwest, so the collection of skinners, tanners, glovers, and leather goods makers whose workshops and stalls made up the southeast quadrant of the city didn't usually pollute the whole of the city. If they had, when Gareth had arrived at the west gate yesterday, he might have turned his family around right then and there.

Gwen was having a more difficult pregnancy this time than with Tangwen, and Gareth knew she struggled to keep down her breakfast most mornings. Fortunately, she was hanging onto it at the moment, even if it meant clenching her fists so tightly her knuckles had turned white.

Gareth put his head close to Gwen's. "Breathe slowly and deeply through your mouth."

She put the back of her hand to her nose. "They say that after a while a person can get used to any smell, but I'm not so sure about this one."

Cedric halted in front of an inn. Like most buildings in Shrewsbury, it was made of wood, not stone, with a thatch roof that had a hole in the center to let out the smoke. It was bigger than most of the surrounding houses and workshops, and a sign out front was adorned with a drawing of what might have been the head of a horse.

"The Boar's Head Inn," Cedric said.

Gwen raised her eyebrows. "They should get you to do the drawing for them, Gareth. Then we'd at least know what its name is supposed to be."

She'd spoken in Welsh and in an undertone, so Cedric, who was purely Saxon for thirteen generations, couldn't understand her. He didn't turn around.

"I'm sure the last thing they need is criticism of their sign," Gareth said, though he touched her hand as he spoke so she would know he understood that she was trying to lighten the mood.

The rush mats on the floor were stained and looked as if they hadn't been changed since before old King Henry died. The tables, benches, and stools were scarred and unpolished, and a young woman was wiping them down with a wet cloth that looked to be smearing the dirt around on the surface of the tables rather than cleaning them. This tavern's trade was definitely of the rougher sort.

At first blush, the inn was less a place to sleep than a drinking establishment. The common room reeked of beer, the national drink of England. Fermented from grains instead of honey, which was the main ingredient in Welsh mead, the scent was unmistakably yeasty. This early in the morning, the smell—mixed as it was with the slightly muted scent of tanning leather—made Gareth gag, and he glanced concernedly to Gwen, whose face had taken on a pinched look, and who was breathing exclusively through her mouth, as he'd suggested.

Gareth sent up a prayer of thanks that he possessed enough status and relative wealth that he hadn't had to stoop to housing his family here. Even if the abbey had been full, he could have stayed at the castle—and would have anyway had he come to England on official business for Gwynedd. If that too had been full, they would have been welcomed by a Welsh family who lived in Shrewsbury. And if all else failed, he would have chosen to stay outside the city and sleep in their tent or under the stars, as they'd done for the past week when no more hospitable circumstance presented itself, rather than stay here.

Cedric appeared not to notice the smell—but then, he'd grown up in Shrewsbury and to him the smell of tanning leather would seem normal. Fortunately the young watchman hurried them through the central room, out the back entrance, and into the courtyard behind the main building. "This way."

Cedric fetched up at the entrance to a long low building that at first Gareth had mistaken for a stable. Upon closer inspection, it bore no real resemblance to one, other than its three separate doors, which faced into the courtyard and which Gareth had confused for horse stalls. They were revealed instead to lead to small but serviceable rooms. Each was furnished with a narrow bed and a washstand—and was far cleaner than the common room they'd just left.

Perhaps the paying guests demanded somewhat more from the proprietor in the way of amenities than the usual tavern clientele. Gareth might have been willing to house his family here after all, if not for the smell and the dead body, which was located in the last room on the right.

Gareth and Gwen gazed at the dead man for a count of five, and then Gwen said into the silence, "Cedric is right. This isn't the body we're looking for."

The man had been well-built, of medium height with reddish-brown hair and beard, approximately in his late thirties. He lay before them on the floor with his hands folded on his chest and his eyes closed as if he'd already been washed and clothed for burial. His face was bloodless, but not because he'd bled out. He was merely dead. From the wound on his neck, it was instantly clear as well, as Cedric had asserted, that he had been strangled. And given the obvious bruises and cuts on his face and hands, he'd put up a good fight for his life.

"Who found him?" Gareth said.

"I did." A man in his late forties moved out of the far corner of the room. Of average height but stocky, he looked like he could hold his own in a fight, and his square jaw bulged as he spoke.

Gareth hadn't noticed him earlier because the only light available came from the open doorway. Perhaps Gareth couldn't be blamed, given that there was a dead body on the floor, but he nonetheless kicked himself for being so unobservant. That was a good way to get himself—or worse, Gwen—killed.

"And you are?" Gareth said.

"Rob Horn, the proprietor."

Gareth gave the man a quick once over, noting that the backs of Rob's hands were clean and unmarred and that he had no wounds showing on his face. Then Gareth crouched by the dead man's side and touched him gently here and there, looking for a less obvious wound that might explain the puddle in the alley—just to make sure they weren't wrong about the cause of death and that this really wasn't the body they'd been looking for.

"He wears no purse," he said to Gwen in an undertone, speaking in Welsh this time, regardless of whether or not it was rude or if it excluded Cedric. At other times, Gareth would have used the next hour as an opportunity to explain to Cedric how he knew what he knew, but with the innkeeper present, he felt a need to keep the discovery process of the investigation to himself for now until he knew the people involved better.

"He could have been murdered for it." Gwen leaned in closer to Gareth, also speaking softly. "Or we were meant to think so."

"It would have been easy enough for a sneak thief to have seen him in the tavern and followed him to his room," Gareth said.

Gwen tipped her head. "The room is cleaner than I would have imagined a simple thief would leave it—and look how this man is laid out east to west."

"The whole scene implies that the killer gave what he'd done some thought. This man's death may not have been planned, but the aftermath—" Gareth nodded his head as he went through in his mind the steps the murderer must have taken in order to leave the room as they saw it now, "—that definitely was."

"What do you want me to do?" Gwen said.

"Nothing in front of these two." Gareth lifted the man's arm and laid it down again. "I'd put his death after midnight and before dawn. He's isn't completely cold, but he's stiff." Gareth looked up at the innkeeper and returned to English. "I gather this man was a guest? Can you tell me his name?"

After a dismayed glance at Cedric, Rob said, "He wasn't a guest."

"We both know him well," Cedric added. "His name is Roger Carter, and he is one of the most important men in Shrewsbury."

5

Gareth

"This man was Adeline's betrothed?" Gareth gazed at the body as if seeing it for the first time. He was having trouble accepting the way his two worlds had just collided.

"Yes, my lord," Cedric said.

"Why didn't you say so when you came to get us?" Gareth swiveled on the ball of his foot to look over at Cedric, who stood to the right of the doorway.

"I didn't think it mattered since I didn't think you would know him," Cedric said. "Obviously, I was wrong."

Gwen was shaking her head back and forth repeatedly, seemingly unable to muster up the appropriate words to convey how she felt.

The questions tumbled over themselves in Gareth's mind, but he asked the first one that leapt to the forefront. "Why would Roger Carter rent a room at this inn?"

"He didn't," Rob said.

Gareth sent him a piercing look, at which point the innkeeper got the hint that his answer wasn't sufficient.

"The room was rented to someone else."

"Who?"

Rob gestured helplessly. "A stranger. Came two nights ago. Kept to himself."

Gareth rose to his feet. "What was his name?"

"Irish, wasn't he? Could hardly understand three words out of ten that came out of his mouth, but he said his name was Conall."

"Did the proprietor just say that the dead man was Irish?" Gwen said in Welsh to Gareth, apparently having lost the thread of the conversation due to Rob's rapid fire English.

Gareth nodded, but he kept his attention focused on Rob. The innkeeper was one of the first men Gareth had encountered who hadn't blinked an eye at Gareth's foreign appearance or his Welsh accent. And if Roger Carter was on the town council, his murder would send shock and panic throughout the town. Gareth didn't know if that would make it harder or easier for him to get the residents to tell him what they knew. "Why would Roger Carter have been in his room?"

Rob shrugged. "I wouldn't know. I never saw Conall but twice: when he paid that first night and when he returned home the second. He let himself out in the mornings before the dawn." His smile was apologetic. "With the tavern, I'm awake past midnight most nights, so I have others to look after the place during the morning hours."

"How many nights did Conall pay for?" Gareth said.

"Just the two," Rob said. "I expected him to have been off this morning—before dawn again, he'd said, so I was coming to see to the room when I found Roger lying there dead."

"Do you know why Conall was in Shrewsbury in the first place?" Gareth said.

Rob shook his head. "At the time, I thought it strange for an Irishman to come to Shrewsbury at all, but he said he had business in the town."

"Apparently, some of that business was with Roger Carter," Gwen said, finding her voice.

Another shrug from Rob. "I wouldn't have said so—no word of them meeting came to my ear—not before today, anyway."

"Might it have?" Gareth said.

Rob raised his eyebrows. "I own a tavern, and people talk. If Conall and Roger Carter were doing business, it's more surprising to me that I didn't hear of it."

"What did Conall say his business was?" Gareth said.

"Wool," Rob said.

"Buying or selling?" Gareth asked.

"Selling."

Gareth grunted. To have an Irishman come to Shrewsbury to deal in wool would be a strange thing, since there were already more sheep in this part of the world than people. Shrewsbury didn't need more wool merchants, a fact so self-evident that he'd even heard people say the phrase *it's like bringing wool to*

Shrewsbury, to imply that a deed was unnecessary and redundant. "Did you believe him?"

"There wasn't anything to believe or disbelieve. I don't meddle in my customers' business. If they pay and don't damage the room, they can stay as long as they like."

"So you don't know the last time Conall was in this room, or if he ever had visitors?" Gareth said.

Rob gestured to the body on the floor. "Other than Roger, obviously? No."

"You didn't hear them fighting?" Gwen said, and Gareth was glad not only that she'd asked the question—since coming from him it might have sounded accusatory—but that she'd been able to follow the continuing conversation. Trained as a musician, and thus already conversant in Latin and French, she had a good ear. He wasn't surprised that she was starting to find her rhythm with English too.

Rob grimaced. He seemed genuinely disturbed by the death of Roger Carter—maybe not for the man himself, but for the circumstances. "The common room is loud. Earl Robert's army could have been attacking out here, and I wouldn't have known."

He genuinely seemed to be trying to help, which under other circumstances might have made Gareth more suspicious of him rather than less, especially given Gareth's experience with Prince Cadwaladr, who tended to overthink things and tie himself up in knots. Gareth found it as hard to trust an Englishman as an Englishman might find it to trust him, a Welshman.

Still, while it was too early to make judgements, Gareth found it unlikely that Rob would have murdered Roger Carter and left the body in his own inn, especially if it was he who called the watchman. Roger was a worthy of the town. Even a man unused to murder would have known to dispose of the body in a far less incriminating fashion. On top of all that, Rob's hands and face bore no marks of a struggle.

"Do we have your permission to question your staff to find out if they encountered Conall more than you did, or if they noticed when Roger arrived last night?" Gareth said.

Rob gestured with one hand. "I have no objection."

"Did you arrange Roger's body this way, or was he like this when you arrived?" Gwen said.

"He was like this."

"Did you have guests in the other rooms last night?" Gareth said.

"I had two merchants passing through with their apprentices, who slept in the stable. The merchants attended a guild meeting that didn't break up until after midnight. The apprentices spent the time until their masters returned in the common room. They all left this morning early, like they'd planned. Heading east, I think."

Gareth groaned inwardly. If he rode from Shrewsbury this very instant, it might be possible to track them down, but if they'd taken a side road, it would be wasted effort. If they were guilty of murder, he would regret letting them go, but it was too long a shot. And in truth, not his problem, as he needed to remind himself again. He was helping out—standing in for John Fletcher who hadn't yet arrived. This was neither Gareth's investigation nor his problem.

Gwen, however, either didn't see it that way, or had forgotten it, and said to Gareth. "Our first step, then, appears to be to track down Conall."

Gareth looked again at Rob. "Can you describe Conall for me?"

Rob snorted. "He looked like a bloody Irishman, didn't he? Red hair, freckles, and skin as white as snow."

"Red hair like Roger Carter's?" Suddenly inspired, Gareth pulled a piece of paper and charcoal from the inner pocket of his coat and drew a quick outline of a face.

"No," Rob Horn said. "Not dark like Roger's—bright like fire."

"Long hair or short?"

"Short—cropped to almost nothing." Rob stepped to Gareth's side to look at what he was doing. He proceeded to answer Gareth's questions about the size of Conall's nose and the shape of his mouth. In a matter of a few strokes of Gareth's hand, a picture of Conall took shape on the paper. Before long, Rob nodded, satisfied. "That's him, all right." Then Rob pursed his lips. "I know you're thinking Roger came here because he had business with Conall and Conall betrayed him, but I never pegged him for either a renegade or a killer, even if he was Irish."

"What makes you say that?" Gareth said.

"He liked to laugh," Rob said. "Come to think on it, I thought I heard his laugh in the common room yesterday evening. I didn't think of it until just now, since I didn't actually see his face. Maybe it wasn't him."

"It seems obvious that Conall is the murderer, but—" Gwen canted her head to one side. "Do you know of anyone else who might want to murder Roger Carter?"

"Now that's a question." Rob barked a laugh. "But what you really should be asking is *who wouldn't?*"

6

Gareth

"What do you mean, *who wouldn't?*" Gareth asked this question even though he might have made a good guess on his own, just from the little he'd heard about Roger Carter from John Fletcher. Gareth distinctly remembered John mentioning that, although Roger had achieved a certain stature in the town, he had a temper. For that reason, few had been surprised when Adeline had run away rather than marry him. Gareth, however, wanted to hear Rob say that himself.

Instead, Rob shook his head and looked down at his boots. "I hate to speak ill of the dead."

This was no time for mincing words. "The man was murdered," Gareth said. "If we are to find Roger's killer, we must know the truth about him, and the only way we're going to find that out is if you, and everyone else, tells it to us."

Rob still didn't seem to want to speak, so Gareth turned to Cedric, eyebrows raised.

Cedric wrinkled his nose, his eyes on Rob, and then shrugged. "Rob's right. Roger had enemies. Many, in fact."

"Why would that be?" Gareth said, again feigning ignorance.

Cedric cleared his throat and then said very clearly, as if reciting a Latin lesson. "Because he was a son of a bitch and a bastard." Then he looked sheepishly at Gwen, though she might not have even understood the English profanity, and added, "or so my father says."

Gareth assumed that Cedric didn't mean either of those epithets literally and waited patiently for either Cedric or Rob to elaborate.

Finally, Rob sighed. "Cedric's right. Roger Carter had a cruel streak and a temper. When he was in a foul mood, woe to the man who stood in his way. From what I heard, he beat his apprentice every other day for his mistakes or for not doing exactly as he was told—or maybe even because Roger liked it."

Cedric nodded. "I heard that Roger was elected to the town council because the other members were afraid of him."

"He threatened them?" Gareth said.

Rob shrugged. "Maybe not in so many words, but he is rich and influential."

"Influential with the sheriff?" Gareth said.

Cedric shook his head. "Not him. The Lord of Ludlow thinks highly of him and his work, however."

"I have to admit, his carts don't lose wheels often," Rob said, "and if they do, he fixes them for no charge. He is rigid, but when he says he will do something, he does it."

"I wouldn't have thought a man could become rich as a cartwright," Gwen said.

"It isn't the carts but the carriages," Rob said. "When the Lord of Ludlow orders a fine carriage for his wife and Roger makes him one fit for a king, more orders follow. He made one for Robert of Gloucester earlier this year."

"Robert of Gloucester supports Empress Maud," Gwen said, "and this city stands for King Stephen."

Rob quirked one eyebrow. "Money is money, miss. It doesn't matter who buys a man's goods as long as someone does. We were for Maud before we were for Stephen, and the Earl is as good as his word and pays well."

Other than a few dark days nearly ten years ago when Shrewsbury Castle, which had been held for Empress Maud, had fallen to King Stephen and he'd had the garrison slaughtered, this region of England had mostly escaped the war between the royal Norman cousins. This close to Wales, when danger came, half the population would retreat west anyway, waiting for the violence to die down before returning to their homes and livelihoods. Many, John Fletcher among them, had Welsh blood, and those who didn't might find that friendship with a Welshman for once came in handy.

Upon their return and the appointment of their new sheriff, the allegiance of the townspeople would have changed from Maud to Stephen, but few of the common folk were much concerned with who sat on the throne in London.

Rob canted his head. "Besides, once Roger started doing well, he looked for ways to invest his money."

Gareth's eyes narrowed. "What does that mean?"

Rob shrugged. "If a neighbor had an idea to start a business, Roger would go in with him on it, as a partner. He wouldn't be the one who would do the work—just someone to put up the money to start it. He had such arrangements all over Shropshire."

Gareth himself had never thought about wealth in that way. When he saved, he stored coins in a bag and either carried the bag with him, or gave it to Taran, King Owain's steward, to keep for him. Taran had a ledger where he recorded every transaction. The idea that Gareth could take what he'd saved and invest it in someone else's business was a completely foreign idea to him. It seemed to make sense to both Rob and Cedric, however.

Gareth pointed with his chin to Rob. "Thank you for your help. If you can think of anything that could assist us in finding Conall, or if you have a thought of the specific name of a man who might want Roger dead, please send word to me at the abbey or to John Fletcher at the castle."

Gareth was of a mind that he'd pulled everything he could out of Rob for now. John Fletcher might want another go when he arrived, but it wouldn't be helpful in the long run to overtax an important witness from the start. If he needed to, Gareth could come back.

Rob gestured to Cedric. "If you like, I could let him know if I remember anything else. Cedric's my cousin's lad."

"That would be fine."

Rob turned to leave the room, but then he hesitated one more time. "What of the body? I'd like to rent the room tonight."

"Unless something else unforeseen happens, he and we will be gone by then," Gareth said.

Rob nodded, looking satisfied.

Cedric moved aside to let the innkeeper leave, and then he took Rob's absence as an opportunity to approach the body for the first time. His eyes were wide, and Gareth just managed to keep a grim smile from his lips. Here was another young man excited by the mystery of violent death, having little experience with it up until now.

It was Gareth's thought that all men yearned to be tested and not found wanting. Even in this time of war, not every man could be a soldier, but every young man desired to be one—until the battle actually began. War made old men out of young men in a day, if not an hour.

"Bad luck for Uncle Rob to have this happen in his inn," Cedric said. "It isn't good for business."

"If he's telling the truth about what happened," Gwen said.

"Of course he is!" Cedric said.

What Gareth wanted to ask was *lad, how long have you been in service to the sheriff?* but Gwen took care of that response for him too. "You know your uncle better than we do, but people lie to us all the time, Cedric. We can't assume anything."

Cedric deflated. "You're right. Of course, you're right. Just because he's my uncle doesn't mean that he wouldn't lie to my face if it would save his own skin."

Gareth raised his eyebrows at Gwen, silently urging her to keep talking. She had a way of getting information out of people simply by being curious. People told her things that they wouldn't tell Gareth.

"That sounds like a very different person from the uncle you were defending a moment ago," Gwen said. "Are you speaking from experience?"

Cedric's expression turned rueful. "My mother doesn't trust him and doesn't like me coming around here. Uncle Rob isn't respectable. He did something a long time ago—not here, somewhere else—that makes my Da almost spit whenever he speaks of him. They've never told me what it was."

It sounded like Cedric's Da was an opinionated man, given that he appeared to have had a similar reaction to Roger Carter. Gareth had never met Roger, but on the whole, Rob seemed a reasonable man.

"But you like him," Gwen said, not as a question.

"He's always talked to me like I was worthy of respect, even when I was a boy," Cedric's brow furrowed. "He isn't as welcoming to me now that I'm one of the sheriff's men."

"How long have you been one?" Gwen said.

"Three weeks. I'm just past my nineteenth birthday." That made Cedric even younger than Gareth had first thought. Cedric looked down at his toes for a moment. "I don't want my uncle to be the murderer."

"It's important to remember that we know very little at this point. The murderer might not be either Rob or Conall," Gwen said.

"Conall is Irish," Cedric said, revealing the English prejudice, though Gareth hadn't noticed when he'd been in Ireland with Prince Hywel years ago that the Irish committed murder any more or less than any other people.

"There's more here than simply finding a dead man in your uncle's inn. Do you notice anything strange about the way the body is lying?" Gwen gestured to the floor. She was speaking to Cedric as she might have to John Fletcher last year—trying to instruct him without seeming to.

Cedric's brow furrowed. "Is it ... because the scene looks arranged? The man wouldn't have fallen exactly like that."

"That's right," Gareth said. "From the wounds on the man's face and hands, he had been fighting, but the man who killed him laid out the body carefully. Why do you think he did that?"

Cedric's brow remained furrowed. "Murder is a crime of passion. Of anger. Wouldn't he leave the body and run?"

"Sometimes men do panic and run for their lives," Gareth said, "but in this case, I suspect we're looking for a thinking man, one who, after the initial shock wore off, wanted to leave us a message about what he'd done."

"That he was sorry?" Cedric said.

"Or that he wasn't," Gwen said.

"I still don't understand," Cedric said.

Gwen shared a glance with Gareth before speaking again. "We won't know the truth until we find him. While the arrangement of the body indicates that the murderer has an organized mind, it looks to me from what else is here that his intent was to clear all traces of himself from the room."

"So not regret, but thought," Gareth said.

Gwen made a sweeping motion with one arm to indicate their surroundings. "The room shows no sign of a fight, which has to mean that the wounds on Roger's face came from earlier in the day or—"

Cedric nodded, seeing where Gwen was going with this, "—or that the murderer cleaned the room, just as he did the body. Which means we won't find anything," Cedric concluded glumly.

"Though we must still look," Gwen said.

Cedric, rightfully, took that statement as his cue to circle the room.

Gwen gestured to the entrance. "You'll note that the door wasn't forced."

Cedric glanced behind him, and when he turned back to Gareth, his eyes had lit again. "Conall invited Roger here!"

"Or at the very least, opened the door to him and welcomed him inside," Gwen said.

That thought made Gareth frown slightly. The laws of hospitality were as important to the Irish as to the Welsh. It would take a truly compelling circumstance for an Irishman to invite a man into his home and then murder him in it, even if that home was temporary, as this one had been for Conall.

"We need more information, clearly. Others might rush to condemn Conall or Rob, but we shouldn't." Gareth crouched again by the body and turned over Roger's hands to look at his palms. The fingers of his left hand showed deep indentations, which experience told Gareth meant he'd managed at some point to slip his fingers between his throat and the garrote.

Gwen bent forward as she had when they'd first arrived, her hands on her knees—not looking at Roger's face, but at his clothing. She reached out a hand to feel the softness of the wool that made up his jacket, and then crouched beside Gareth to look closer. "This is finely done, Gareth. Feel it."

He swept his gaze down the length of Roger's body. "Everything about him speaks of money. Given what Rob said and that he served on the town council, it should come as no surprise that he was a wealthy man."

Footfalls came on the cobbled walkway that led from the tavern to the room, and Gareth turned to see John Fletcher standing in the doorway.

"One of the wealthiest, in fact," John said.

7

Gwen

Gwen could tell that John was shocked by Roger Carter's death, but he was containing himself admirably. For such a young man, he'd lost more people he knew to foul play than most people four times his age. Though he'd made clear to Gareth when they'd met him last year in Wales that he was inexperienced in solving murder, he was certainly growing more experienced with every hour that passed.

"I'm sorry, John." And Gwen was—though, even as she said the words, she found herself puzzled by her detachment. Usually, when confronted with a murder, she became almost too emotionally involved. Not today. She'd followed along with Gareth, curious about what had happened—but she felt neither outrage nor horror at Roger's death.

Now, as she outwardly comforted John, she had to acknowledge that something really was wrong with her. In the last few hours, she'd stood first over the puddle of blood, and then Roger's body, talking about who he was and how he'd died—and hadn't taken a single moment to acknowledge the loss, which meant nothing more to her than a puzzle to be solved. *When had she become so insensitive to murder? How could she find justice for a victim when she no longer cared about him or saw him as a person?*

John took a moment to regain his composure, during which time nobody but Gwen looked at him, and then he said, "How did Roger's body get from that alley to here?"

"It didn't," Gareth said, and then he explained that the blood couldn't be Roger's because that wasn't how Roger had died.

"So we have two incidents in Shrewsbury today." John was aghast.

"So it seems," Gareth said. "What can you tell me about Roger Carter?"

John spread his hands wide. "He was a worthy of the town, on the council, and influential. Rich."

"He was also Adeline's former betrothed. Could her death have anything to do with his?" Gareth said.

"Unless Prince Cadwaladr was somehow involved, I can't see how." Then John frowned as he looked between Gareth and Gwen. "There is another thing that ties the events of four months ago to today, you know."

"What is that?" Gareth said.

"You."

Gwen put her hands on her hips, her unease put aside in the face of John's assertion. "You can't seriously think that Gareth had anything to do with Roger Carter's death?"

John held up both hands defensively as if staving off an attack. "I didn't mean that Gareth murdered Roger. I only meant to suggest that if Roger knew more about Adeline's death than he told me, someone might be worried to see you here, Sir Gareth. The murderer could have acted hastily—killing Roger—in hopes of preventing Roger from speaking to you."

Gareth straightened from where he'd been crouching beside the body. "You imply that my reputation as an investigator has preceded me."

"Yes." John cleared his throat. "I might have spoken of you a time or two, and certainly the whole town would know of your arrival by now."

Gareth closed his eyes briefly as if gathering his strength, before opening them and speaking again to John. "With two investigations ongoing, your men are going to be spread thin, but I would say that Roger Carter's death takes precedence over the possible death of someone we haven't identified. We need to determine Roger's whereabouts over the last day—and we need to break the news of his death to his family."

John heaved a sigh. "That falls to me."

"I will come with you, if I may," Gareth said. At John's relieved look, Gareth turned to Gwen. "I can't send you out to question townspeople on your own, and I don't think now is the time to introduce the woman who looks just like Adeline to Roger's soon-to-be grieving family."

"I will return to the monastery," Gwen said. "If you give me a sketch of Conall, I can start showing it around."

"And the rosary too." Gareth handed the beads to Gwen. Then he pulled out the picture of Conall and sketched a copy for himself, from which he could make other copies later when he had time. When he was done, he looked up. "Cedric?"

"I'll escort her," Cedric said, though his eyes flicked to John as he spoke.

Gwen had the sense that Cedric was torn between chivalry and wanting to stay with Gareth and John. Gwen would have relieved him of the duty of escorting her if she could have, but she understood why Gareth didn't want her wandering about Shrewsbury on her own, and that he wouldn't have liked it even if her face wasn't so like Adeline's. "Come on." She poked at Cedric's arm.

He sighed and assented, and they left the room.

Gwen liked leaving Gareth even less than Cedric did, but Gareth was right, and she had the additional duty of checking up on Tangwen. Gwen would have brought Tangwen's nanny, Abi, on this journey, which would have meant that Tangwen would have been safe to leave for days at a time. Unfortunately, only a few days before they were to set out for Shrewsbury, Abi had received word that her mother had fallen ill and needed tending. Gwen could hardly insist that Abi neglect her mother and, after further consideration, decided that it was for the best. Abi had never been outside Gwynedd in her life—and had hardly traveled more than ten miles from Aber itself. The trip then became an opportunity for Gareth and Gwen to be together with their immediate family, just the five of them.

She and Gareth hadn't yet told anybody at Aber what the future held for them, not with the risk of miscarriage so high and the mourning still ongoing. Even if Gwen would have loved to break the somber mood that filled the great hall like smoke from burned cooking, she didn't feel it was her place to do so.

Some—Queen Cristina among them—might also have thought that Gwen's pregnancy should have precluded her coming on the journey—which was another reason Gwen hadn't said anything about it to anyone earlier. She'd had no intention of being left behind. When Gareth had taken her and Tangwen to their small house on Anglesey in February, Hywel had recalled them to Aber after a few short weeks. But even that brief absence had made her see how important it was to get Tangwen away from the grief that hung over Aber.

Once back at the monastery gate, Gwen let Cedric go, and with a grateful wave, he hastened back towards the east bridge and into Shrewsbury.

Gwen then walked into the courtyard, expecting to find her daughter and Gwalchmai there, in the guesthouse, or at the very least in the adjacent garden. A quick search revealed no sign of them, however. Before she had to quarter the entire abbey to find them, however, a monk exited the church, and the sound of Gwalchmai's tenor poured into the courtyard through the open door. Mocking herself, because she should have known he would find his way to the place with the best acoustics in Shrewsbury, she entered to see her brother standing before Abbot Radulfus himself.

Gwen hoped that Gwalchmai had asked permission before he took up his position in the center of the nave, but perhaps it didn't matter, given the abbot's rapt attention. Her brother's soprano voice had been known to make grown men cry, and even though his voice had deepened with manhood, it had lost none of its quality, timbre, or tone.

As Gwen hovered in the doorway of the church, Gwalchmai stood in the middle of the transept and filled the space with song. The abbot, meanwhile, sat on the step below the altar, Tangwen beside him, and Gwen didn't think she mistook the disguised movement that swept a tear from his cheek.

Her brother was well on his way to becoming one of the greatest bards Gwynedd—or maybe all of Wales—had ever produced. But despite that fact, and his enormous natural talent, he never allowed the adulation to go to his head. He seemed to view the act of singing in front of an audience as a service to them and to God rather than behaving, like some bards did, as if he were a lord bestowing a gift on his people.

Few professions were more celebrated in Wales than that of bard. The role cut across all classes, all types of people. This was one of the reasons that Gwen, a bard's daughter and a musician in her own right, had been allowed more freedom during her childhood and early womanhood than almost any other woman she knew. A bard could go anywhere, be forgiven anything (except maybe murder), as long as he could sing.

Gwalchmai knew all that. He'd been treated like the heir to the throne his whole life. He could have behaved like a spoiled child—or at the very least like an entitled princeling—but he did neither. He could sing for his audience of two with as much joy—more joy even—than when he'd performed the previous summer for half of Wales at Prince Hywel's festival in Ceredigion.

Gwen waited until Gwalchmai had finished his song before moving through the nave to the altar where her daughter sat. At the sight of Gwen, Tangwen toddled over to her, holding out her arms so Gwen could pick her up. Radulfus rose to his feet too, though not without a slight grunt of effort and the crack of aging knees.

"Father." Gwen bent to scoop up Tangwen.

"I have been enjoying your brother's music. It is an honor to hear such a voice raised in God's praise in my church. And for him to sing as he does in Latin—" Radulfus broke off, shaking his head, though in awe not in dismay.

"My father is the court bard for King Owain Gwynedd, and he instructed both of us," Gwen said, deciding not to take offense that Radulfus might have believed them more ignorant than they were—because they were Welsh, or just because he didn't encounter many lay people who knew Latin. "He was the first teacher to Prince Hywel of Gwynedd as well."

"I'm sorry to say that most of the brothers here do not know Latin beyond the recitations of the hours, and none of the laymen are lettered." Abbot Radulfus bent slightly at the waist. "I had no idea until now who had favored my abbey with a visit. It is our charge as God's servants to treat all who come through this abbey equally, as we are all God's creatures. And yet, it would be a waste of talent and time not to use what He has given us. I apologize for mistaking any of you for less than you are." He looked past Gwen to Gwalchmai. "It is my hope that you will sing during mass on Sunday."

"I would be honored to do so," Gwalchmai said, though his brow furrowed. "Are you sure? Nobody has ever asked me to sing during mass before."

"I am sure." Abbot Radulfus pressed his lips together in a thin line in displeasure—or maybe simple disbelief.

It was true that while bards were renowned throughout Wales, they weren't often called upon to sing in church, singing being viewed in this context as a more secular activity. Gwalchmai had become friends with Aber's new priest, a jovial man who liked his mead, who had taught Gwalchmai several hymns of praise because singing was what Gwalchmai did for fun. But even Father Elis hadn't asked Gwalchmai to sing at mass, believing it the purview of the ordained.

"Please see me in the sacristy before mass, and we can discuss the order of the service."

Gwalchmai bowed. "As you wish." He beckoned with one hand to Tangwen, who wriggled to get down from Gwen's arms in the boneless way of a two-year-old.

Gwen could hardly have continued to hold her if she'd tried, and she let Tangwen run across the floor to her uncle. They left together. Then Gwen turned back to Radulfus. "Thank you."

Radulfus didn't pretend to misunderstand. "Oh no. It is I who should be thanking you. It has been many years since I heard a voice such as his. It is my understanding from a few words he let slip that Gwalchmai used to have a surpassingly beautiful soprano."

"It is true. I wish we could have preserved it somehow, just to hear it one more time" Gwen said.

"Like a treasured vintage of wine. Yes," Radulfus said. "Wouldn't that be a feat? Alas, such is the condition of man that we cannot return to our younger selves. As it is, perhaps a child's voice is more precious, like life itself, in that it is fleeting."

Gwen smiled. "Honestly, I'm surprised my father didn't say anything to you about Gwalchmai when we arrived. He is so very proud of what Gwalchmai has become."

"As any father would be." Radulfus gestured towards the rear door, indicating that they should walk towards it. "As our Father in heaven surely is as well. But I have a feeling you did not come here to discuss your brother and his music, no matter how beautiful."

Gwen took in a breath. "No, Father. There's been a murder. Maybe even two. What's more, one of the dead men is Roger Carter, a member of Shrewsbury's town council."

"My dear, what are you saying?" Radulfus halted before the door. "Roger Carter has been murdered?"

"Strangled, I'm afraid."

"How is it you came to know of it?"

Gwen took in a quick breath. "John Fletcher, the Deputy Sheriff, has asked my husband to consult on the matter."

Radulfus rubbed his chin. "Sadly, we are no stranger to murder here, as we've witnessed several over the years, but I'm afraid that with the sheriff absent, we may be much at a loss in solving it until he returns."

"That is why my husband has become involved," Gwen said, trying not to take offense. "He has a regrettable amount of experience in that regard, and he is assisting John Fletcher with his inquiries even now." She paused, looking searchingly into the abbot's face, hoping for a sign that he understood her English, which she felt was failing her as she tried to explain. "Gareth was hoping you wouldn't mind if he sent the body here to await burial and—" She hesitated again.

"And what?" Radulfus' face remained a mask Gwen was struggling to read. It was generally accepted that the Welsh were expressive and the English impassive. Radulfus was Norman and also had noble blood. He had probably learned in his cradle how to prevent his emotions from appearing on his face.

"I am asking this of you with the idea that housing the body here would allow Gareth and John Fletcher to examine it without inconveniencing anyone or offending the family," Gwen said. "The fact that Master Carter was an important man in the town complicates matters."

"Has the family been notified?"

"Gareth and John Fletcher are doing it now," Gwen said. "Gareth sent me to you instead."

Radulfus bowed his head, pursing his lips and staring at the ground.

"I'm sorry," Gwen said. "Did you know Roger well?"

Radulfus looked up. "No. Not personally, but his family has had enough troubles this year, what with Adeline's death—" He gestured to Gwen.

"I know. I look like her."

"I'm glad you came to me. I agree that it would be best if Roger awaited burial here. His family will want to see him and to see to him, of course."

"Gareth will be discreet, I promise you," Gwen said. "His family won't have any objections to his treatment, though—" Gwen found herself pausing again.

Radulfus canted his head, waiting for her to continue

"Roger's neck is bruised," Gwen said. "Strangling is an ugly way to die, and it isn't possible to hide it."

"I will speak to Martin and his wife when they arrive and make sure they understand the severity of Roger's wounds. Perhaps a few of the brothers could take from them the burden of washing the body for burial." Radulfus' gaze was piercing. "It is kind of you to think of Roger's family. Meanwhile, I will see that a room is set aside for the body."

"Thank you," Gwen said.

Radulfus made a motion as if to suggest that the interview was over and that he intended to return to his other duties, but then he hesitated too. "Didn't you say there were two deaths?"

"The possibility of the first is what brought John Fletcher looking for Gareth this morning—except, all that we've found so far is a pool of blood and no body," Gwen said.

Radulfus studied her. "Your news grows more disturbing by the moment. I am also concerned about your continued use of the word *we*. Don't tell me that you have been a party to these events?"

"Not a party so much as an assistant to my husband in his investigation," Gwen said, and at Radulfus' continued stare, she added. "I have served Prince Hywel in that capacity for several years, alongside Gareth, of course."

Radulfus blinked, but he didn't object further, merely straightened his shoulders. "Prayers will be said for these poor souls—and those who sent them to an early grave—beginning immediately."

Gwen would have expected no less, and she was glad that Radulfus wasn't openly objecting to her participation, for now anyway. "Thank you, Father." She reached into her purse and pulled out the string of rosary beads she'd found. "Do you recognize these as belonging to one of your people?"

Radulfus took the rosary in both hands and inspected it before glancing up at Gwen. "We, as an order, decry individual possessions, but that doesn't extend to rosaries, and every monk possesses one. This is roughly made, which I would expect from a monk's rosary. Though I don't recognize it specifically, I wouldn't deny that it could belong to a member of my order. Where did you find it?"

"We discovered it in the alley where the pool of blood was found," Gwen said. "As you can see from the smoothness of the ends, if the victim lost it as he was running, it wasn't because it broke but rather because it became untied. It could also have been there for some time and wouldn't necessarily have belonged to the victim."

"Did you clean the beads before you put them in your purse?" Abbot Radulfus asked.

"Not beyond picking a few leaf scraps from between them," Gwen said, somewhat warily. "Why?"

"If the rosary had lain in the alley for some time, as you suggest, the wood and leather would have become stained, don't you think?" Radulfus gestured to Gwen herself. "You wear a gold cross on a chain. How long could it have lain in the street before dirt would have adhered to it?"

"Not long. I see now that what you said is true: you are no stranger to murder."

Radulfus gave a slight laugh. "It isn't murder I know, but rosaries."

That prompted a smile from Gwen. "Perhaps you can help me with this, too." She reached again into her purse and pulled out a sketch of Conall that Gareth had made on the guidance of the innkeeper. Gwen was inordinately proud of Gareth for his artistry, which was among the many skills he'd developed over the years on the way to bettering himself, such that he'd risen from a man-at-arms to become the captain of Prince Hywel's guard. They wouldn't know if the sketch was a good likeness, however, until they found Conall.

"Would it be possible for me to inquire among the brothers, guests, and lay workers if they've seen this man? He's

Irish, going by the name of Conall. Finding him might go a long way in helping us discover the reason for Roger Carter's death."

"He is the murderer?" Radulfus studied the image.

"Roger Carter's body was found in a room let to Conall. Although the image can't show it, he had fiery red hair, white skin, and freckles."

Radulfus grunted and handed the picture back to Gwen. "I do not know him, nor have I seen him, but if he has been staying in Shrewsbury itself, likely he would have attended mass at one of the town churches."

Gwen accepted that assessment without comment even though she personally thought it optimistic of Radulfus to think the man would have gone to any church at all. It wasn't her place to express her disbelief to an abbot, however, so she simply nodded and put the sketch away.

"I will instruct my charges to answer your questions, and I will find someone to accompany you. Brother Julian, I think," Radulfus said, "and I would appreciate it if you would keep me apprised of what you find."

"Of course, Father," Gwen said, "but I don't want to take anyone away from his duties."

"I insist," Radulfus said. "Sadly, I have loaned our one Welsh brother, with whom you could have conversed and who would have made an excellent translator, to Ludlow, to tend to the Lacy heir who is very ill."

"Perhaps before too long it won't matter," Gwen said, giving way, though she wondered if the real reason Radulfus wanted someone to accompany her was because he didn't want a woman speaking to his monks without supervision. "Gareth speaks English better than I do, and I'm hoping that with a few more days here, my speaking and comprehension will be greatly improved."

"You already speak English very well," Radulfus said.

Gwen scoffed under her breath as she walked with the abbot out of the nave and into the afternoon sun in the courtyard. "Far be it from me to accuse an abbot of speaking untruths."

Radulfus' footsteps faltered yet again, but this time when he turned to her, he was laughing.

8

Gareth

Telling a family that they'd lost a loved one was never easy, but today it was made far worse by the twitching and fidgeting that was going on in the body of John Fletcher as he walked beside Gareth towards the cartwright's yard.

Finally, when they were one street away, Gareth stopped and turned to the younger man. "Talk to me."

John pulled up. "What?"

"Don't try to pretend with me," Gareth said. "We've been through too much together in our short acquaintance for me not to realize when you are troubled by something, and I'm thinking it's more than finding Roger Carter dead—difficult as that must be for you."

John took in a deep breath. "It's my sister. I fear what the shock of Roger's death could do to her, coming hard on the heels of the loss of Adeline."

As explanations went, it was plausible, but Gareth didn't think that was all that was bothering John. Gareth studied John's face and was about to let him off the hook when John sighed and said, "I lied to you before."

Now they were getting somewhere. "About what?"

"About how I felt about Adeline," John said.

"Ah," Gareth said. "You did love her."

"I loved her my whole life," John said. "I begged my father to make an offer to her father for me, but he refused, thinking her beneath me. I didn't have the courage to defy him, and then Tom Weaver gave her to Roger."

"Did Adeline love you? Were you lying about that?"

John looked away. "No, or if she did love me, it was only as the brother of her friend. But she would have chosen me over Roger."

"And by doing so condemned you to a loveless marriage," Gareth said. "It would have been the same kind of marriage Roger would have had. Death spared Adeline that fate, as her death spared Roger, though I suspect he cared about love less than you. Your father may have forbidden the marriage for the wrong reasons, to your mind, but that doesn't mean he didn't have your best interests at heart."

John nodded, still looking away.

Gareth stepped closer and gentled his voice. "Now Roger is dead, and Adeline is dead. We found her killer, and we will find Roger's. Take comfort in your duty. We need to speak to Roger's family before the rumor of his death reaches them."

John nodded jerkily and continued walking. The cartwright's home was in the center of Shrewsbury, south of the castle and equidistant between the inn where Roger's body was found and the alley where the pool of blood had by now soaked into the earth. Gareth gave that coincidence a moment's thought and then dismissed it as inconclusive. Even for such a large town as Shrewsbury, no place could be more than a quarter of an hour's walk from anywhere else and still be within the city walls.

The cartwright's yard sat on the corner of a block on an expanse of level ground at the base of the hill upon which the castle perched. A two-story house, which was large enough to contain at least two rooms on the lower floor and possibly more than one on the upper, fronted the street. The yard was accessed by a driveway that ran between the house and the neighboring shop. At night, a wide gate would block it, but as it was during business hours, the gate was fully open.

For a business inside the town, the lot was large. But as had been made clear to Gareth, Roger Carter had been a wealthy man, and he and his brother, Martin, had a thriving business. They needed the space to house the carts and equipment necessary for their work.

"In here." John led Gareth down the driveway to the back of the house.

The yard consisted of a house to the left, which fronted the street; a small chicken run on the far side of the property; a two horse stable; a large workshop, twice the size of the house, where the actual work was done; and a similarly sized carthouse. The carthouse's double doors were open, allowing Gareth to peer inside to the rows of carts, big and small, lined up in it.

At their entrance, a man came out of the workshop, which was open on all four sides, giving Gareth a good view of the orange fire of a forge, necessary for crafting the iron rims and fittings for carts. Another man remained in its depths, a dark silhouette against the glow of the flames.

"Hello, John," the first man said, indicating to Gareth that this was Martin, Roger's brother. He was, even to Gareth's eyes, Hywel-handsome, though he looked nothing like Hywel. He had hazel eyes, unruly short brown hair, a narrow nose, and high cheekbones. Gareth would never have guessed that he and Roger were brothers, and Gareth wondered if they shared only one parent. "Jenny has gone to the market."

As Martin was married to John's sister, it made sense that he would think John was here to see her, but John made a dismissive motion with his hand. "Now that I'm here, I'm glad she isn't."

Martin's eyes went past John to Gareth and turned curious, but then he returned his gaze to his brother-in-law. "What's wrong, John?"

John took in a deep breath and seemed about to speak, but then he hesitated again and no words came out. Gareth should have realized that John had never before delivered news of a death to a loved one. He put a hand on John's shoulder and spoke to Martin. "What John is trying to tell you is that we found the body of your brother, Roger, this morning. I'm sorry, but he is dead."

"Wha—" Martin's face paled, and he stuttered as he looked from Gareth to John and back again. "What-what did you say?"

His voice, when he managed to speak, had gone high. People weren't capable of paling on command, which meant Martin's reaction was genuine. He was shocked by the discovery of his brother's body.

The man still inside the shop gave up what he was doing and approached, hesitating in the space between light and dark at the edge of the shop. "Sir?"

Martin threw out a hand, but Gareth wasn't clear on whether Martin meant for this second man to leave or to stay. The man came forward anyway, his brow furrowed. He was John's age or younger, taller and very well built, with huge arm muscles as befitted one who worked with his hands. He had intelligent brown eyes and brown hair pulled back in a thong at the base of his neck.

Gareth cleared his throat reflexively, since John still wasn't speaking. "Who are you?"

The man looked Gareth up and down—and then surprised him by answering in fluent Welsh. "Huw, Roger's and Martin's apprentice. Who are you?"

"Gareth ap Rhys, of Gwynedd."

That prompted a widening of the eyes and a quick nod that was almost a bow. "What's happened?" Huw looked from Gareth to Martin, who was gazing past John as if he didn't see him.

"Roger is dead," Gareth said shortly. "Perhaps you could tell me when you last saw him?"

Huw blinked once, pausing with his mouth open as if he was going to speak to Martin, but then turned to Gareth instead.

He spread his hands wide as he answered Gareth's question. "Yesterday evening sometime. He left me to close up."

John moved closer to Martin and found his voice enough to speak gently, "Martin, do you mind telling us when you last saw Roger?"

"Last night at supper." Martin spoke almost reflexively, and it was clear his mind was not on his answer. Then the nature and specificity of John's question seemed to hit him. "Why do you ask me that?"

John bit his lip. "Roger was murdered, Martin."

Martin's mouth made the shape as if he was going to say, "What?" again, but no sound came out.

Huw was more expressive, looking away and swearing in his native language. Then he turned back. "How?"

Gareth glanced at John to see if he was going to answer or if Gareth should, but John was in control of the interview now. "He was strangled, down at Rob Horn's Inn."

"Strangled." Martin spoke as if he didn't know the word's meaning.

"We found him in one of the rooms," John said.

Martin's brow furrowed. "How unlike him. Roger was never one to rent a room by the hour."

Huw looked at Martin with a puzzled expression on his face. Gareth didn't think the apprentice understood what Martin was implying: that the reason Roger had been at the inn was to be with a whore. That hadn't been Gareth's first, second, or third assumption, and from the quick glance John sent him, it wasn't where his mind had gone either.

Gareth was quick on the uptake though and asked, "Does Rob rent rooms by the hour?"

"No, not normally, but why else would Roger be in a room at an inn? He lives here. He would have brought any respectable woman here."

Huw took a step back, finally understanding what Martin had meant. The puzzled expression remained, but it was now accompanied by a half-smile and a head shake. Gareth had never been a merchant's apprentice, but he'd been a man-at-arms not too long ago. It was the assumption among the lower echelons of any profession that it was they, not their superiors, who best understood the workings of day-to-day life. Huw was discovering, in this case, that he didn't know as much about his masters as he'd thought.

"We assumed he'd gone to meet someone who was staying at the inn," Gareth said. "Would you know anything about that?"

Martin's eyebrows were almost to his hairline as he shook his head. "No. Nothing. He said nothing to me last night."

"To me either," Huw said, now speaking in English.

"Do you know this man?" Gareth pulled out one of the sketches he'd made of Conall. "He would have had red hair."

Martin pursed his lips as he gazed down at the image. Then he looked up at Gareth. "Did you draw this?" At Gareth's nod, he added, "You're quite good. We can always use a man like you in our line of work, because a customer likes to see what he's getting before he buys. My brother and I—"

For a moment there it seemed that Martin might be offering Gareth a position, but with his own mention of his brother, Martin broke off as his face went gray again, and he handed the sketch to Huw, who took it without speaking.

"As far as I know, this man hasn't been to the yard, is that right, Huw?" Martin said.

"Right," Huw said.

Martin nodded, as if agreement from his apprentice was a given. "But if he has red hair like you say, and he was in Shrewsbury for very long, someone is sure to remember him." He paused. "I just realized you're showing his picture to me because you think this man killed Roger."

Gareth accepted the paper from Huw and pocketed it again. "It is really too early for us to think anything. Again, I am very sorry for your loss."

"Please give my condolences to Jenny," John said. "I know that she was fond of Roger, and that he was kind to her. I'll be by later this evening to see her."

Martin nodded. "Thank you." He coughed. "Wh-where is the body?"

"Still in our custody," John said. "He's on his way to the abbey right now, and you can contact the brothers there about burial."

Another nod. "Thank you." Martin turned away.

Gareth and John did too, striding down the driveway and out into the street. Gareth didn't say anything for a dozen paces, not wanting to taint John's first impressions with his own. They headed east, towards the monastery, which John's watchmen should have reached with the body by now. After two streets, however, John pulled up. "Can I tell you what I'm thinking?"

"I hoped you would," Gareth said.

"Three things," John said. "The first is that Martin didn't say outright that he didn't recognize Conall—did you notice that?" John didn't wait for more than a nod from Gareth before continuing. "He said only that Conall hadn't come around the yard that he knew."

"Likely, that's the truth, which is why—if he is, in fact, lying about knowing Conall—he tried to distract me by complementing me on the drawing." Gareth jerked his chin. "What's the second thing?"

"There's not a lot of sadness inside Martin at the loss of his brother, is there? He looked ashen when we told him, but he was all business afterwards and almost offered you a job. That isn't the act of a grief-stricken man." John's eyebrows lifted for an instant and he flashed a brief, satisfied smile. "For whatever reason, Martin knows more than he's telling."

"And the third?"

"I know for a fact that Roger beat his apprentice, and yet, to my eyes Huw expressed more concern at his death than Martin did."

"I am hardly the man to instruct another in how to grieve, but I think you're right on all three counts." Gareth clapped a hand on John's shoulder. "We'll make a sleuth of you yet."

9

Gwen

Showing Conall's image to the various monks and lay workers at the abbey was something Gwen could do with Tangwen by her side. Shrewsbury Abbey was laid out in a pattern similar to other monasteries Gwen had visited over the years, though she had the sense that the Abbey of St. Peter and St. Paul was more prosperous than many—if not all—abbeys in Wales.

It had been built of red sandstone at the end of the last century, as had the castle, and had been expanded upon since then to include the multitude of buildings and extensive grounds it owned today. The church was magnificent enough for an archbishop's seat: the guest house and monks' quarters were large, with big windows that faced south to take advantage of whatever warmth the sun offered; and the gardens were well kept and fruitful. It was peaceful here too, with a little brook that gurgled by as it headed towards the Severn River.

With the picture of Conall in one hand and the rosary beads in another, Gwen trailed around the abbey for nearly an hour with Brother Julian, a bright young novice in his early twenties, a few years younger than Gwen. They fell into a pattern where Julian would introduce her, explain what she was doing, and then Gwen would show the man in question the rosary and the sketch. From cooks to laborers to monks in the scriptorium, everyone was polite and wanted to be helpful, except that nobody could. The people she encountered were also, without exception, men. If not for the abbot's countenance, she couldn't have spoken to any of them.

"How about you?" Gwen said to Julian. "Are you ever given permission to enter the town?"

"Every now and then. You must understand that I was raised here. The abbey is my home, and I have never known life outside it."

"You're a foundling?" Gwen had heard of such a thing, but as a bard's daughter, and then a knight's wife, Gwen had traveled the length and breadth of Wales and couldn't imagine staying in one place always. The very thought gave her the shudders. Being a woman, even a spy and a sleuth, she also hadn't had a great deal of experience with monastic men.

"My mother left me on the doorstep a few days after my birth," Julian said. "One of the women in the Abbey Foregate became my nurse."

"I don't mean to imply any sort of criticism, but are you ... happy being a monk?" Gwen said. "You don't want some other kind of life for yourself—a wife and children, for instance?"

Julian smiled and gestured expansively with one arm to indicate the whole of the abbey. "I work. I am useful. I serve God.

What more could I want? Besides, a man like me doesn't just find himself a wife, you know. I have no land, no money, and no profession beyond the labor I do here."

"And what is that labor?" Gwen said.

"I work in the scriptorium," Julian said.

"So you're lettered!" Gwen said. "You could work for a lord or help merchants with accounting."

They had been walking along a pathway in the garden. The day had continued fine to the point that Gwalchmai had taken Tangwen to wade in the brook. Gwen could hear Tangwen's squeal of delight in the distance. Even if she couldn't see her daughter, Gwen knew she was safe in Gwalchmai's hands.

Now, Julian stopped and gazed at her with something close to a condescending smile. "And how would that be better than what I have here? My family is here."

That Gwen could understand. She bowed her head. "I know I was prying. I'm sorry if I offended you."

"I am not offended." His serenity reminded her very much of Abbot Radulfus.

It wasn't until she'd questioned twenty men that she hit upon the first one, a lay worker who labored in the fields for the abbey, who could tell them something they didn't already know. "Aye, I seen 'em."

Julian was skeptical. "You're sure, Al?"

"Red hair like that? Hard to miss, especially on a sturdy fellow who's a stranger. I was working in the fields near the mill race when I saw him ride past not three days ago, coming down the road from Atchem. Fine horse he had too." Al lifted his chin to point to a stand of trees to the southeast of their position. "It was just past the abandoned mill yonder."

Gwen couldn't see a mill, abandoned or otherwise, from where she stood, but the landscape was more treed and hillier in that direction. She hadn't realized the abbey lands were so extensive.

She also hadn't thought to ask at Rob's inn about a horse, though as a traveler come all the way from Ireland, it made sense that Conall would have ridden here. Maybe Gareth had remembered to ask the innkeeper about it after she left. That Conall had come down the east road also meant that whoever was on guard at the gatehouse three days ago might also recognize her sketch.

Red hair wasn't unknown among either the Welsh or the English, but given the very similar reactions of both Rob and this lay worker, Conall's coloring was still uncommon enough for people to notice and comment upon.

"Thank you. You've been very helpful." Gwen made to turn away, but the laborer stopped her.

"Was that your brother I heard singing earlier?"

"It was," she said.

"I could hear more of that," he said. "A real gift, he has. My mother was Welsh. Been a while since I heard a real bard. These Saxons don't know how to sing."

Gwen smiled. "The abbot asked that Gwalchmai sing in the church on Sunday. You can hear him again then."

The man pointed with his chin to where Gwalchmai was now gamboling among the garden paths with Tangwen. "All I have to do is stay here, I think. He'll break into song soon enough."

Then Julian tugged on Gwen's elbow, indicated she should look towards the entrance to the monastery where Gareth and John Fletcher had finally arrived. From the end of the path where they were standing, Gwen could just see the main courtyard. A cart was parked half out of her sight, and she assumed it had brought Roger's body to the abbey.

Despite her husband's arrival, Gwen continued her questioning of the abbey residents, fruitless as the rest of the afternoon turned out to be. She didn't seek Gareth out until the examination of Roger's body had to be nearly finished. She hadn't needed a warning look from Gareth to know that she didn't want to be present for it, not only as a balm to the sensibilities of the monks—though Radulfus seemed like an eminently reasonable man—but for the sake of her stomach.

Over the last few weeks, Gwen found herself with a growing sympathy for her friend, Mari, who'd birthed two sons within as many years of marriage. Having witnessed twice what Mari had endured for nine months, Gwen comforted herself with the knowledge that her ability to stand upright and retain the contents of her stomach at this moment was better than any day Mari had experienced while pregnant.

Besides, Gwen was overjoyed to find herself with child again. In the aftermath of Rhun's death, she'd thought she was pregnant, but it had only been the same sickness that had laid

King Owain low. She'd recovered much more quickly than the king had, however, and must have fallen pregnant sometime around the Christmas feast, which meant the baby would arrive in early autumn.

Having finished her quest for now, she said goodbye to Julian, who headed off purposefully towards the scriptorium, and Gwen made her way back to the courtyard. She had just entered it when Gareth exited the doorway that led to the cloister, John Fletcher beside him.

Gwen hastened to them. "How did it go?"

John raised his shoulders and let them fall. "We told Martin Carter, Roger's brother, of his death."

To Gwen's eyes, both John and Gareth were looking drawn and worn, which she could understand given the tasks they'd undertaken.

"I just spoke with the abbot," Gareth added. "He promised to send word to Martin that he could see the body now. What did you discover?"

Gwen told him about the day laborer's belief that he'd seen Conall enter Shrewsbury three days ago.

John nodded. "I will speak to whomever was on duty as soon as I leave here. Maybe someone saw him depart the city too."

"Did the innkeeper mention Conall's horse?" Gwen said.

"I did ask before we left," Gareth said. "He had a horse, and it is still there."

Gwen bit her lip.

"Yes. Odd." As he spoke, Gareth was turning something over in his fingers.

Gwen looked down at his hand. "What do you have there?"

"Oh." Gareth clenched whatever it was in his fist, as if it was occurring to him only now that Gwen might be interested in what he'd discovered. He glanced ruefully at John, and then opened his hand to show her. "It's a wooden coin."

Frowning, Gwen took the coin from his palm. "Was it on Roger's body?"

"Actually, no. It turns out that Conall left a few belongings behind—a small bag he'd placed underneath the bed at its foot—and this was in it."

She turned the coin over in her hand. "What is its purpose?" It had an etching of a woman on one side and a shoe on the other. As she peered closer at the etching, she realized that the woman wore no clothing. Gareth still hadn't answered, so she looked up at him. "What don't you want to tell me?"

"This is a coin to gain entry into an establishment called *The Lady's Slipper*." Gareth sighed. "It's a brothel, *cariad*."

10

Hywel

Hywel cupped his hands around his eyes, shielding them from the glare caused by the setting sun behind him. Mold Castle would be his within the hour, and Hywel was roiled by a stew of emotions—jubilation, anticipation, as well as the anger that never left him. They were within days of the official end of the four month peace he'd agreed to with Ranulf, the Earl of Chester, and that was close enough for him. He was finished with the *enduring* he'd been doing since Rhun's death.

His father might never recover from Rhun's loss. Hywel might never either. But this—this battle—was one thing he knew how to do.

"Fire!"

Hywel and his next oldest brother, Cynan, sent the shout into the sky at the same time from opposite ends of the field. Cynan was with the cavalry, who were waiting in a stand of trees at the foot of the road that led to the castle.

A heartbeat later, the arrows from two hundred archers' bows arced through the air and disappeared over the castle's battlements.

At nearly the same instant that the archers loosed the arrows, a handpicked group of some of the bravest men Hywel had, Cynan's younger brother, Madoc, among them, moved the siege engine forward, driving it up the road towards the gate. They were protected front and back by shields and wooden barricades, designed to deflect any enemy arrows that might come from the walls, and to prevent their own men from killing them from behind with stray arrows.

Hywel wished he had a way to communicate with Madoc and Cynan, but he had to trust that his brothers knew what they were doing. The trees in which Cynan and his men were hiding lay a hundred yards from the castle, and the cavalry were waiting for the moment the gate was battered down to charge. The bulk of the army Hywel had brought to Mold were spearmen, and they remained as they had been, crouched low to the ground in front of Hywel and his archers, also making sure to keep out of their direct line of fire.

Hywel's army had been given four months to stockpile arrows, and his archers did him proud now. They fired barrage after barrage at Mold Castle, successfully forcing Ranulf's soldiers to keep their heads below the level of the wooden balustrade, unable to counter the steady progress of Hywel's siege weapon.

Hywel could have ordered the arrows to be lit, but that would have defeated half the purpose of this endeavor. His father wanted Mold Castle taken intact, so he could fortify it against the English. Hywel would burn it to the ground if he had to—if he were desperate and it was the only way to win it—but he was a long way from desperate just yet.

"The door is weakening, my lord!" Cadell, the youngest of Hywel's brothers currently on the battlefield, reined in beside Hywel, his eyes wild with excitement and anticipation of victory. He was smaller and slighter than Hywel and his other older brothers, and now that he was past twenty, wasn't likely to grow more.

"I'm glad to hear it, Cadell." Hywel secretly thought that Earl Ranulf, whose castle this was, had known Hywel was coming and had made a strategic decision to put up only a token resistance, so as not to waste men and resources on a lost cause. But Hywel wasn't going to ruin Cadell's pleasure by telling him so.

Maybe Ranulf really had all but abandoned Mold to Hywel. Maybe they could have walked right into the castle without any bloodshed at all. Hywel hadn't wanted to risk that, however, and neither had any of his brothers. Hywel hadn't even shown a flag of peace that would have offered terms to the castellan of Mold. They'd come too far and suffered too much since Rhun's death to be satisfied with taking the castle without a fight.

Rhun couldn't be avenged today, and it wasn't the Earl of Chester who'd seen to his death, but ensuring the fall of Mold Castle to an army from Gwynedd was as good a place to start as any.

"I wish I was with Madoc!" Cadell was still circling around Hywel, restless energy in every line of his body.

He had begged earlier to be in the siege engine, but Hywel had forbidden it. Hywel understood Cadell's excitement, just as he understood his need to be in the thick of things. If they'd been fighting on an open field, both of them would have been at the forefront of the cavalry, but sieges weren't the purview of a commander, and Hywel's men would have been more hindered than helped by his presence. They would have felt the need to protect him. It was one of the many changes in his life since Rhun's death and his rise to the station of heir to the throne of Gwynedd.

Thus, it was Hywel's fate as *edling*, and Cadell's as his squire, to let others do the fighting today.

"This is the first real battle you've ever been in," Hywel said soothingly. "It is better to learn by watching this one time. You have plenty of wars in your future."

"You were younger than I am when you fought in your first battle!" Cadell threw the words at his brother.

Hywel didn't take offense. "We were fighting for our lives in Ceredigion, Cadell. My aunt had just been hanged from the battlements by the Normans. Any man who could walk was on the field that day."

"Rhun died—"

"He did, but not by Ranulf's hand, and Ranulf does not threaten Gwynedd today. This is a skirmish," Hywel said. "Perhaps

I should have let you fight, to get your feet wet, but I thought it would be foolish to risk you in such a little war."

Cadell subsided, perhaps slightly mollified. Hywel wished he could see better what was happening, and he stood in his stirrups, both hands shielding his eyes.

Then, without further ado, the front gate collapsed in on itself and, with a roar, Madoc's company surged forward, past their siege engine and into the castle. Up until now, the archers had been aiming over their heads so the arrows would fall inside the castle. Hywel released a piercing whistle, and the firing ceased.

That was also the signal for the waiting cavalry to break cover. They charged up the road, anxious to support the brave souls who'd broken through the gate. The spearmen who'd been resting in front of the archers surged to their feet too and ran straight for the castle entrance. Not a single arrow came from Mold's battlement. Perhaps Ranulf really didn't have anyone able to fire one.

Hywel let them all go before urging Glew, his horse, into a trot, Cadell at his side. The younger man's brown hair was mussed, and he'd taken off his helmet somewhere along the way. At this point, Hywel didn't think it mattered what Cadell wore. Neither of them was even going to have to use their swords.

"Should I send word of the victory to the king?" Cadell said, looking around to see who was available to send. All of Owain's sons had reverted to formality when referring to their father these days. He had made himself unapproachable—even—and maybe especially—to Hywel, as if it was somehow Hywel's fault that Rhun had died.

Hywel blamed himself for Rhun's death, it was true. He should have been the one to ride after Cadwaladr that day. But at the same time, Hywel knew within his heart that to blame anyone other than Cadwaladr was to deny Rhun's right to act on his own behalf. Rhun had demanded the responsibility of hunting down Cadwaladr. There had never been anything Hywel could have done or said to dissuade him, and no amount of wishing was going to change the past.

"Let's make sure the castle is really ours, first," Hywel said, finding himself amused rather than annoyed by his younger brother's enthusiasm.

Another half-hour, and the standard of Gwynedd waved from the top of the keep, proclaiming that Mold Castle had been taken in a single day—in a single hour—by the forces of King Owain. Hywel told himself to remember this day, to remind his future self what could be achieved with enough time and planning.

It had taken four months to reach this moment: four months of heartache, grief, and rage, such that often Hywel didn't know where one emotion ended and another began.

He did know, however, even as he rode through the demolished front gate, that he'd been lucky. Only a few weeks ago, on the last day of February, Prince Henry, the son of Empress Maud and the rival to the throne of England, had landed a thousand men on England's east coast. Naturally, King Stephen had marshalled an army to counter the young prince's force.

Once Earl Ranulf's spies had reported the landing, Ranulf had taken Stephen's occupation with Henry as an opportunity to march an army of his own across England to besiege Lincoln Castle, which King Stephen had taken from him earlier in the war, back when Ranulf was playing both sides against the middle.

Hywel had lost track of how many times Ranulf had shifted his support from Maud to Stephen and back again in the last ten years. Now, however, Ranulf had forsworn all allegiance to any side but his own. If Earl Robert, Empress Maud's general and half-brother, hadn't been weakened by illness, Ranulf might have found himself fighting both Stephen's forces and Maud's at the same time. As it was, both sides appeared to have decided to treat him like a particularly annoying gnat, to be swatted at but not squashed.

Not yet, anyway.

In turn, Hywel, who'd simply been waiting to attack Mold until the ending of the peace between Gwynedd and Chester, had force-marched his own men across Gwynedd. They'd crossed the Clwyd Mountains yesterday, learned that many of the castle's defenders had been called away east, and decided not to wait another day to take the castle. Because they weren't quite at the end of the four-month peace period, Hywel hadn't notified Lord Morgan of his presence—though surely he knew of it by now—and the only men in his company were those he'd brought from Aber. It seemed somehow fitting, since it was their hearts that had been broken.

They'd assembled the siege engine, the pieces of which they'd hauled from Denbigh in carts, and begun the assault, knowing that this evening's descending sun would be shining in the defenders' eyes.

And, at last, he had a victory to share with his father.

Cynan came forward to hold the horse's bridle while Hywel dismounted in the courtyard of the castle. Cynan's younger brother, Madoc, was there too. The two brothers were built similarly—squat and muscular—but with opposite coloring, Cynan being light to Madoc's dark.

Once Hywel was on the ground, Cynan tipped his head to indicate the English soldiers, who were all that was left of the garrison, standing off to one side. "What should we do with them, brother?"

"Strip them of their gear and send them home to Chester on foot," Hywel said, without even stopping to think about his answer. He'd taken the castle, which was what he'd wanted and needed. Killing men who'd surrendered was unnecessary in this instance.

In addition, Ranulf had left only twenty men behind to garrison Mold. The eight who'd fallen were just the latest casualties in the ongoing war. If Hywel guessed right, from the look of the dozen men before him, Ranulf had left these few here because they were his least competent soldiers—the oldest and the youngest, the unfit for duty or the drunk. None of the men were worth ransoming, and they would cost Hywel more to feed than they'd be worth in ransom, even if Ranulf would consider it.

"What are our losses?" Hywel asked Cynan.

"Four, my lord." Cynan couldn't keep the grin off his face. "Four. Bards will sing of this day for generations to come."

Hywel smiled too. "I will sing of it myself."

But then Cynan's brow furrowed, and he lowered his voice. "There is one thing, Hywel. I am loath to mar our victory, but Madoc found something in the castellan's quarters I think you should see."

"No gold, I assume," Hywel said.

Cynan shook his head. "We didn't expect it. Ranulf stripped Mold of everything valuable before he took his men east. No, it isn't that." He still hesitated, whatever was bothering him held on the tip of his tongue.

Hywel knew his brother better than he had four months ago. For the whole of Hywel's life, he and Rhun had been natural allies. While they'd been different in some ways as two brothers could be, they had also been born two years apart to the same mother. They'd been blood brothers in fact and life, and for Hywel the loss of Rhun had affected him as if he'd cut off his right hand and left it on the ground at the ambush site.

These other brothers—Cynan, Madoc, and Cadell—though relatively close in age to Hywel, hadn't been part of his life until recently. He was far closer to his foster brothers—seven of them— the sons of his foster father, Cadifor. Some of them were also here, called to Hywel's side since Rhun's death. Initially, Hywel had sent for them because he couldn't bear to let any brother out of his sight, and then afterwards, he'd used them with intent.

Hywel, who had spent his life sniffing out intrigue among his father's enemies could smell it now among his allies. They saw weakness in the king, and even if King Owain had loosened hold on his mind and the reins of Gwynedd, Hywel himself was by no means willing to let go.

Hywel and Cynan had ridden together to oust their uncle from his lands in Meirionnydd, and then—unable to bear the silence at Aber—Hywel had ridden south to Ceredigion to see Mari and his children and to bring them north with him when he returned, installing them at Rhun's former castle of Dolwyddelan. Throughout, Cynan had never left his side.

He wasn't Rhun, but he was doing his level best to be the brother Hywel needed. Despite Hywel's grief and an underlying resentment of anyone who tried to fill Rhun's shoes, Hywel was grateful.

Hywel himself was trying to do the same thing for his father, and he knew that he too was failing.

"Spit it out, Cynan."

"It is a letter from the Sheriff of Shrewsbury to King Stephen." Madoc stepped forward from where he'd been talking to Cadifor. "Ranulf appears to have intercepted it—and very recently. It's dated this month."

Hywel held out a hand to take the paper Madoc presented, even as the grave expressions on all three of the men who faced him had him feeling very wary. He looked down at the paper. To his dismay, his eyes swam with tears. He blinked them back. Hywel didn't know if Madoc saw his distress, but he continued to speak, telling Hywel what was in the letter so he didn't have to read it.

"It says that Cadwaladr was seen in the vicinity of Shrewsbury on St. Dafydd's Day, though the sheriff calls it the first of March. He describes in detail the events of last November and asks for guidance as to how he should proceed, since he doesn't know if the king intends to shelter Cadwaladr or return him to Gwynedd for justice."

Hywel's eyes had cleared as Madoc had been talking, and he was able to read the words for himself. Hywel's comprehension of written English wasn't good, but this had been written in Latin.

He looked up. "How far is it to Shrewsbury from here?"

"Fifty miles by road," Cynan said. "But surely you're not thinking of going? The men are tired."

"The men may be tired, and deservedly so. But I am not—and I shouldn't take an army into England anyway," Hywel said, making an instant decision. "You and Madoc need to stay and consolidate our victory. I will ride with Cadell and a handful of men. We can make better time that way."

His brothers now looked so concernedly at Hywel, it was almost comical. Hywel tried to suppress his smile at the sight.

Then Cadifor stepped forward. "My lord, I offer my services."

Now Hywel smirked, whatever anxiety he'd felt earlier at the mention of Cadwaladr completely dissipated at the sight of his foster father's craggy but earnest face. "I accept your offer—but not from anyone else." He looked with fondness at his family, warmth overtaking the anger for once. It was such a foreign emotion that he almost didn't recognize it for the love it was. "Don't worry about me. I'll bring ten men, including Evan and Gruffydd, just in case. Besides, Gareth is in Shrewsbury, remember? He knows how to keep me in line."

Cynan's expression actually cleared a little at the reminder, and now Hywel really did laugh out loud. They trusted Gareth more than they did him, as well they might. His brothers had probably spent some time every day during the last four months on their knees, thanking God that Hywel hadn't yet behaved rashly in his desire to bring his uncle to justice.

As much as Hywel would have liked to have done exactly that, his family was wrong in thinking that he couldn't contain his anger. He was a realist, and he knew that he was hampered by two inconvenient truths. The first was that he didn't know exactly where his uncle was and was having difficulty finding out. Cadwaladr didn't appear to be anywhere in Wales; Hywel's Danish spy, Erik, had found no sign of him so far in Dublin or Ireland; and Hywel's spy network in the March and England was sadly deficient.

And secondly, his father was at peace with both King Stephen of England and Robert of Gloucester. If Cadwaladr had sought sanctuary with either party, despite Hywel's personal desires, he had sense enough not to jeopardize that peace with ill-considered action.

Like a cat stalking his prey or a snake lurking in the grass, Hywel could bide his time, waiting for the opportune moment. And then he would strike.

11

Gareth

"This was in his bag?" Gwen turned the coin over in her fingers.

"It was," Gareth said, "which immediately begs the question—why didn't Conall use the coin or take the bag with him after he murdered Roger? He cleaned the room, so why leave the bag?"

"It isn't the obvious answer," Gwen said, "but it's been what I've been thinking: what if Conall didn't kill Roger?"

"Then he shouldn't know that Roger is dead," John said, "which means he should have come back for his bag."

"Maybe he returned to the inn while we were there, and one of the workers told him what had happened. He preferred to abandon his possessions rather than face watchmen in a strange town who would be suspicious of any stranger."

"John and I questioned the workers," Gareth said, with a glance at John, who nodded. "None had seen Conall since yesterday morning when he left the inn."

"Then I have no answer." Gwen held up the coin. "But at least we have a place to start asking questions."

"Where would that be?" Gareth said, though he had a sinking feeling he knew what his wife was going to say next.

"The brothel," Gwen said, as if it was obvious.

John jeered. "You? In a brothel?"

Gareth put a heavy hand on John's shoulder, hoping to get him to tone down his outrage. After they'd found the coin, John had expressed astonishment to Gareth that he would even consider allowing Gwen to accompany them. Had they been in Wales, Gareth would have taken her with him as a matter of course. But then, had they been in Wales, they wouldn't have been investigating a brothel either.

The lack of brothels wasn't because men were any more virtuous in Wales, but because families tended to be more closely tied together among themselves and to their lord. It was a rare woman who could fall through the cracks like these whores must have done. Because of those connections, and the way everybody knew so much about everybody else, Gareth was having a hard time picturing any family—or any girl—so desperate that a father would think selling her to a brothel was the only option. Or, furthermore, would be allowed to.

Even the camp followers who'd traveled with the army last year didn't sell themselves in the same way. Most had men with whom they were associated, even if they hadn't married them. And since illegitimacy was no disgrace in Wales, a child wouldn't be rejected by his father just because he was a bastard.

John still looked amused and horrified at the same time, but at Gwen's sudden fierce look, Gareth said in a gentle voice, "It is the one place in the entirety of Shrewsbury you cannot go."

"Why not?" Gwen said.

"You are a lady, the wife of a knight, even if you are Welsh," John said. "Surely you can see how uncomfortable your presence would make everyone feel."

Gwen made an exasperated sound. "You can't be serious. I investigate murder!"

"Not in any of Shrewsbury's brothels," John said.

Gwen was still looking daggers at the deputy sheriff, but Gareth had questioned John about this before, and it seemed there was no arguing with him. So instead, he tried to deflect them both. "You're saying that there's more than one brothel in Shrewsbury?"

John rolled his eyes. "And she can't enter any of them."

Gareth shook his head. "That's not what I meant. Shrewsbury is a market town, with a charter from the king. All commerce is controlled, which means the brothels are under the authority of the town council. They have strict hours of operation, and only single men are supposed to frequent them. So ... technically, I'm not supposed to enter one either."

"Are those rules enforced?" Gwen said.

"They are supposed to be enforced by the Council," John said, his expression clearing as they moved on from the more delicate subject of Gwen's participation, "not by the castle, which would become involved only if lawbreaking occurred."

"Like, for example, murder," Gwen said.

John made a noncommittal noise in the back of his throat. "The Council is mindful of the need to contain what goes on in the brothels and to enforce certain restrictions. If it passes ordinances that are too restrictive, however, the proprietor might simply close the business and open it somewhere else, out of the Council's reach."

Gareth nodded. "It is my understanding that in other places brothel owners have been known to move beyond the limits of the town. Wales is only seven miles away, and laws there are very different."

"Has money exchanged hands, then, between the owner of this brothel and the Council or the sheriff?" Gwen said.

Gareth had been thinking that such an exchange might be more normal than not, but at the shocked look on John's face, he realized that wasn't the case.

"Of course not!" John said. "What do you take us for here?"

Gwen put out an appeasing hand. "I'm sorry. I'm very sorry, but I felt I had to ask, and by your reaction, I'm glad I did."

For a moment John looked as if he was going to stalk away and not accept Gwen's apology. This conversation had started badly, and Gareth didn't want it to end badly too. He clapped a hand on John's shoulder. "What Gwen just did is what we do when we interview people during an investigation. Your unguarded response—angry as it was—revealed the truth far more than a considered straight denial ever could have done."

John settled back on his heels, his expression clearing. He even managed a laugh. "That was well done." He bowed to Gwen.

"Remind me to let you interrogate all my suspects before I let my men at them."

Gwen laughed. "See—this is why you need to include me when you visit the brothel."

"To continue—" John took in a breath, seemingly determined to ignore Gwen's quip, "—laws outside of Shrewsbury are very different and enforced differently. The sheriff's writ runs through the whole of Shropshire, but he is under the authority of the Earl of Ludlow, who has no mind to prevent any legal commerce in his lands, as long as the businesses pay tax to him."

"Brothels are allowed in most places, as long as upstanding citizens can continue to pretend they don't exist," Gareth said. "If a brothel is prosperous, I could even see the earl encouraging the proprietor to move it from Shrewsbury, from which he receives no taxes, to the countryside."

"One here already has." John gestured to the coin still in Gwen's hand. "This coin grants admittance to two brothels: the one I told you about by the west gate, and also to one to the west of Shrewsbury, both owned by the same people. The one outside the town is called *The Dancing Girl*." Then his brow furrowed. "Come to think on it, the one in town isn't far from where we found the pool of blood."

"Nothing in Shrewsbury is far from that pool of blood," Gareth said.

John shrugged. "The brothel outside the town is less convenient for patrons. But, as you say, it has the benefit of being beyond the council's jurisdiction."

"And this coin could be used to enter either of them?" Gareth said.

John nodded. "Conall still had it, though, so he may never have visited either one."

"Or he could have bought it for a repeat visit." Gareth held out his hand to Gwen, who gave the coin back to him, though clearly with some reluctance. "We won't know until we show his picture around and ask."

"I still don't see why I can't come with you." Gwen's hands were on her hips. "Do you really think the women who work there are going to talk to you more than they would talk to me?"

Gareth studied his wife before answering. John was horrified at the thought of her visiting a brothel, which for all his explanations, Gareth thought was more a gut response rather than a rational assertion. Gwen was a married woman, soon to be the mother of two children. John knew she investigated murders and, surely, whatever went on in a brothel was no worse than standing over Roger's dead body this morning. Still, John was determined to prevent her from coming with them, whether or not he was justified in doing so, and Gareth didn't feel he was in a position to overrule him.

"I don't know," Gareth said, finally. "John is right that whores tend to avoid respectable women because they feel they are being judged."

Gwen wrinkled her nose at him. "Which they usually are."

"In which case, speaking to a man would be more normal for them," John said, looking pleased with this sudden conclusion.

"For now, let Gareth and me do this. If our luck fails us, I promise I will consider other options."

"We should go right now," Gareth said. "The trail will never be warmer than it is at this moment."

But before John could agree or Gwen could protest further at being left out of the investigation, Cedric appeared, his expression grave, loped towards them from the gatehouse, and came to a panting halt in front of John.

Gareth bent his head, knowing what was coming.

"We found the body of a woman in the river."

John raised his eyebrows at Gareth and Gwen. They both shrugged as their only response and started towards the gatehouse.

Cedric actually looked disappointed that his news had caused neither surprise nor consternation—but simply resignation at the inevitable. But then, like the good soldier he was, he hustled after them to lead them to the body.

Gareth had figured it was only a matter of time until they found the body associated with the pool of blood. As he kept insisting, and murderers kept not realizing until it was too late, bodies weren't so easy to get rid of.

For one thing, they were heavy. Once a person was dead, his body made a very awkward burden for a single man, no matter how strong that man was or how small the body. Two, there were few good places to leave a corpse where it wouldn't ever be found and the murder discovered.

In his time, Gareth had seen murderers try to get rid of
bodies by, among other things, burying them, dropping them in a
pond, and leaving them to desiccate inside an abandoned house,
just to name a few instances. Eventually the bodies were found,
and the murderer caught. Maybe it was hubris on Gareth's part to
think he was good at his job, and perhaps dozens of people whose
bodies hadn't ever been discovered had gone missing in Gwynedd
in recent years, but Gareth didn't think so.

To Gareth's mind, making a body difficult to dispose of was
God's way of allowing justice to be done, even if it was many years
after the fact.

When they arrived at the riverbank to the south of the
town, two watchmen were in the process of wading in the shallows
off the north bank of the Severn River, soaking themselves to the
waist. At a nod from John, they grasped the body and lifted it.
With the slow meander here, once the body had begun to float, it
had caught on a branch hidden just below the surface of the water
and hung there.

All dead bodies had a nasty tendency to float to the surface
eventually. Given the blood in the alley, this girl had been dead
before she went in and chances were she'd never sunk at all. The
river hadn't been the easy place to dispose of the body that the
murderer had thought it.

"Look at all the blood on her skirt, Gareth," Gwen said.

Gareth breathed deeply through his nose and let it out. The
murder of a woman set Gareth's teeth on edge—though the

murder of a child would have been far worse. He was grateful he'd so far been spared such a death.

Gwen seemed far more matter-of-fact about the dead woman than Gareth, and even made a motion as if to move down the bank towards the men carrying the body. Gareth put out a hand to stop her. "Stay back, Gwen."

If nothing else, he didn't want her to slip on the wet grass and mud and land on her back. She was with child, and sometimes she acted before she thought. Earlier, Gwen's arrival in the alley had raised some eyebrows among John's men, but they hadn't balked at her presence, and they weren't now either. Maybe they thought women investigators were an odd peculiarity of the Welsh. Gareth himself didn't care what they thought, but John's authority was tenuous enough without having additional questions asked about his judgement. Gareth had brought Gwen because he wanted her there, but he didn't have to flaunt that fact in front of these Englishmen.

She glanced at him and nodded, stepping behind him and allowing him to be the one to haul the body up the bank instead of her.

Gareth glanced at Cedric. "Who found her?"

"One of the town boys we sent to look along the river," Cedric said. "Someone would have seen her soon enough, seeing how she was bobbing up and down in the shallows."

Gareth was impressed. "That was a clever idea. Good for you to have the foresight to send them."

Cedric gestured to John. "It wasn't my idea. It was his."

"Here we all grow up with the river. It's the lifeblood of the town, and these boys are in and out of the river all day long." John shrugged, though Gareth could tell he was pleased with Gareth's praise. "Especially with the warm spring we've been having, they can't stay away. I remembered our conversation from this winter about disposing of dead bodies and thought that if the murderer tried to get rid of the body from the alley that way, we might find her quickly if we looked hard enough. Though—" he amended, "I didn't know it was a her then."

Gareth put his hands on his knees and bent to look more closely at the woman, who the watchmen had settled face up in the grass. Gwen looked with him, and said, after a moment, "Back at the inn, I wondered if Roger's murderer could be a local man because of how the body was oriented east to west. This implies local knowledge too."

"We have no indication that this girl is connected to Roger," John said.

Gwen shot him a wry look. "When was the last murder you had in Shrewsbury?"

John rubbed his nose with his palm. "Adeline, I suppose, though she didn't die here. Before that—it's been a year at least."

"In that case, it's hard to believe that two in one day could be a coincidence," Gwen said.

"We should assume nothing as yet," Gareth said, feeling like he was mediating between them again.

John glanced around somewhat furtively. The two watchmen who'd removed the body from the river had been dismissed to find dry clothes, and the others who'd come to watch had moved away to control the few onlookers—or simply because they felt uncomfortable with a dead woman on the ground. At the moment, there was nobody within hearing distance but Cedric, Gareth, and Gwen. "Perhaps we have a third murder to consider. We can't be sure that this girl is connected to the blood either."

"I grant you that we can't be sure yet about her connection to Roger, not without even knowing her name, but—" With a heavy heart, Gareth moved into a crouch beside the girl's body. It wasn't that she looked like anyone he knew—praise the Lord—but simply that now he was really looking at her, he saw how young she was. From her unlined face and hands, she was more a girl than a woman. "—we can determine easily if the blood was hers by finding a wound."

The girl's skirt was stained with blood, but even more, it had been jaggedly ripped, as had the girl's underskirt. Pulling the fabric aside revealed a gruesome gash in her upper thigh, the tissue mangled and torn, with the remains of splintered wood still in it. It gave Gareth the shivers just looking at it. "I don't think you need to concern yourself that there's been a third murder, John."

John moved closer to Gareth, his expression pained. "The crate slat from the alley—"

Gareth nodded. "A major avenue for blood flows just below the surface right where she was wounded. When a cart overturned in a river last year and I lost my belongings, one of the men went with it. He fell on the rough corner of the cart bed as it splintered on hidden stones beneath the water's surface and bled out before we could get to him."

"That's horrible." Gwen's shoulders convulsed with the same shiver that had gone through Gareth, and her eyes were sad. "No wonder she bled so much."

"That means that whoever killed her and dumped her in the river knows something about the human body," John said.

Gareth put a hand on Gwen's shoulder and squeezed. "We'll find him."

"I almost don't want to." Gwen shook her head. "He must be as cold as Cadwaladr inside."

"We should get her to the monastery," John said. "She can lie in the room with Roger until her burial. Hopefully, we will have a name for her by then."

Gwen felt at the cloth of the girl's dress. "Her dress might have been pretty before the river water spoiled it and leached the color."

"She was a pretty girl." Gareth stood and looked north, his hand shading his eyes as he inspected the course of the river. The Severn River meandered as it flowed, such that it passed the west gate going south, looped around Shrewsbury and the fields adjacent to the town—common land for the production of fruits and vegetables in small plots, each worked by a family in the town—and then turned north.

At that point, it flowed under the east gate bridge and past the castle on its eastern side, before finally turning east again. After leaving Shrewsbury, the Severn continued to meander north and south in long circular loops for many miles until it straightened out somewhat in its ultimate journey south to the sea.

"If the girl ended up here, near the southernmost point of the river," Gareth said, "she would have gone in the water somewhere upstream, likely near the west gate, which wasn't far from where the pool of blood was found."

"I will make sure my men pay special heed to activity or footprints by the river along that side," John said.

"I don't understand how the murderer got her out of the town," Gwen said. "What did he do—throw the body over the wall?"

"Oh—you don't know." Gareth looked down at her. "Many of the houses abut the river and have access to it through narrow doorways and gates."

Gwen frowned. "Doesn't that defeat the purpose of the wall? What kind of protection can it provide if just anybody can walk through it?"

Gwen had been speaking in Welsh, which John understood, and he made a *maybe* motion with his head. "People need access to the river. They do their washing in it, they cook with it, the town boys swim in it. Besides, the private gates are inspected annually for their security and sturdiness, and it would be impossible to truly batter any down with a siege engine, seeing how the river prevents access."

Gwen gave an unladylike snort, as skeptical as Gareth, who'd already had this conversation with John. Still, when King Stephen had attacked the town nearly ten years before, he hadn't tried to force the river and instead had taken it from the castle side in the traditional manner. So maybe there was something in what John was saying. One or two spies sneaking in a back door could disable the guards at the main gates and let in an army, but that weakness was always the worry for a defending force, regardless of how many holes in the fortifications they had to contend with.

The vagaries of Shrewsbury's defenses weren't Gareth's problem today. They had two murders now, a missing Irishman, who was looking less like a suspect and more like a third victim with every hour that passed, and a murderer who, as Gwen had said, might have a heart as cold as Cadwaladr.

Gareth hadn't thought that anyone could be cold as the traitorous prince. Without a doubt, they had a villain on their hands.

12

Gwen

As John's men loaded the dead girl into the cart, Gareth turned to Gwen. "What have you heard from your father?"

"Nothing." Gwen had been trying not to think about her father all day. He'd left the monastery early that morning, after John Fletcher's boy had come to fetch Gareth about the pool of blood and just before Gareth had sent for Gwen herself. Here it was, getting on towards evening, and she still hadn't seen him.

"Should I ask John Fletcher where Adeline's father has his shop?" Gareth said. "I hadn't thought to inquire."

"I was with my father when he spoke to the prior, so I have an idea where it is." Gwen tucked her hand into Gareth's elbow, and they set off behind the cart, back through the main gate that allowed access into the town from these fields and the southern sweep of the Severn. "Maybe we should walk by it on our way to the monastery."

"On second thought, this is your father's business," Gareth said. "You shouldn't meddle in it unless he asks you to. When he is ready to talk about it, he'll come to you."

"You seem very sure of that," Gwen said, not liking Gareth's advice but knowing he was right. They were here in Shrewsbury for her father, even if she and Gareth were using it as a cover for Prince Hywel's inquiries. Adeline may have been Meilyr's daughter, and even if Gwen had been her half-sister, she had fewer rights to her than Meilyr, and she certainly needed to respect his privacy for one day at least. She could always pin him down later and make him tell her what had gone on in his meeting with Tom Weaver. "There was a time he wouldn't have told me anything at all."

"He is no longer that man," Gareth said, "and you are no longer that daughter."

Except, a moment later, Gareth was proved wrong as a very familiar voice, raised in song, came to Gwen's ears. It wasn't Gwalchmai this time, singing praises to God for the abbot's pleasure, but her father, bellowing out a bawdy ballad. Fortunately, he was singing in Welsh, which would at least reduce the number of people who understood the words.

After entering the town, Gareth and Gwen had been following the river road towards the east gate, but now Gareth guffawed and started forward at a quicker pace, darting down a different street that led more to the center of town. "Meilyr boxed Hywel's ears once for singing that song in the hall."

"How did you know that?" Gwen hustled to keep up with Gareth's long legs as they left the cart behind them. "You weren't at Aberffraw back then."

Gareth glanced down at her. "Hywel told me about it just the other day."

Gwen laughed with genuine pleasure. The prince's mind had been closed to her since Rhun's death. That Hywel had told Gareth about his childhood meant that Hywel might speak to Gareth about his thoughts and feelings when he was ready.

They came around a corner, some distance now from the east gate, and spied Meilyr weaving on his feet in the middle of a street. Even drunk, his voice was impressive, rich in tone and fully supported, so it wasn't any wonder a crowd had gathered around him to listen—and maybe to see what spectacle he might create of himself next.

Gwen approached Meilyr from the front, to make sure that he saw her and didn't startle away or become angry. "Father, it's time to return to the monastery."

"Don't want to go home." Meilyr sounded like Gwalchmai when he was five and hadn't wanted to leave the warmth of the hall for his bed.

Gwen moved closer and cautiously put a hand on his arm. "You don't have to go home if you don't want to. Perhaps you and I can walk a bit instead." She hadn't seen her father drunk like this in years, though at one time it had been a nightly occurrence. A rush of memories returned to her, mostly of the despair and sadness she and her father had felt after her mother's death.

They'd grieved separately, however, and that, more than anything else, had created the rift between them that hadn't healed until a few years ago.

Meilyr had sought relief from grief in mead and wine. At times, Gwen had been relieved to see him drinking, because he wasn't a sour or angry drunk, as some men were and which she might have expected, given his normal gruff personality. Instead, alcohol softened him around the edges and made him easier, rather than harder, to deal with.

Still, it hadn't helped his singing or composing and, in retrospect, Meilyr blamed too much mead for his falling out with King Owain after old King Gruffydd's death. It wasn't that he'd said things he'd regretted. He'd been sober when he'd argued with the king. It had been his slow incapacitation for which Owain had held no patience.

Thankfully, Meilyr responded now to Gwen as he had then, most of the time anyway. His belligerence faded, and he put a hand on her cheek. "Daughter, you look just like your mother."

Gwen smiled. "Yes, Father."

She met Gareth's eyes and gestured with her chin towards the east, indicating that Gareth should continue as they had been, returning to the monastery with the girl's body while Gwen handled her father. Gareth, seeing that she did, in fact, have things in hand, nodded and turned away. John Fletcher had stopped the cart at the bottom of the road where they were standing, and Gareth raised a hand to him, indicating that he could now continue.

The onlookers, seeing that the concert had ended, dispersed as well, though not before several took a second look at Gwen herself. She would have explained to them who she was if they didn't already know, but right now her father was her first concern.

Gwen glanced upwards, noting how low the sun had fallen in the sky. She wasn't worried about their safety on the streets of Shrewsbury, but she knew that at some point the guards closed the gates and were reluctant to open them again to just anyone. She steered her father in the direction Gareth had gone.

"Has something happened, Father?"

"I spoke with the weaver."

Gwen heaved a sigh, grateful that she wasn't going to have to beg him to tell her what had happened that day. "What did he say?"

"He wasn't Adeline's true father."

"Oh." Gwen didn't know whether she was happy or sad to hear it. Either way, Adeline was dead, and Gwen would never know her now. "Does that mean—"

Meilyr shook his head back and forth in the way he did when he wanted to say 'no' and was too drunk to realize he was still doing it. "He doesn't know who her father was. Said he didn't mind telling me, seeing as how I might have been him."

"So he didn't resent you coming to talk to him?"

Her father shook his head again, and this time the motion made him weave on his feet such that Gwen was afraid he might fall over.

She gripped his arm tighter to steady him. "Who was Adeline's mother?"

"He hardly knew that either. He met the woman one night at a tavern. She had the baby with her. This was when he was still working a cart, peddling his wares from place to place and weaving on a small loom. He didn't have a wife—didn't have anyone. They spent the night together." Her father's words came in a long stream with no inflection and barely any pause. He said the last sentence as if it was of no more importance than the first.

Gwen's brow furrowed, confused by the disjointed way her father was telling the story. "So, the woman fell pregnant, and Adeline was Tom's child?"

"No, no." Meilyr shook his head forcefully. "He awoke the next morning to find the woman gone and the baby left behind."

Gwen stopped in the middle of the street and turned so she could see his face. He was only a few inches taller than she, so she barely had to look up. "You're telling me that Adeline's mother left her with Tom Weaver and didn't look back? He never heard from her again?"

The fresh air and the pointed questions were sobering Meilyr up. He took in a deep breath, looking away as if he was collecting his thoughts, and then said, "He asked at the tavern about her, but nobody there claimed to have seen her before, and Tom only knew her as Rhiannon, which might not have been her real name."

"So then what?"

Meilyr raised both shoulders in an exaggerated shrug. "He decided then and there that he would keep the child and settle down. He came to Shrewsbury and put out that his wife had died at the baby's birth."

Gwen gaped at her father. Of all the outcomes he might have learned, this was the least expected to the point that she had never even considered it. "Where did all this happen?"

"Down south near Abergavenny."

"The weaver is Welsh?"

"No," Meilyr said. "He was selling to the lord there. A Norman."

Abergavenny had been held by the Normans against the Welsh almost from the day the Normans had come to Wales, and no Welsh king had yet had the wherewithal to wrest it from them.

"Did-did you ever—"now Gwen was glad her father had drunk too much because she could never have asked this of him when he was sober, "—know a woman named Rhiannon?"

"No."

"Did Tom Weaver describe her to you?"

"She was a woman. Brown hair, brown eyes. Tom didn't really remember. It was so long ago, and he'd been drunk himself at the time." They'd reached the east gate, and Meilyr was now striding along, making it difficult for Gwen to keep up with either him or his thoughts. "I will never know if Adeline was my daughter."

"No, it doesn't seem so." Gwen saw no reason to pretty up the truth with a lie. "Not unless we find Rhiannon."

Her father shot her a sour look. "How am I to find a woman from Abergavenny or thereabouts who may or may not have been named Rhiannon and who left her baby with Tom Weaver over twenty years ago?"

"It's impossible, I suppose." Gwen said. They were almost to the bridge across the Severn.

"It is the very definition of the word." Meilyr tipped his head to the street they'd just come down. "Tom would like to meet you tomorrow, if you would. I said I'd bring you by after breakfast."

"I would be happy to meet him," Gwen said, which was no less than the truth. Maybe, thanks to Gwen's experience with questioning people during the course of her investigations, she could encourage Tom to remember something else, some small detail, that would help them find Rhiannon.

"Father, what you said to me just now made think—could Mam and this Rhiannon have been sisters?"

"Your mother didn't have a sister."

"I know that's what we thought, but who knows how far back in time this goes? How well did you know her family?"

Gwen was realizing only now, at the late age of twenty-five, that she knew even less about her origins than she'd thought and far less than she should. The Welsh were known for their preoccupation with family and ancestors, but Gwen's family had always been a bit of an unknown to her.

With her father a wandering bard, and all of her grandparents dying before she was born, she'd never had much of an extended family. Gareth, too, was an only child, raised by an uncle after the death of his parents when he was five years old. The uncle himself had died before Gwen had met Gareth. It was as if the two of them existed on a little island of their own, surrounded by a vast continent they could never reach.

"Her brother, Pawl, was a womanizer and a wastrel. I didn't want your mother to have anything to do with him, and I feared he would come looking for her if he knew I served King Gruffydd."

"So you distanced yourself." Gwen nodded, determined to get at as much of the truth as she could while her father was still willing to talk. "Is he still alive?"

"Pawl died when you were young. You wouldn't remember the mourning."

"What about your family?"

"My parents died before I married your mother. I was already singing by then," Meilyr said.

Gwen had known that, but she hadn't ever asked how they died, and she was horrified at herself for her lapse. At ten, when her own mother died at Gwalchmai's birth, she'd been too young to ask these questions. Caring for Gwalchmai had fallen to her, at which point, she'd been too busy, as well as too estranged from her father. She'd assumed that his family had died from disease, but from the look on his face now, that wasn't the case.

"How did they die, Father?" she said softly.

"My family was killed in the fighting between King Gruffydd and the Normans. King Henry of England was trying to curb Gwynedd's power and our croft was in the way—" he broke off, staring unseeing at the ground in front of him.

Gwen stared at her father, horrified. She'd experienced enough death and war over the years to have some idea what her father was seeing in his mind's eye.

King Gruffydd had lost his throne to the Norman invaders three times before ripping it from their hands for a fourth time with the help of his Danish and Irish allies. His ancestry, like King Owain's and Hywel's, was a combination of Irish, Danish, and Welsh—and so mixed up with lineages of kings that Hywel could have claimed three thrones at once if he'd had a mind to.

Then, nearly two decades after Gruffydd had finally achieved the throne of Gwynedd, King Henry, wary of Gruffydd's growing power and reach, had attacked Gwynedd's eastern border, much as Earl Ranulf of Chester had done last year. The war had been short, and while Gruffydd had sued for peace, he hadn't lost any land.

He had lost people, however—among them, it seemed, Gwen's grandparents.

Then Meilyr blinked and looked up at Gwen. "Don't be sad for me, *cariad*. It is past—that song has been sung."

Gwen took in a breath. Her father hadn't called her *cariad* since before her mother died. She leaned forward to kiss his cheek. "Let's go home, Father."

13

Gareth

"Two in one day, a man and a woman." John sighed. "It's the same as it was in Clwyd in the autumn."

"Heaven forbid this turns out to be anything like the same circumstance." Gareth's initial examination had begun with a slightly more cursory mindset than was usual for him, since he found his thoughts returning again and again to whatever might be going on between Gwen and her father. It was just as well that he had planned from the start to leave most of the actual work to John. If John was going to be a competent deputy sheriff, this was something he needed to know how to do.

And they were trying to hurry, since the monks, whose job it was to prepare the dead for burial and to do the actual washing and laying out of the body, were waiting.

"We've had no sign of Prince Hywel's uncle, leastwise," John said. "That has to be good, right?"

Gareth tsked through his teeth but otherwise didn't answer. He was focusing instead on getting the clothing off the girl—always a difficult task with a dead body. He ultimately decided to cut the dress off of her rather than try to wrestle her out it.

"Look at this bruise!" John lifted the girl's arm, now free of the dress, and spoke with dismay.

Gareth had already noted her condition and felt equally disturbed. "I wish I could say I'd never seen anything like it, but that wouldn't be true."

"Is there any way this could have happened after she was dead?"

"Dead people don't bruise," Gareth said, with regret.

"To know that her murder had been preceded by pain makes this all the worse. You can see the imprint of his thumb!" John put his hand to the girl's upper arm, which he was able to circle almost entirely with his own fingers.

"Now that you've seen her up close, you still don't know this girl?" Gareth said.

"I've never seen her before in my life." John looked up at Gareth. "She would have been beautiful."

"Yes. Any man would have remembered her, which makes me wonder why has nobody come forward to say that she's missing?" Gareth touched the girl's hair, noting, now that it was drying, the way the blonde highlights in the brown caught the light of the candles burning around the table.

John's eyes widened. "You know how Roger and Conall both had red hair, even if Roger's was much darker?"

"Many have red hair," Gareth said, "including your own sister."

John raised one shoulder, dismissing that coincidence as immaterial. "What if someone came to Conall's room to murder him, but Roger was waiting there to do business with Conall, and the murderer mistook Roger for Conall and killed the wrong man?"

Gareth gaped at John, caught between consternation and laughter—and real surprise that John might be on to something. "That would be a scenario worthy of Cadwaladr."

"But it could be true," John said eagerly, warming to the idea, which undoubtedly he'd thought up only a few heartbeats before he told Gareth about it.

"It would certainly be coincidental that of all the reasons Roger could be murdered, in the end it was by mistake," Gareth said.

"Perhaps the girl died by mistake too," John said. "We have no reason for her death at all."

Gareth shook his head. "Before we make any assumptions about her, tell me why a girl might come to Shrewsbury on her own?"

John pursed his lips and reined in his enthusiasm. After a moment, he said, "She could have run away—from a husband or a master. Shrewsbury is a free market town. If a churl lives here for a year and a day, uncaught, she is free."

Gareth had heard of that law, if only because it was yet another English custom that had no equivalent in Wales. Churls in England were tied to the land and could not leave without the owner's permission. They weren't exactly slaves, but they weren't free to move about either. A lord might lose his position, be hanged or beheaded, but the people who worked his land would stay where they were, regardless of what new lord ruled them.

In Wales, churls were called *taeogion*. They owed their lord tithes of food and services. Because of the rugged terrain that made most of Wales poor for crops, being tied to the land was less of an issue. The Welsh were more herders than farmers. Gareth himself owed service to his lord, so in a sense, all men were *taeogion,* though Gareth appreciated the distinction between choosing that service and being forced into it by birth.

Gareth also understood that, in his time, King Gruffydd had kept actual slaves, and even traded the freedom of some of his own people in payment to the Irish and Danes for helping him gain his kingdom. By contrast, King Owain had bowed to the precepts of the Church, and since he'd come to the throne, slaves had become few and far between in Gwynedd. Because of the Church, or their own sensibilities, the Normans had forbidden slavery in England from the moment they set foot in Kent eighty years ago, even if, to Gareth's mind, the difference between an English churl and a slave was a line too fine to draw.

"But surely, were she caught, she would be hauled back to her home, not killed," Gareth said.

"One would think." John stared down at the girl's body.

Gareth sighed. "We should make a record of her injuries and see if we can find any clue among them as to who killed her."

"I found nothing in her clothing," John said.

They worked in silence for another quarter of an hour, until John turned away. "I have duties at the castle that cannot wait."

"Go on. I'll finish up here." Gareth pulled out a piece of paper and began to sketch the girl's face. With Conall's sketch, he'd had to go off of the memory of the innkeeper. This time, the difficulty was to take her slack features and return them to what she would have looked like in life.

It took only a few moments and then, his mind full of what had driven the girl to bleed out in the alley, Gareth turned the body over to the monks and left the room. As he took his first step into the fresh air of the courtyard, the bell tolled for supper.

Gwen was waiting for him in the doorway to the guest house. Vespers—the monks' prayers at sunset—had come and gone. There would be one more service at nine o'clock before the monks went to bed. Guests were not required to get up in the night for lauds or matins, however, and thus the kitchens had prepared a light meal for them, here at the end of the day.

Gareth put a hand on his belly, realizing that he couldn't remember the last time he'd eaten.

"What did you find?" Gwen spoke at the same instant that Gareth said, "How is your father?"

Then they both laughed and clasped hands briefly (though Gareth wanted to touch her longer than that). As they walked towards the guest hall where supper would be served, Gwen related the gist of her conversation with her father, including what she'd learned about the deaths of Meilyr's parents and about her mother's brother, Pawl. Meilyr wouldn't be dining with them, having been put to bed with a supper tray in his room, since he needed to sleep off the alcohol he'd consumed and couldn't be trusted with a meal in the guest hall. Meilyr, thankfully, had given way without protest.

"Where is everyone?" Gareth said to the monk who put a carafe of wine in front of him. Unlike the previous night, when there had been a half-dozen other guests, only two others dined with them tonight.

"We are not often as full as we were yesterday," the monk said. "When the war was at its height, we went weeks without any guests at all, though now that things have calmed down here in the west, that lack has become rarer."

Gareth thanked him and looked down the table to the other diners: two men, a few years older than he was, in close conversation. Gareth thought about asking polite questions, simply to know more of them and because he was curious that way, but unless they were involved in these murders they weren't his concern. He would rather spend the dinner with his family. It would be rude, however, not to say something.

Gareth stood, a hand to his chest, and bowed. "I'd like to introduce myself. I am Gareth ap Rhys, companion to Prince Hywel of Gwynedd." Then he introduced Gwen, Gwalchmai, and Tangwen.

Faced with a knight, even a Welsh one, both stood themselves. "I am Flann MacNeill, of Oxford," the first man said. He was middle-aged and balding, with the look of someone who'd had enough to eat his whole life, "and this is my companion, Will de Bernard." Will had the presence of a nobleman, though that might simply be because he was wealthy. He was of similar age to Flann, but leaner, with brown hair and a full beard.

"You're Irish?" Gwen said to Flann.

Flann turned to her with a slight nod. "By birth, only. I have never been to Ireland." Both men sat, and they all continued with their meal.

Tangwen perched decorously beside Gwen, having decided at some point in the last three days that she was a lady like her mother and should eat like one. The mind of a two-year-old girl was completely beyond Gareth, but he appreciated the absence of the antics of six months ago, when Tangwen couldn't sit still for longer than the time it took to cut and butter a slice of bread.

"Gwalchmai will be singing in church on Sunday," Gwen said.

Gareth raised his eyebrows, recognizing Gwen's ploy for what it was—an attempt not to talk murder in front of Tangwen—and he played along. "Are you, Gwalchmai? That will be something to look forward to. Have you told your father?"

Gwalchmai, however, knew himself to be a man now and was having none of it. "Gareth, is it true what they're saying?"

Gareth scoffed under his breath. They should have known better than to keep anything from Gwalchmai. Given his incredible voice, perhaps it wasn't surprising that he could hear around corners too. "Probably not. What are they saying?"

"That a member of the town council is dead, and a girl's body was found in the river?"

Gareth glanced at Tangwen, but if his daughter was listening, she gave no sign that she was disturbed. Thus, Gareth spoke normally, so she would continue to think nothing was amiss. "Yes, I'm afraid that's true." He reached into his coat and pulled out the sketch he'd drawn of the girl's face, along with the one of Conall. "See for yourself."

Gwalchmai took both images to study. The two men at the other end of the table had looked up at Gwalchmai's question. Deciding it would do no good to whisper when their ears were already perked, Gareth gestured to Gwalchmai that he should pass the sketches down the table. "Do you recognize either of these people? The girl had light brown hair, and the man's hair was red, if that helps. We know he was Irish too."

"You don't say?" Flann took the sketches from Gwalchmai. "They're both dead?"

"Only the girl," Gareth said. "The man is missing."

Flann frowned and looked closer. His companion bent nearer too, and some kind of look passed between them before Will sat back in his seat and Flann half-stood, shaking his head, to hand the pictures back to Gareth.

"You don't know them?" Gareth had been sure there for a moment that he'd seen recognition in Flann's eyes.

"No, no, of course not. You don't know their names?"

"The man is named Conall," Gareth said. "The girl's is unknown."

Again, a look that Gareth couldn't interpret passed between the man and his companion, but then Flann made a dismissive motion with his head and said, "We live in troubled times."

"We do, sir." Gareth didn't mention that he was assisting the Deputy Sheriff in his inquiries, though the fact that he had sketches of the two people in question should have given it away. Gareth might believe that Flann had never been to Ireland. He might even find the fact that he didn't know Conall or the girl credible, but his presence in Shrewsbury as another Irishman when there weren't that many around, begged for questions.

Which fortunately, Gwen wasn't afraid to ask. "What brings you to Shrewsbury? You're a long way from Oxfordshire here."

Flann had started in again on his vegetables. He stabbed a turnip and held it before his lips as he spoke. "We're merchants."

"Oh, really? What of?" Gwen said.

Flann swallowed. So far Will seemed disinclined to speak at all. "Leather."

Gwen nodded and returned to her own meal. Flann's answer was a safe one, since Shrewsbury was known for its leather working, and his words might even be true. But the hairs on the back of Gareth's neck were standing up, and he'd learned something over the years about listening to his instincts.

They could be wrong. They were sometimes wrong, but he would lose nothing by finding out more about these two strangers to Shrewsbury, especially since Conall had been a newcomer too.

He was marshalling his thoughts to ask more about their business when both men stood. Flann tossed a last uneaten crust of bread onto his trencher, nodded at Gareth and Gwen, and left the guest hall with Will.

Gareth immediately bent close to Gwalchmai. "Go after them, will you? I want to know if they leave the monastery—but do not leave it with them! Return to me instead."

Gwalchmai's mouth was full of food, but he swallowed quickly and nodded, his chin firming with sudden purpose. "Yes, sir!"

"Take Tangwen with you," Gwen said. "She's a good excuse to be loitering in the courtyard."

"You have a devious mind, sister." But Gwalchmai had a grin on his face as he scooped up his niece, who was still holding her buttered roll, and hurried out the door after the men.

Once they'd gone, Gareth leaned back in his seat. "Did you see—"

"—the looks they exchanged?" Gwen said. "If they meant to disguise the fact that they knew Conall, they didn't do a very good job of it."

"You thought it was Conall they knew?" Gareth said. "I thought the second man, Will, paid particular attention to the sketch of the girl."

"Either way," Gwen said, "those two know more than they're saying."

Gareth rubbed his chin. "I don't know how we're going to get it out of them. I can't compel them to talk. And John—"

Gwen nodded without Gareth having to finish his thought. More and more often, particularly these last weeks as they'd spent nearly every waking moment together, they'd developed a habit of finishing each other's sentences. Gwen already had his heart, so Gareth was pleased that their minds had connected so completely as well.

"John means well, and in time he might make a good investigator, but menacing he isn't," Gwen said.

And then Gwalchmai came rushing back, Tangwen on his hip with her arms around his neck. "They've left the monastery!"

Gareth pushed to his feet. "Did you see which way they went?"

"West. I followed them a little way, thinking I didn't have time to come back here to tell you, but they're walking slowly towards the English bridge. You might just catch them if you hurry. I'll mind Tangwen until you return."

"Thank you, Gwalchmai." Gwen started for the door. "I'm glad I wore my cloak to dinner."

Gareth might have objected to her assumption that she was coming with him if it wouldn't have meant wasting his breath. It was entirely his fault that Gwen was involved in the investigation, since he had sent for her in the first place. He could hardly complain that she wanted to leave the monastery with him. Besides which, if he'd refused to take Gwen with him, he would have found Gwalchmai looking at him eagerly instead.

He consoled himself with the idea that a married couple such as they would look more innocuous strolling through

Shrewsbury than he would alone, hurrying as he would be after two English merchants as if he wanted to rob them. Men tended to look askance at a full-on Welshman wandering about after dark by himself.

Like Gwen, Gareth had worn his cloak to the meal, since the dining room wasn't heated, and the temperature was hardly different outside than in. The night was clear and the moon shone down. As they hurried through the monastery gatehouse and down the road to the bridge across the Severn, they could see well even without a torch. When they spied the merchants, the two men were just passing the watchman at the east gate.

Gwen and Gareth were far enough behind that the men didn't notice them. Nor did they turn around to see if they were being followed. Fortunately, as Gareth and Gwen came across the bridge themselves, Oswin, one of the young watchmen from the alley, arrived from a different direction, with the intent of showing the guards one of Gareth's sketches. He looked up at Gareth's approach, his expression brightening, and then introduced him to the guardsmen.

"We are following two men, who just passed through here," Gareth said. "Did you see which way they went?"

"They headed west," one of the guards said. "Should we stop them?"

"No," Gareth said. "This is simple curiosity. I think."

"It might be late before we return," Gwen said. "Will you be on duty then? Will you let us pass through? We're staying at the monastery."

The guard glanced at Oswin, who nodded, though Gareth wouldn't have said that the younger man had any more authority here than the guard. "Of course, madam. The wicket gate is always available, but we must be careful about who comes in and out at night. These are troubled times."

"We understand your duty," Gwen said appeasingly, though her brow furrowed.

Gareth had also noticed that the guard had repeated the same phrase Flann had used earlier.

Then Gareth and Gwen were off again, wending their way through the mostly deserted streets. It wasn't that late, not quite nine in the evening, but the residents of Shrewsbury rose early to open their shops in order to take advantage of every daylight hour given them.

They were nearing the west gate, an area that Gareth was growing more knowledgeable about, since this was near where the pool of blood had been found, when he saw the men stop forty feet away before a three-story house. It was one of those among the inner ring of houses and shops that lined the interior of the palisade, and Gareth wondered all of a sudden if it had gate access to the river. These houses weren't backed up right to the wall, like might occur in a castle, but had yards and stables behind them that the wall enclosed.

The men stopped before the door, below a sign showing a picture of a woman's shoe, and spoke to a man standing in the doorway.

"That's the brothel!" Gwen said in a breathless whisper.

Gareth gripped her arm tightly, just in case she had a mind to go closer. Meanwhile, Will pulled something from his pocket and showed it to the guard, who nodded, and then the two merchants entered the house. As they passed through the doorway, another man was just coming out, tugging his cloak tighter around his shoulders as he did so.

All three men nodded at each other, not necessarily because they knew each other but out of politeness, since they were passing in a tight space, and then the newcomer left the shelter of the stoop. The road was well lit by both the moonlight and the many torches shining from the buildings along the street, so Gareth could easily see the face of the man.

It was Luke, the skeptical watchman.

14

Hywel

H is men could ride fifty miles in a day, but even Hywel had to concede that their horses couldn't keep going that long. They'd come fifteen miles since sunset, which left thirty-five for tomorrow—not an unreasonable distance to cover in one day, especially with a small group of men whose horses would once again be fresh.

Throughout the evening hours, as the miles from Mold had unrolled beneath him, Hywel's mind had been occupied with what lay before him in Shrewsbury and what he might find there. It was as if an invisible thread was pulling him forward.

It had been an impulsive move to leave the newly captured Mold in the hands of his brothers, as capable as Cynan and Madoc were, but Hywel had a good feeling about this trip—maybe *because* it was impulsive. He'd been playing the good son, the reasonable prince, for far too long. He hoped Rhun would forgive him for being himself this one time.

Coming from Mold, they'd ridden directly south, staying within the territory his father now claimed for Gwynedd. Ahead of them now was the little village of Llangollen, which nestled alongside the River Dee. Above it, on a rocky plateau twelve hundred feet above the valley floor, sat the castle of Dinas Bran. These lands were controlled not by Hywel's father, King Owain of Gwynedd, but by King Madog of Powys. Madog was of an equally ancient lineage as Hywel, and guarded his lands of Powys as jealously as Hywel's family did Gwynedd. He was also married to Hywel's aunt, his father's sister, and thus happened to be Hywel's uncle, though not by blood.

As Prince Cadwaladr was Hywel's uncle by blood, and he had betrayed the family far too many times, Hywel tended to give a man's lineage less weight than his deeds in assessing his worth. But he didn't know this uncle well, and though Powys and Gwynedd were currently at peace, it remained to be seen whether animosity still festered below the surface in his uncle's heart.

On the whole, that seemed likely. Madog's family had hated Hywel's for far too long to have that division mended by one marriage, even if it was to Owain's sister.

Dinas Bran had been the seat of the kings of this region for as long as Wales had existed. Hywel pointed out the ancient earthen ramparts, which encircled and protected the wooden castle, to Cadell, who'd never been here before.

"Are you sure coming here was wise, my lord?" Cadifor said. "We could have slept peacefully in a thicket."

"We could have. We probably should have. But if Madog learned of our journey afterwards, he would be rightfully angry that we hadn't asked for his hospitality." Hywel clicked his teeth. "Rhun would have asked for hospitality."

"Rhun wouldn't have come on this journey at all."

His foster father spoke under his breath, and though Hywel was sure he meant for him to hear, he didn't call Cadifor out for it. He wasn't wrong, and they all knew it. But Hywel was right about Rhun.

That was one of the hardest things about trying to fill his brother's shoes: behaving like him, like an *edling* should, when he didn't naturally think like him, and when his instincts were always telling him to do something different. When Rhun was alive, it had been far easier to let his elder brother be the ambassador, to give the dignified response, while Hywel went around the back and did what needed to be done.

Rhun had relied on him to do exactly that. Hywel was struggling with how, now that he was the *edling*, he was going to do both.

The approach to the castle was impressive, particularly by the light of the not quite full moon that shone down upon them. The ramparts were arranged such that any rider to the castle was required to ride along the full length of the palisade to reach the gate located on the southeast side. Unlike at Mold, it would be impossible to bring a siege engine to bear on this gate, not unless the castle was already taken—in which case using a siege engine would be pointless.

Not for the first time, Hywel wondered at the Norman tendency to build castles on the flats and not the heights. The

Normans could build all the moats and walls they chose, but nothing was ever going to change the fact that the high ground was everything in war, and, nine times out of ten, the army that held it was the victor in any battle. With their mountain castles, the Welsh had held off first the Saxons and then the Normans for nearly a thousand years. Then again, the Normans had taken England and held it for nearly eighty years with their castles built on flat lands.

Maybe they did know something Hywel didn't.

Despite the fewness of their numbers, Hywel's small company was obviously armed for war. Thus, Hywel made sure, as they rode along the pathway, that the flag of Gwynedd was clearly visible on its pike above his head, so the watchmen on the palisade could see it.

Again, Cadifor urged his horse closer. It was he who held the spear that showed Hywel's banner. "What did I say? Can you see the arrows trained at our backs?"

"I don't need to see them to know they're there." Hywel laughed low. "Be sure to announce us in a loud voice long before we reach the gate. The last thing my father needs is a letter from my uncle regretfully informing him of the loss of two more of his sons."

Cadifor nodded and, straightening in the saddle, he lifted his chin so his voice would carry. "It is Prince Hywel ap Owain, *edling* of Gwynedd, who seeks shelter this night from his uncle, the great Madog, King of Powys!"

It may have been that the guards thought the riders coming towards them were messengers only because Cadifor's words elicited a flurry of activity on the palisade, indicating to Hywel that they hadn't been prepared to receive someone of his stature. It couldn't be that they hadn't seen them. The giant wooden gate swung open to admit his troop of ten, and Madog's steward, a man named Derfel, himself caught the bridle of Hywel's horse.

"My lord! We believed you to be at Aber. What brings you here at this hour?"

Hywel allowed his voice to project throughout the courtyard. "I was at Mold. We took it not five hours ago. Gwynedd now stretches from Arfon to the Dee."

"We are honored that you took it upon yourself to bring us this news in person," Derfel said, with another bow.

Hywel dismounted, pleased that Derfel was behaving in appropriately courteous manner. Hywel had never stood on ceremony when he'd come here in the past, but he hadn't been the *edling* of Gwynedd then.

As to Derfel's misunderstanding of the reason for his journey, neither Cadifor nor Cadell contradicted him. Cadifor had been advising kings since before Hywel was born and knew when to keep his mouth shut, and for all that Cadell had not known Rhun well, he had suffered with all of Gwynedd at Rhun's loss and then through the pursuit of Cadwaladr that followed. He'd learned, as they all had, to hold his tongue when he was unsure of another's loyalty or intentions.

Because there was a painful truth behind the courteous exterior: Derfel—and Madog—had every reason to distrust, if not Hywel, then his father. Although Madog had married Hywel's Aunt Susanna, Powys and Gwynedd remained in an uneasy peace, in large part because of instances such as Mold, where Gwynedd had expanded its territory in one bold move.

It was Chester who'd lost land this day, but Madog wouldn't be wrong to think that it could be Powys tomorrow. Hywel's Uncle Cadwallon had died in 1132 right here in Llangollen, fighting against his own kin at the behest of his father, King Gruffydd, whose relentless pursuit of more land and power had been legendary. Madog's father had died that same year. While his death could not be laid at Gwynedd's feet, rumor had it that Madog believed the long years of battle and betrayal by his kin had shortened his father's life.

Hywel knew this history like he knew the shape of his own hand. He knew, too, that his father had a similar thirst to spread the influence of Gwynedd across the whole of Wales. In the past, it had been Rhun at the forefront of Gwynedd's military actions. But even as the second son, Hywel had fought in many battles in the years since he'd become a man.

It had been Hywel, after all, whom King Owain had sent to Ceredigion to eject Cadwaladr from his lands. Now as the *edling*, Hywel had already fought in Meirionnydd and in Mold. His father could decide to send him to Powys next, and Hywel would obey as he always did.

The activity continued unabated in the courtyard of the castle as Derfel attempted to quickly accommodate ten new men and horses. Hywel handed his horse off to one of his men, to be taken away and cared for in the stable, and Derfel led Hywel, Cadifor, and Cadell towards the hall.

Unlike Mold Castle, the purpose of which was to dominate its region of Gwynedd and to control the people who lived there, Dinas Bran was a palace. Its purpose was to provide a home to far more people than simply a garrison of twenty men. The hall, adjacent living quarters, and kitchen occupied the northern third of the courtyard, but within the palisade also lay a barracks, huts for his uncle's servants and craftsmen, a blacksmith works, and a stable. Other than being at the top of a mountain, Dinas Bran closely resembled Aber Castle or Aberffraw.

The night air wasn't cold, but the light and warmth coming from the open door into the hall was inviting, and smoke rose from the hole in the center of the roof, indicating the central hearth was blazing. Hywel could smell roasting meat, and his stomach growled, reminding him that he'd consumed nothing but a few bits of dried meat and a flask of water since leaving Mold.

"When was the last time you were here? Do you know King Madog well?" Cadell said in an undertone as they stepped through the doorway. Even at this late hour, the hall was full of his uncle's people. The meal had ended long ago, but people remained behind, drinking and talking.

"I stopped here on my way home from Newcastle-under-Lyme a few years ago. But I can't say that I know my uncle well, and certainly not well enough," Hywel said.

Cadifor spoke from behind them. "I remind you that he fought with your Uncle Cadwaladr at Lincoln on behalf of Empress Maud five years ago and has Norman leanings."

Hywel made a slight motion with his chin to indicate he'd heard him. "We all need to be wary. Follow my lead, Cadell."

"Assuredly." Cadell nodded his head vigorously, causing Hywel to wonder again at the impulse to ride to Shrewsbury with this least experienced of his brothers. Was it really because he felt that Cynan and Madoc deserved the reward of consolidating the hold on Mold, or was it because he didn't want their more experienced counsel?

But then, he had brought Cadifor, after all, and his foster father had never been one to hold his tongue when he didn't approve of what Hywel was doing. Hywel glanced at the older man, who drew abreast as they approached Madog's seat.

"Your father regretted this marriage, you know," Cadifor said.

"I know. At the time, it wasn't his place to object," Hywel said.

"That didn't seem to stop you in the case of your sister," Cadifor said.

Hywel almost gave himself away by hesitating in mid-stride, but he managed to keep going and skirted the central hearth. "The match between Susanna and Madog was intended to improve relations with Powys."

Hywel didn't see how it was possible for Cadifor to know about the role he'd played in disrupting his sister's marriage to the King of Deheubarth, but somehow he seemed to. Or he'd been guessing, and Hywel had just given himself away. Hywel would have laughed right then and there at his foster father's audacity in bringing up the issue in this moment, but they'd reached the high table at the far end of the hall, and King Madog had risen to his feet, requiring Hywel to make the necessary obeisance.

"Uncle."

"Nephew."

Then Aunt Susanna left her seat and came around the table to embrace him and speak in his ear, "I am so sorry about Rhun."

Hywel found himself squeezing his aunt tightly. "Thank you."

She was slender and blonde, much the same in appearance as Hywel's sister, Elen. Hywel thought Elen was happier, however, having recently married a lord from Lleyn instead of the king for whom she'd been originally intended. At one point, there had been talk about marrying her to Cadell, the current King of Deheubarth, but nothing had ever come of it.

Susanna released him and stepped back, a small smile on her lips. "We are all proud of the man you've become."

Hywel felt himself undone. His aunt might be the Queen of Powys, but she was a mother too, and understood his heart almost as well as Hywel himself, whose own mother had died at his birth.

Susanna patted his hand. "We'll talk later."

Hywel returned his gaze to Madog. "Uncle, we have taken Mold from Ranulf."

Madog was a man of middle age and middle stature, ten years older at least than his wife, with dark hair shot with gray and shaved clean like a noble Norman. He had several sons, though Hywel didn't see any of his cousins in the hall tonight.

Madog had a stare, too, that was hard both to look at and to look away from. Not for the first time, Hywel wondered how his aunt had made the best of a bad situation, and if she loved her husband at all. He hoped, for her sake, that her marriage was like that of many nobles, meaning a bit of both.

"I am honored that you would have ridden all this way to tell me this," Madog said.

"It seemed the proper thing to do, seeing as how Gwynedd now occupies your northern border," Hywel said, and then hurried on because his choice of words hadn't been the most politic. "I assure you my father has no intention of bringing his forces any farther south."

"Today, anyway," Madog said dryly.

Hywel didn't try to deny it. "As you say. I ask for your hospitality for tonight only. We will be off early tomorrow."

"Again, I thank you for bringing the news of the fall of Mold to me in person," Madog said, "but surely the news could have been sent by a messenger?"

Hywel could have lied outright, but in the end, chose not to. He wore Rhun's shoes now, and his brother would not have lied. "We journey south."

A flash of irritation appeared in his uncle's eyes. "May I ask to what end?"

"Shrewsbury, my lord," Hywel said, "on business for my father."

That *was* a lie, and Hywel mentally shrugged off the admonition he heard in his head in Rhun's voice, telling himself he wasn't going to fill his brother's shoes overnight.

His foster father stirred beside him, recognizing as Hywel had, the animosity in Madog's expression, but then he settled back on his heels.

Hywel was careful to keep his hand away from the hilt of his sword. He clasped his hands behind his back to make sure they wouldn't stray accidently in that direction and bowed again. "Do we have your countenance, my lord?" He hoped that this speedy conclusion to the audience wouldn't make him appear rude, but he didn't think prolonging this conversation was going to end well for anyone.

His uncle didn't speak for a count of five, which was a terribly long time when one was standing before a lord in his completely silent hall. Then Madog pressed his lips together in an almost-smile. "Of course, nephew. I am delighted you are here and honored that you have given us a chance to provide you with hospitality. Let me say also, now that I have you here in person, that I am sorry for the loss of your brother. He was a valiant warrior. We have been much grieved here."

It was his uncle who was lying this time. Hywel was a hundred miles away from Aber, however, and was backed by too few men to call him on it. Lying was part of what lords did. Hywel was generally very good at it and, in the past, had taken pleasure from a verbal back and forth with an adversary.

Somehow, tonight, the interplay wasn't nearly as enjoyable. If his father ever woke from his stupor, he might turn his attention to Powys, and Hywel wasn't looking forward to bringing his men to besiege his uncle's fort. And yet, he knew that his father couldn't be sad forever and, when he stopped mourning, it would be anger he would be feeling. That anger would have to find a direction. It was as likely as not that he would direct it outside Gwynedd's borders.

Thus, his uncle wasn't mourning Rhun, not really, because he would know this too. And he would know that Rhun would have been sent against him eventually, just as they both knew that it would be Hywel who would be sent in Rhun's place.

"Thank you," Hywel said.

"I would hope you might sing later, after you've dined," Madog said. "My people would view me as much remiss if I didn't ask you."

Hywel almost said no, but a quick look at the eager expressions on the faces of the people seated on either side of his uncle, all of whom were looking at him, had him reconsidering. It was the least he could do, especially given the suddenness of his appearance tonight. If nothing else, it might well-dispose his uncle's people to him. There might come a time when he was glad he'd done his uncle's bidding.

Again, Hywel bent his neck to Madog. "Thank you for asking. I would be honored to sing."

To Hywel's relief, he was dismissed.

"I will ask about Cadwaladr among your uncle's guardsmen," Cadifor said in an undertone before he went to his seat next to Cadell at one of the lower tables. "Discreetly. As for you, my lord, don't let the name pass your lips. Now that you've started down this path, better not to give the game away."

"Thank you." Hywel then went to join his aunt and uncle at the high table for what was bound to be an uncomfortable meal, especially since they'd be watching him eat, having already eaten themselves.

His aunt was gracious, however, sending for more wine and fruit tarts for everyone to enjoy. Hywel had been here often enough in his younger days to know that she didn't condone a rowdy hall and would ration the wine most evenings, making available only very watered down mead that couldn't get a four-year-old drunk.

"How is Mari?" Aunt Susanna said as Hywel sat down next to her.

"She is well, aunt," Hywel said. "We have two sons now, who keep her busy."

"When did you see her last?" Susanna said, understanding, as she could, being a wife of a king, the long separations of a noble marriage.

"It has been a mere two weeks," Hywel said. "She had been in Ceredigion, but she and the boys now reside at my castle at Dolwyddelan."

Susanna laughed. "I hope it's in better condition than when I last saw it!"

"Rhun saw to that," Hywel said.

Susanna pressed her lips together. Their shared grief was just below the surface, and there was no need to comment on it. "Not ... Aber?"

Hywel could tell that his aunt had tried to phrase this question delicately, not asking outright, as she could have, how it was that the wife of the *edling* of Gwynedd didn't reside in the same household as the king.

"She likes being the mistress of her own house," he said.

"Understandable," Susanna said, without asking for a better reason.

Hywel didn't know if rumors of the full extent of his father's current malaise had reached this far east. He had to assume they had—that and the fact that his stepmother, Cristina, ruled Aber with an iron fist. The latter, at least, was well known to the whole of Gwynedd.

As to his father's illness, it was very much their luck that Gwynedd's Norman enemies were otherwise occupied, or else Hywel's forces would have been retreating from Mold rather than taking it. Up until now, Gwynedd's Welsh allies—namely Cadell of Deheubarth and Susanna's husband—had been respectful of their grief. Hywel didn't suppose that was going to last very much longer.

Susanna shot a look at her husband, who was deep in conference with his steward, so she took the opportunity to lean closer to Hywel. "Cadwaladr came here, but he left again, before we knew what he had done. I cannot tell you his whereabouts now."

As Susanna started speaking, Hywel had taken in a breath of surprise, but now he eased it out. *Cannot* did not mean that she didn't know, but he understood that if her husband had ordered her not to speak of Cadwaladr to Hywel, she would not disobey. Hywel would expect no less of Mari.

"Thank you, aunt," he said. "We have heard little but rumor as to where he has gone. Alice, his wife, claims not to know."

"But you seek him," she said, not as a question.

Hywel opted for the truth, and not even against his better judgement. "I can do nothing else until my brother's death is avenged."

15

Gareth

"What are you doing—" Gwen closed her lips on her protest before it was fully realized, and allowed Gareth to tug her out of the street and around a corner.

Gareth stopped a little way down the alley, keeping his arm around her and his head bowed in the darkness until Luke passed. The wall behind him felt cold at his back, and he tried to ignore the rank smell in the alley. As he held Gwen, his overriding need was to protect her from where this investigation was heading. More than when they'd gone to Newcastle-under-Lyme and found themselves saving the life of Prince Henry, he felt out of his depth in this English town.

After Luke had gone by, Gareth stayed where he was through another count of ten, and then he finally released Gwen.

She looked up into his face. "Am I to guess what this is about, or do I already know?"

"You said it earlier," Gareth said. "That's the brothel, the one that goes with the coin we found in Conall's room. According to John Fletcher's information, if I show it to the man at the door, it will gain me entrance."

Both of them peered around the corner of the alley again, looking towards the house where the doorman still stood in shadow, watching the street and obviously on guard.

"We aren't far from where the girl died," Gwen said. "Are you thinking what I'm thinking?"

"I sincerely hope not and fear to ask," Gareth said.

"What if nobody will admit to knowing the girl because she worked at this brothel?" Gwen gestured towards the house. "How many of the townspeople with whom we spoke would willingly admit they knew her from there?"

"Not many," Gareth said. "The town council and the good citizens of Shrewsbury tolerate whores out of necessity, but they don't like them."

"If she was a whore, and she escaped, why kill her? Why not simply bring her back to the brothel?"

"I don't know."

"And why the bruising?"

Gareth didn't want to answer, but it wasn't information he felt he could keep to himself. "From what I understand, not from experience but from what others have told me, that guard we see there in the doorway is employed by the brothel to keep the girls who work there in line."

Gwen contemplated that piece of information for a few heartbeats. "In case any decide they want to earn their living another way?"

"Yes. Beating would not be outside his purview," Gareth said. "Such men also are called upon to control unruly patrons."

"Oh." Gwen nodded. "They probably serve mead in there, don't they."

"Wine and beer, rather, since we're in England." Out of a desire to fleece the men who patronized them to the fullest extent, brothels served alcohol as well as women, but too much beer in a violent man could be dangerous to a woman, a fact which Gwen would have seen for herself often enough.

Gareth closed his eyes briefly, forced for honesty's sake to add a final comment to the conversation. "It isn't uncommon for girls to be forced into this life, Gwen, and once in it, they have no means of getting out. They're whores. Who's going to marry them?"

Gwen chewed on her lower lip as she studied the house in front of her.

Except for the guard, the brothel looked nothing out of the ordinary. This was probably on purpose, so the worthies of Shrewsbury could walk by without having to think about what went on inside.

"Here in England, a child produced out of wedlock is such a shame that it might leave a girl without a home," Gareth said. "Or the child herself might be abandoned. Alternatively, a father might be so in debt that he sells his daughter to free himself of it."

Gwen drew in a breath. "I feel like a child who's just discovered that the puppets at an Easter fair aren't real but hang on strings pulled by men."

SARAH WOODBURY

"I don't see it that way, Gwen," Gareth said. "It's just that you have no experience with a town like Shrewsbury, with all the darkness that goes on beneath the surface here."

"I investigate murder!" she said. "How could I not have known any of this before?"

Gareth put his arm across her shoulders and turned her away from the brothel, heading back towards the east gate and the monastery. "We have done what we came to do tonight. I will speak to John Fletcher in the morning."

"And it will be with John that you visit the brothel—in daylight," she said. "Without me."

"Without you, *cariad*," he said to her. "I cannot express to you how unwilling John was to take you in there. I confess, I'm starting to share his opinion."

To Gareth's relief, Gwen gave way. "I will not argue. Is it possible, however, to discover how many girls don't want to be there? Is there any way to free them?"

"You can't save them, Gwen," Gareth said. "We are strangers here, and those are questions I cannot ask, not even for you."

Gwen looked down at her feet as she walked. While a Welsh woman could divorce her husband if he beat her, in English law, women had no rights at all. These women weren't wives, but at one time they might have been. Certainly they'd been daughters. The dilemma preoccupied them both for the whole of the walk back to the east gatehouse.

As they passed through the wicket gate, Gareth said to the guardsman on duty, the same one they'd spoken to earlier on their way into the town, "I'm going to walk my wife to the monastery, and then I intend to return. I need to speak to John Fletcher at the castle."

"Of course, my lord."

"You're going back to speak to John?" Gwen said as they headed across the bridge towards the monastery. "Can't it wait until morning?"

"I don't think so. Spare me that long." Gareth lifted a hand to Gwalchmai, who was hovering in the entrance to the monastery. At the sight of them, he hurried out.

"Tangwen's asleep," he said before Gwen could ask where her daughter was. "I've been waiting for hours!"

"Hardly," Gwen said. "We weren't gone that long."

"What did you find?" Gwalchmai's expression was eager.

Gwen looked at Gareth, and then she put her arm around her brother's shoulder and turned him underneath the archway. "Let's get inside, and I'll tell you everything." She glanced back over her shoulder at Gareth.

"A quick word with John, and then I'll come home to sleep. I promise," he said.

Gwen let go of Gwalchmai and came back to her husband, standing on tiptoe to kiss his cheek. "Do what you must. I will be waiting." She disappeared into the darkness of the courtyard.

With a lighter heart, Gareth turned on his heel and paced along the road back to the bridge. The guards admitted him without argument, and soon the imposing bulk of Shrewsbury Castle rose up before him. Even at this late hour, the gate was open and the portcullis was up, and the guards, seemingly recognizing Gareth, waved him through.

As he approached John's quarters, however, Gareth heard the bark of an angry voice coming through an open doorway. It cut off almost immediately as if the owner had thought better of his words.

Gareth quickened his pace, and as he turned into the last corridor, he came face-to-face with Martin Carter.

Both men pulled up short, and then Martin ducked his head. "Excuse me, my lord." He brushed past Gareth and disappeared around the corner Gareth had just turned.

Curious, Gareth stepped back in time to see Martin disappearing into the courtyard. With concern furrowing his brow, he continued onto John's rooms, where he found the deputy sheriff seated behind a table, his feet sprawled out in front of him, staring at the fire.

"What was that about?" Gareth said.

John released a low groan. "Martin Carter came here asking for details of the investigation, and he was angry that I wouldn't give them to him. I don't blame him for that."

"He had to have known you couldn't tell him much," Gareth said.

"Apparently not."

John had a rumpled look to him that made Gareth think the investigation was getting the better of him—and it had been only one day.

"Never mind him. Tell me what you've discovered." John straightened in his seat. "I know you've discovered something, else you wouldn't have come."

Gareth eased onto a cushioned bench near the fire. The stone walls of the castle kept the interior far colder than if they'd been wood. A chill hung in the air that had Gareth tucking his cloak closer around himself, glad he'd worn it, for all that the day itself had been warmer than normal.

"I've just come from the brothel." Gareth held up the coin, which he'd been carrying around in his purse since they'd discovered it. If he hadn't been with Gwen just now, he probably would have presented it to the guard in the doorway of The Lady's Slipper. "Gwen and I followed two merchants, who are staying at the monastery guest house. They went directly there and, as they entered, your watchman Luke was coming out."

John's expression didn't change. "He is a single man." But he turned to look into the fire for a moment before moving from his seat behind the table to a chair nearer to Gareth.

"He's a watchman," Gareth said, unable to keep his suspicions to himself. "Don't tell me that it wouldn't be in keeping with Luke's character to take payment in kind for keeping the council and the sheriff from bothering the brothel or its patrons."

As before, John looked affronted at any maligning of his sheriff's honor. "That is not the way we function. We don't take payment, in kind or otherwise. As long as those involved break no law and keep to themselves, we don't bother them."

"Yes, but Luke may have told them a different story," Gareth said. "Your sheriff has been gone over a week. *The mice are merry—*"

"*—where there's no cat.*" John sank lower into his chair, his hands dangling between his knees. "The English have that saying too."

"Something more," Gareth said. "One of the merchants goes by the name Flann MacNeill. He says he's never been to Ireland, but he is an Irishman. It's a connection to Conall—not a strong one, I admit, but I can't ignore it."

John's brow furrowed. "That is more worrisome than anything you've said so far. I can't say I've met more than one or two Irishmen in the whole of my life, and now we encounter two in the space of a day? Is that too much of a coincidence to be believed?"

"Coincidence is always possible, but Conall had a coin to that brothel, and now Flann and his partner, Will, have gone to the brothel," Gareth said. "Is the owner, by chance, Irish?"

John shook his head. "No."

"Who owns it?"

John licked his lips. "The Lady's Slipper is owned by a group of merchants in the town who went into business together."

Gareth threw back his head and laughed. "You're telling me that by day these men are respectable business people? Was Roger Carter by chance one of them?"

"No!" John looked shocked.

Gareth raised his eyebrows. "Can you get me their names?"

"I-I don't know them all."

"But you can find out?"

John nodded. "I confess that I am in no way looking forward to questioning them."

"It will have to be you who does it," Gareth said. "You can't leave it to one of your men, or even to me. They'll appreciate your discretion, I'm sure."

"And every one of them will report back to the sheriff the moment he arrives." John sighed.

Gareth couldn't think of anything to say that would make John feel better, so he said, "Shrewsbury has other brothels, correct?"

"Two more in the town and, as I said, a third beyond the town limits."

"Owned by the same group that owns The Lady's Slipper," Gareth said, remembering.

"Yes," John said, and he drew the *s* out in a long hiss. "You and I will attend to this together in the morning. The manager of the brothel will be less wary then and won't be angry because we disrupted her customers. I will collect you."

Gareth rose to his feet. "As you wish."

"Can I convince you not to bring your wife?" John looked up at him hopefully.

"It's hard for us to understand why visiting a brothel is worse than investigating murder, but—" Gareth snorted laughter, "I have already persuaded her."

The look on John's face was one of pure relief.

16

Hywel

Like most nights—and most knights—Hywel dreamed of violence, much of it directed at him. Tonight, he woke with a start just as he blocked an opposing knight's sword, which had been aimed at his head.

It was a relief to wake, but as Hywel lay in bed, breathing quietly to himself in the dark, he realized that it hadn't been his imminent demise that had woken him, but something else: a noise. He heard it again, the scrape of a shoe in the corridor and then the creak of wood. The room in which Hywel lay with Cadell and Cadifor wasn't completely dark, as they hadn't closed the shutters against the cold night air, and the nearly full moon made a square of light on the floor as it shown through the open window.

As he listened, hardly daring to breathe, Hywel felt motion to his right and was in no way surprised to see Cadifor already crouched beside his pallet on the floor. Hywel had never been able to put anything over on his foster father, who seemed to sleep with one eye open.

Cadifor gestured with one finger, a quick slash to the left, to indicate that he should wake Cadell, with whom Hywel was sharing the bed. Hywel obeyed, rolling over and slipping a hand over Cadell's mouth before putting his lips to his ear and saying as softly as he could, "Wake up."

Cadell was a sound sleeper, still more a child in that than a grown man, but his eyes popped open instantly, and they widened to see Hywel hovering above him. "What is it?"

"We don't know." Hywel lifted his chin to point at Cadifor, who had by now moved off his pallet to the end of Hywel's bed.

Hywel had removed only his shirt and boots before getting into bed—not because he expected treachery from his uncle, but because he didn't need a specific lesson to know not to trust where it hadn't been earned. He slipped his shirt over his head and reached for his boots. He was trying to be as quiet as possible, while at the same time hurrying, even as he cursed to himself that they'd been caught so unawares.

Cadifor, meanwhile, had cat-walked to the door, which remained closed. With his boot knife in his right hand, a wicked long blade that Hywel had been afraid even to hold as a boy, he put his back to the wall beside the frame. If someone came through the door, Cadifor would be right there to stop him.

Cadell hastily pulled on his boots too, while Hywel drew his own knife from its sheath. In the confined space of the room where a swinging sword might end up hurting Cadifor or Cadell, a knife was the better weapon.

Hywel peered out the window of the room, looking for an escape that didn't require them to go through the door. The barracks, in which their room was located, abutted the wooden palisade that encircled the castle. Unfortunately, while their room was on the top floor, the window faced south instead of overlooking the wall. Hywel could have had a more spacious room in the main living quarters of the castle next to the hall, but he'd insisted on sleeping with his men, who were mixed up among Madog's men in the dormitory one floor below. He hadn't wanted to put anyone out. That instinct was looking near-to-prescient now.

Unfortunately, it wasn't an easy drop to the ground, and since the window didn't give them access to the exterior of the castle, they couldn't actually *leave* like every muscle in Hywel's body was screaming at him to do.

"Hywel."

Hywel turned back at Cadifor's breathy warning. The latch had clicked and the door swung open on greased hinges. The room was shadowed enough that all Hywel saw at first was the glint of a knife coming through the door.

His second boot still in his hand, Cadell bounded forward without waiting for Cadifor to move first. The sight of his prey, upright and alert instead of lying in bed, even if he held a boot instead of a sword, gave the intruder a moment's hesitation. That was all the time Cadifor needed to thrust his knife through the man's back and turn with him so that the body was between

Cadifor and the door. The move saved his life since a second man had come through the door behind the first.

This man was better prepared for opposition than his companion, and he launched himself towards Hywel with a muted grunt. The two men fought silently and yet brutally, in quick hand-to-hand combat, Hywel countering the man's knife with his own.

Meanwhile, a third man sprang upon Cadell and backed him up against the bed, followed by a fourth, who didn't get past the doorway because Cadifor was right there to stop him, having dropped the first man he'd killed to the floor. Hywel finally managed to get his knife under his opponent's guard, and he shoved it through the man's chest. Like the first man through the door, this intruder wasn't wearing armor. Perhaps he knew that leather creaked and mail clinked, and he'd been aiming for a silent attack.

Before the man could even fall to the floor, Hywel pulled his knife from his body, spun around, and drove it into the back of the man who was fighting Cadell. While Hywel had been busy with his own opponents, Cadifor had already killed two more.

Then Cadifor shouted a warning, and Hywel turned again to see yet another man coming through the door. This latest attacker was too much for Cadifor, however, and he was forced backward, causing him to trip over one of the bodies behind him. Hywel leapt over his foster father in order to slice through the man's neck.

That man collapsed and Cadifor, thankfully still breathing, scrambled to his feet to rejoin the fight. Containing the attackers within a foot of the doorway was their best option, and the two of them fought shoulder to shoulder. Unfortunately, as the next man went down beneath one of Hywel's thrusts, the blade of Hywel's knife snapped. When he held it up, only the hilt and two inches of jagged blade remained, since the rest of the blade remained in the man's body.

Cadifor shoved at Hywel's shoulder to get him out of the way, just as two more men attacked simultaneously. Cadifor was pressed hard by the first and thus unable to stop the second from chasing after Hywel, who skidded across the bloody floor to his sword, which he'd propped in the corner by the window. He grabbed his sheath, but wasn't able to pull out his sword before his opponent raised his own, prepared to bring it down on his head, just like in the dream—except Hywel had no sword this time to counter it.

Crash!

The man with the sword keeled over, and Hywel found himself facing Cadell, who held a piece of the washing basin in each hand.

Hywel gaped at him, finding uncontrolled laughter overcoming him. "A wash basin? Where's your knife?"

Cadell looked ruefully down at the heavy pieces of pottery he held and then gestured with one of them to where his knife lay on the floor under the window. "He was on you so fast, I grabbed the first thing to hand."

Cadifor grunted as he poked his head into the hallway. "More are coming!" Feet pounded on the stairs, and men shouted from the common room below.

Hywel raced forward to help Cadifor drag the dead men away from the door so it would close. He eased the door shut, making sure it didn't bang, though it was probably very much a matter of tuning a harp after a string had already broken. "My uncle didn't think very much of our skills if he sent only ten men to kill us. He should have sent two dozen."

"He may have, since more are coming." Cadifor crouched next to one of the men, feeling along his body for weapons. "My guess, we were supposed to be dead asleep, thanks to the potency of the drink he served us."

He found a knife in the man's boot, a sharp one, sturdily made, which he tossed to Hywel, who caught it and slid it into his empty sheath.

"Should we kill those who aren't dead?" Cadell said.

"Not in cold blood." Even counting the fight in the room, Cadell hadn't yet killed a man in battle, and seeing how the attackers who weren't dead were unconscious, they posed no threat. Hywel saw no reason for Cadell to cross that particular barrier today.

"We need to get our men and get out of here," Cadifor said.

"Any suggestion as to how we do that?" Hywel said. "We have more of Madog's soldiers coming up the stairs, wondering where these men have got to, and a barracks full of enemies between us and the exit. I imagine if our men aren't yet dead, they soon will be."

"Likely," Cadifor said, without emotion, though Cadell looked stricken at the thought. In response, the older man held out his arm to Cadell. "I'm happy to fight at your side any time, my lord."

Cadell had been raised by his own mother, so he had never met Cadifor and his sons before Hywel had requested that they join his *teulu*. But even short acquaintance had Cadell coveting Cadifor's approval, as well he might. Cadell wanted to be a warrior, and nobody could mistake the experience and wisdom in Cadifor's craggy face.

Thus, Cadell eagerly grasped Cadifor's forearm, prompting Hywel to roll his eyes, though he made sure he was slightly to the right and behind Cadell when he did it so that only Cadifor could see.

Then Hywel straightened, pushing aside the loss of his companions, Evan and Gruffydd among them, whom he'd left to their own devices downstairs, and forcing himself to concentrating on saving Cadell and Cadifor.

"Why aren't they attacking?" Cadell said.

"Because they're followers, Cadell, and not used to thinking for themselves, not in Madog's domain." Hywel worried at his lower lip with his teeth. He recognized one of the dead men as the captain of Dinas Bran's garrison. What he wasn't was the leader of Madog's *teulu*. Where that man was, Hywel didn't know, and it could be that Madog was endeavoring to keep certain hands clean.

At this stage, however, Hywel didn't see why he was bothering. Murdering the *edling* of Gwynedd was going to start a war, no matter who did it.

Then again, maybe that was Madog's plan. If he believed Hywel's father to be weak beyond reason, by killing Hywel, he would leave Gwynedd rudderless and ripe for the taking.

That wasn't quite the ending for his life Hywel had envisioned. Certainly, he wasn't ready to die with Cadwaladr unpunished. With sudden resolve, he moved to the oil lamp that lay on the table beside the bed and lit it with a strike from the fire starter that had been left beside it.

Just as the wick flared, more shouts came up from the common room below them, along with the unmistakable clash of metal on metal. Hywel picked up the lantern. "It appears, Cadell, that they aren't waiting." Hywel met Cadifor's gaze, the lamp in his hand. "Yes?"

"I'd say so, my lord."

While Cadell's eyes widened, Hywel dropped the oil lamp onto the bed, and then flung his arm out across Cadell's chest to stop him from leaping forward.

"What are you doing?" Cadell said.

"Getting us out of here," Hywel said.

The lamp had tipped onto its side, spilling oil onto the bedding, which immediately lit where the oil had pooled. It was a matter of a few heartbeats for the fire to get going, at which point Hywel gathered up the rest of his belongings, his sword among them, while waving a hand at Cadell that he should buckle on his own sword.

Cadell obeyed, his eyes never leaving the flames, which in those few moments spread across the bedcover to reach the hangings.

Cadifor jerked his head. "Time to go."

Trying to breathe without tension, Hywel waited in front of the door for Cadifor, who stood to one side of the frame as he had earlier, to open it. At a nod from Hywel, he swung it wide and Hywel bounded through it, driving his new knife into the chest of a man on the other side, who from his awkward position looked like he'd been about to put a boot through the door.

A moment later, Cadifor and Cadell were through too, their swords bare in their hands, and it was chaos in the corridor and the stairs as the three men from Gwynedd fought their way down it.

The passage was narrow, and the stairs circled around to the right, which gave the advantage to right-handed men, but forced the men coming up to defend left-handed. Hywel was so focused on the men coming towards him that he didn't glance back at the death behind him, though he had made sure to leave the door ajar, so the air would feed the flames as it flowed through the door and out the window they'd also left wide open. He gave a passing thought for the men they'd left unconscious in the room. He was still glad not to have murdered them outright. They had a fighting chance, which was more than they had aimed to give Hywel, Cadell, and Cadifor.

Cadifor skewered the man in front of him, and they all leapt over the body in turn as they thudded down the last few steps to ground level and came out of the stairwell into a room seething with fighting men, straining and hacking away at each other in the dark, since the windows in here had been left closed for the night. Then the front door opened—perhaps bringing reinforcements, perhaps bringing someone who'd gone out to relieve himself.

It didn't matter why. Hywel felt the gust of air whoosh past him, moving up the stairs towards the fire which was greedily consuming everything in its path.

Boom! Something crashed to the floor—a section of the roof, Hywel guessed.

Cadifor took the noise as his signal to leap into the fray, though not to fight. "Fire! The barracks are on fire!"

He'd always had a voice that carried, though by this point, even the most intent or dimwitted could smell smoke and feel heat from the flames raging above them.

"Move! Move!" The leader of the garrison might be dead upstairs, but he had an able second, and that man urged his men out the front door. Several who'd been fighting Hywel's men fought shoulder-to-shoulder with each other instead to be the first to escape out the door.

"Our turn," Hywel said, but he didn't follow where Madog's men had gone. On the far side of the room there was a second door, which opened towards the stable. "This way, men!"

In the dark, Hywel's people wouldn't be able to make out his features, but all of them should recognize his voice. Those who could walk struggled after him. On the way, Hywel scooped up one of the younger men, who was on his knees, bleeding heavily from his right side. Flinging the man's arm across his shoulder and grasping him around his waist, Hywel staggered with him out the door, which Cadell had reached first. Smoke billowed everywhere around them and, in an unorganized bunch, they hurried across the gap between the barracks and the stable.

With the fire lighting the sky above them, the moon shining stolidly down, and the torches blazing from sconces at the gatehouse and from the great hall, it was nowhere near dark. But the few men from Gwynedd were lost amidst the chaos in the courtyard as men ran to and fro, waking the castle to the threat. The whole of Dinas Bran was built in wood, and there was a very real danger that the fire in the barracks would spread to adjacent buildings, not to mention the palisade.

"How many did we lose?" Hywel said as they found refuge in the darkness of the stable, having come into the stable through one of the side doors. There were three doors in all—one on each end and a main, double doorway on the long front side facing the courtyard of the castle.

The horses were whinnying and rearing, smelling smoke and fearing it. Cadell ran from one to another, freeing them. Stable boys were helping, and with the smoke and the darkness, nobody looked closely at Cadell or wondered why he was still alive and not dead on the floor of his room in the barracks.

"Four, my lord," Cadifor said.

Hywel nodded, accepting for now what couldn't be changed. Evan, Gareth's close friend, was one of the other survivors, and he took the arm of the man Hywel had carried from the barracks and eased him to the ground. He felt at the man's neck and then looked up at Hywel. "Five, my lord."

"Leaving the five of us." Hywel shook his head, even as he ripped at the tail of his shirt to staunch the blood flowing from a gash he'd just discovered on his upper arm. "This is my fault."

"Recriminations are for later, my prince." Gruffydd, Rhun's former captain, approached and took the cloth from Hywel in order to wrap it around Hywel's arm. The wound wasn't deep, and later it would hurt, but it didn't now.

Hywel acknowledged that it was no coincidence that the two most experienced men in his company were the only two to survive the attack in the common room. He was glad beyond measure that Cadell had been sleeping with him, or the youth would have been among the dead too. Madog's men had nearly finished the job. "We must leave now."

Cadell came running back from the main entrance to the stable. "The front gate is open."

"It would be. They can hardly fight this fire bringing up one bucket at a time from the well," Cadifor said.

Hywel took in a breath and looked at the others—fellow warriors, friends, brothers. "We ride out that gate, and we don't stop for anyone or anything."

"Except for me."

Hywel spun on his heel to see his Aunt Susanna standing in the doorway that led to the courtyard, her hand to her chest, recovering her breath. Likely, she'd run here from the hall. All of the horses but their five were out of the stable now, so they were alone.

"Aunt," Hywel said.

"You can't go out the front. There are too many men between you and safety, but you can lead your horses out the postern gate. I've sent the guard away to help fight the fire. It's just through here." She hastened across the stable towards a far doorway, opposite the one they'd come in from the barracks, and waited for them while they hastily collected their horses.

The blacksmith's shop was adjacent to the stable, on the opposite side from the barracks. Behind a stack of kindling for feeding the forge lay a narrow gateway, just wide enough for a horse to pass through.

Hywel glanced back. The fire had consumed the barracks' roof. He wouldn't have said that a thousand buckets of water could contain the blaze now and thought Madog would be better off soaking everything around the barracks instead of the barracks itself. Meanwhile, Susanna opened the gate, and the others filed through it. Hywel was last, and he hesitated as he reached his aunt, who was waiting for him. "Thank you."

"I guessed what my husband planned to do, and I didn't warn you," she said. "I would never have forgiven myself if you'd died."

Hywel leaned forward and kissed her cheek. "I regret that I will repay your loyalty with war against your husband."

"I know," she said. "I'm counting on it."

That took Hywel back apace. Her hatred for Madog had to be immense to say such a thing. "And your sons."

Susanna took in a deep breath. "I beg you to spare them, if you can."

Hywel's heart filled with pity. "You have my word."

17

Hywel

None of the others had suffered anything more in the fight than sore muscles and a few bloody scrapes, which was fortunate, because the postern gate opened onto the narrowest track Hywel had ever seen. Its poor state of repair had to be deliberate, since of course Madog didn't want anyone coming up it.

The main road wended its way to the castle from the southwest and the village, and he supposed it was a good thing it wasn't daylight now because, by the light of the moon, they could make out only the outlines of what they had to contend with to escape. He honestly didn't want to know what broad daylight would have shown them.

The track led them down the north slope of the mountain, and they slipped and slid along it in their frantic descent away from Dinas Bran. Hywel cursed himself the whole way for being naïve, for thinking that his uncle wouldn't take this ultimate step to gain power, and for allowing himself to be buttered up enough by praise to sing late into the night. While he'd known enough to drink sparingly, which may well have saved his life, he was more tired that he ought to be, and that was affecting his judgment.

The track switched back and forth across the mountain's face. At one point, though Cadifor was in the lead and Hywel at the back, they reached a point where they were face-to-face as they passed one another going in opposite directions.

"I'm sorry, my lord," Cadifor said in an undertone. "I should have warned you that something like this might happen."

Hywel scoffed. It was just like Cadifor to deflect blame onto himself when it was really Hywel's. "Did you have some forewarning that my uncle would take to murder?"

"No, my lord—"

And then he was past his foster father, huffing and puffing along with the others as fast as he could away from the castle. The horses could see better in the dark than they, and Hywel had his fingers woven through Glew's mane, the better to keep himself upright.

On the next switchback, Hywel had time to say, "Then the blame belongs to me, not you. The lives of my men rest on my shoulders, and I let you all down by bringing you here."

"It isn't your fault either, Hywel." Cadell was walking behind Cadifor, and couldn't help but overhear. His tone was uncharacteristically tart. "If anything, my brothers and I should have heard something of your uncle's unrest, seeing as how Denbigh is far closer to Dinas Bran than Aber or Meirionnydd."

"Gruffydd and I had no inkling of what was to come either," Evan said from in front of Hywel. His normally blond hair was dark with soot. "We ordered the men to drink sparingly, as is always warranted in a strange hall, but Madog's men were very disciplined. They gave nothing away."

Gruffydd, walking in the exact middle, grunted his assent. As Rhun's former captain, he'd been nearly as lost as Hywel these last months. Hywel had folded him and the survivors of the ambush that had killed Rhun into his *teulu*, now dramatically expanded to a full fifty, with enough men left over to garrison the various castles around Wales that were now his responsibility. "We failed you, my lord. Evan and I were taking turns sleeping, but even with our precautions, they attacked so suddenly, I had time only to leap to my feet and shout a warning before they were on us."

Hywel was bringing up the rear, so he could see Evan shaking his head up ahead of him. "What is it, Evan?"

"Madog has to realize what he's started, doesn't he? This means war."

"I said as much to my aunt as we were leaving. Madog must believe that the time is ripe for rebellion against my father. Since Rhun's death, the king is seen as weak." Hywel heaved a sigh. "Father has been weak, but Madog was a fool to think I was."

"That's why he tried to kill you, my lord," Evan said, "to get you out of the way."

"Back in the room," Cadifor said, "I said that I thought Madog may have put something in our drink. I still feel that's true."

"We drank from communal cups," Gruffydd said. "I made sure of it."

"Were any of the men sitting beside you at the table sleeping beside you in the barracks?" Cadifor said.

There came a hitch in Gruffydd's step. "Come to think on it, no."

"Madog has enough men that he could afford to let a few sleep out the night so that others who hadn't been affected could fight," Cadifor said.

"So how did I survive?" Cadell said. "I drank quite a bit."

"I know you did, boy, despite my warning," Cadifor said. "Why do you think your wine was so watered? I swapped out our carafe for one from another table."

"I shared a cup with my aunt," Hywel said, "and when I was given my own when it came time to sing, I didn't touch it."

"Luck," Gruffydd growled.

"Good training," Cadifor said.

"Except for me." Cadell's shoulders hunched.

"Lesson learned then, son," Cadifor said.

"I have a further worrisome thought, my lord," Evan said. "Madog may have acted tonight on his own, but I wouldn't put it past him to be in league with Cadwaladr."

"My aunt implied that might be true," Hywel said. "I will believe anything of Madog now."

Their conversation, undertaken piecemeal and in low tones, had carried them three-quarters of the way down the mountain. Hywel glanced back, expecting a sign of pursuit and seeing none, but he didn't allow himself to breathe easier—and wouldn't—

until they were well away from Dinas Bran.

Hywel had known that treachery was a possibility before he'd brought his men up to Dinas Bran, though he hadn't truly believed that his uncle would violate the peace of his own house. But if Madog was in any way allied with Cadwaladr, which now that Hywel thought about it seemed more than likely, Hywel had also underestimated the tenor and quality of his hatred—which, along with the promise of a magnificent reward, could be the only thing that would have made Madog risk open war with Gwynedd on the chance that he could murder Hywel and get away with it.

Unless, as was sometimes the case with Cadwaladr, he hadn't seen it as a risk. The move against Hywel had been both bold and calculating. But like many of Cadwaladr's schemes, Madog also had reached too far and hadn't counted on the betrayal of his own wife—or that Hywel would have surrounded himself with men who slept with one eye open, if they slept at all.

"Our deaths, coupled with Father's grief could provide an opening for Cadwaladr to return to Wales," Cadell said.

Hywel nodded, though they'd reached a straight stretch and Cadell, walking second behind Cadifor, couldn't see him. The comment was, at first blush, uncharacteristically insightful for Cadell. And yet, while Hywel's brother might be young, he'd grown up a prince of Wales. Even a man with a sweet nature like Cadell learned intrigue by necessity, or he didn't survive.

Except for Rhun, who'd risen above it. But Rhun had been the *edling,* and he'd had Hywel always at his back, protecting him and allowing him to take the high road. Now that Rhun was dead, Hywel could admit that when he was younger, he'd sometimes resented their differing roles. His father's countenance and favor had been bestowed on Rhun. Hywel had been the second son— loved, but not respected or adored in the same way as Rhun. But as he'd grown older, he'd come to appreciate the way Rhun protected *him.* Hywel would give anything to have him back.

The thought of his brother had Hywel stepping a bit faster down the trail. Surely they had to be near the bottom by now.

In years to come, Hywel would retain very little memory of their descent out of Dinas Bran beyond overwhelming emotion: a fear of being followed, as images of Madog's men snapping at their heels like dogs at a boar consumed him; an embarrassing and unexpected fear of heights that had his heart pounding and his knees weakening almost more than the far more real danger of discovery; and a raging anger at himself that he'd led his men into danger and had been able to lead only half of them out of it.

That rage, which they all shared, was ultimately what kept them upright as their legs trembled from the sharp descent and as the stew of emotions in their bellies left them sick at heart. The fire in the stable must have spread to other buildings, because it continued to blaze above them, sending the smoke east with the wind that always blew on the top of the mountain. And still, nobody followed them out the postern gate.

Hywel could only hope that his aunt was discouraging anyone from looking for them there, and it would take some time for Madog to realize that they'd gone and hadn't died in the rubble that was all that was left of the barracks.

A heart stopping hour later, they found refuge in a stand of trees two miles east of the castle. The decision to head east had been the result of cold calculation on Hywel's part. If Madog were to look anywhere for them, it should be west back to Aber or north to Mold, not east into England.

"On to Shrewsbury, then?" Evan was taking in big gulps of air.

They'd kept to the shadows, staying off the road whenever possible. It had meant that they'd had to lead the horses rather than ride them and risk the sound of hoof beats echoing through the hollows and bluffs that surrounded them. That could change now that they'd reached the plains of England.

"Where else?" Hywel said.

While neither he nor Cadell should be wandering the roads and byways of England, and certainly not with so few men to accompany them, nobody in England knew who they were either. With his perfect French, thanks to years of lessons with Meilyr and Gwen, Hywel could pass for a Norman if he tried. While his companions looked and acted very Welsh, here in the March, a Norman lord often had Welsh retainers.

"We've come this far. If Madog decides I was telling the truth about where we were going, and that I would continue on to

Shrewsbury despite the loss of my men, he can't follow us there. Shrewsbury is in England, and his writ doesn't stretch that far."

"If anything, we've picked up Cadwaladr's scent now even more than at Mold," Gruffydd said, and there was a fire in his eyes as he spoke.

"It's also possible that what prompted Madog to act tonight was the knowledge that you intended to ride to Shrewsbury today," Evan said. "It could be that Cadwaladr really is there, and Madog knows it, or that Cadwaladr has been there recently enough that if we go there we have the possibility of tracking him."

"It's the closest we've been to Cadwaladr in months," Gruffydd said.

"It would be good to know if Cadwaladr has allied with Madog before we make war on Powys," Cadifor said. "Cadwaladr has been banished from Gwynedd, but he still has support in other regions of Wales, and many a lord would rather that a weaker king sat on the throne of Gwynedd."

Hywel glanced up towards where Dinas Bran perched on its mountain. "Madog must have been so gleeful when he learned that he had me in his lair. He's probably been dreaming since Rhun's death of what he would do to me once he had me."

"Kill you," Gruffydd said dryly.

Hywel snorted laughter. "Indeed."

Cadell spoke into the general amusement. "I have bad news." He'd been tending to his horse rather than participating in the conversation, and now he straightened. "His hock is bleeding."

Cadifor tsked through his teeth and went to look, squinting at the wound in the murky light. Dawn wasn't far off now, and they needed to be on their way before the sun rose. "The wound isn't deep, and he should be fine to walk, but Cadell can't ride him to Shrewsbury."

Hywel sighed and ran a hand through his hair, coming away with ash, which he shook off his hand with an impatient flick. "One wonders if this isn't a sign that I'm headed in the wrong direction. Father needs to know of Madog's treachery."

"He does, but who's to say he will listen or care," Cadell said.

"Whether he does or not, my brothers and I have a new war to prepare for," Hywel said. "Even now, Madog could be marshaling his forces to march against Gwynedd."

Gruffydd went to the edge of the trees and gazed out across the fields. A mist hovered just above the ground. "I will see Cadell to Mold. He and I can ride two on my horse, with the lame horse in tether. Our progress will be slow, but we could make Mold by the end of the day. And then I will personally ride to your father at Aber." He came back to Hywel and spoke in an undertone. "I want revenge against Cadwaladr as much as any man here, but the most important thing is to get you away, and we may all do better if we split up."

Hywel offered Gruffydd his forearm, and he grasped it. Perhaps all of them should return to Mold and forsake this possibly fruitless quest. But while Gruffydd could make Mold today, so too could Hywel make Shrewsbury. "If Cadwaladr is in the vicinity, Gareth will know about it. By tomorrow evening, I could have collected him and be riding home to Aber."

Cadifor rubbed at his chin, nodding slowly at first, and then with genuine enthusiasm. "By then, if Madog was preparing to march on Gwynedd, all of Powys would know. We could bring word of his plans and the disposition of his men to your father, and thus do Gwynedd a great service."

"You'll have to travel through Powys the entire way," Gruffydd said. "That's Madog's territory."

"We'll have Gwen and the others with us," Hywel said. "Nobody will bother a family group, not if war in the north is on their mind. But if it's any comfort, we'll ride through England to Shrewsbury and lose all pursuit that way. Ranulf is off away to Lincoln, along with most of his fighting men. We should have free passage north and south."

"It is true that in England, the roads are flatter and more straight," Gruffydd said, though his expression was dubious—as if flat, straight roads were a mark against a country. Both he and Cadifor shared the same healthy distrust for all things not Welsh.

In the distance, a rider came out of the mist, and by his shape and seat on his horse, Hywel had a sudden thought that he was Gareth. But then he passed by without stopping or seeing them, and Hywel knew him for a stranger.

No, Gareth was thirty miles away in Shrewsbury. Hywel was going to have to manage this next stage with just Evan and Cadifor. He could only pray that it would go better than the last one.

18

Gwen

Gareth had returned from his meeting with John and told Gwen all about it—confirming that he and John would be visiting the brothel the next day without her—and then she'd slept untroubled for the whole of the night.

Even she thought her ability to sleep despite having seen two dead bodies that day was unusual, but since having Tangwen, sleeping through the night had been a rare gift. She wasn't going to waste the opportunity on other people's troubles over which she had no control.

The next morning, leaving Gareth to his brothel and to question the entire town of Shrewsbury if that's what it took to discover someone who might recognize the girl or tell him where Conall had got to, Gwen returned to Shrewsbury with her father, Tangwen on her hip. Few spring days could have dawned as brightly as this morning had, and even two murders and the prospect of presenting herself before Adeline's father couldn't tarnish Gwen's good mood.

Adeline's father lived and worked on a street Gwen hadn't been to yet. But as Gareth had pointed out the day before, Shrewsbury wasn't so large that any place was very far from anywhere else. Tom Weaver's shop lay on the west side of the town, among other merchants selling similar wares. As with the alley, this was a relatively flat part of the town, near the river. All the houses and shops along this stretch were on the level, and thus had room at the back for warehouses or craft halls, and space enough to keep chickens and horses.

As they approached Adeline's father's home, Meilyr put a hand on Gwen's shoulder. "All will be well. He simply wanted to meet you."

Gwen took in a breath and nodded, glad she had brought Tangwen with her. The girl could provide a good distraction in case Tom became emotional. Or in case Gwen herself did. She might have been accepting of the deaths of two people in Shrewsbury, but Adeline had died in part because she looked like Gwen. That wasn't something she could sweep under the rushes and ignore.

Meilyr rapped on the door, which opened instantly.

"I saw you coming." Tom, a large man, with shoulders like a side of beef, stood in the doorway, his eyes on Gwen as if she were a large cup of beer and he was parched.

She dipped into a brief curtsey. "Hello." Then she frowned as her gaze went to a fresh cut above his left eye.

Tom noted where she was looking and put a hand to it. "Even in my own house, I sometimes forget to duck my head under the doorframe."

Gwen smiled, and then Tom did too, instantly breaking whatever ice that could have formed between them. Tom stepped back, gesturing that they should enter his house. "Come in."

Gwen had spent much of her life in castles, but she had her own little house on Anglesey too, and hers resembled this one, with its main single room containing a long table scrubbed smooth, a bench, and several mismatched chairs. A loft above was reached by a ladder. A bed big enough for two sat in a far corner, covered by a patchwork blanket, and in another corner a curtain was pulled back to reveal an empty space behind it. It occurred to Gwen that the private space might have been Adeline's before she died, and that Tom had rearranged his house to get rid of her bed, but he had left the curtain as a reminder of what had been.

Tom pulled out a bench, gesturing that they should sit. "So you saw her? My girl?"

Gwen sat, Tangwen on her lap. "I did. Yes, sir."

Tom took in a deep breath through his nose before crouching on a low stool at the end of the table. He put his elbows on the table and his hands in his hair, hanging there for a moment before straightening. "I'm glad someone was with her at the end."

"She's buried properly in a churchyard," Gwen said, without mentioning that she herself hadn't actually been present as Adeline had died. She didn't know if Tom realized that or not, but it was hardly something she was going to bring up now.

"Up near Mold, is it?" Tom said.

Gwen nodded, though she didn't give him the Welsh name of the village. It would mean nothing to him.

"Where are my manners?" Tom stood again, tipping over his stool. He flushed as he righted it. "I have food and drink prepared." He disappeared out the back of his house, which gave Gwen and her father an opportunity to take a deep breath themselves. Tangwen, for once, wasn't squirming to get down, and instead leaned back against Gwen's chest. Maybe Gwen was going to be so lucky that Tangwen would take a short nap.

"You're doing well," Meilyr said.

Gwen smiled. "What about you? Is your head all right?"

Meilyr scoffed. "I remember now why it has been such a long while since I drank that much. I'll recover. It serves me right."

Gwen hadn't been going to say it, but she was glad that her father seemed to have recovered from his melancholy. Then Tom returned, a forced smile on his face, but still a smile, and he offered them fresh bread with butter and watered mead. "You're Welsh. I thought you might prefer it."

"We do," Meilyr said. "Thank you."

Tom raised his cup. "To Adeline."

"To Adeline," Gwen and Meilyr repeated.

Gwen took a small sip, but Tom drained his cup in a long series of gulps, and when he set it down, his eyes were clearer than before. He filled his glass again. "That's good!"

Tom didn't quite get drunk as he consumed cup after cup, but he became more talkative, making the meeting less awkward than Gwen had feared. She had thought to avoid talking about the specifics of how Adeline had left Shrewsbury, in order not to offend Tom, but Tom's openness encouraged her to try. Besides, having taken a short nap, Tangwen had woken refreshed and run off to chase the chickens in Tom's courtyard, under the watchful eyes of Tom's journeyman and apprentices. Thus, Gwen didn't have to worry about the little girl overhearing something Gwen would prefer she didn't.

"At the end, before Adeline left, did you ever see her with a Welshman?"

"Are you asking if I saw her with the one that died with her, who looked like your husband?" Tom said.

Gwen shot a quick glance at her father, who nodded. "I told him about Gareth."

"I don't mean to bring up bad memories but, while it is true that I was wondering about that man, I also want to know about another man, maybe one obviously wealthy, who might have swept her off her feet."

Tom snorted into his cup. "You're talking about the big, blond, fancy man who wore a sword, though I didn't think he knew how to use it."

"You saw her with him?" Gwen tried to keep the urgency that filled her out of her voice.

"From a distance. He was coming down the street having visited the castle when he came upon Adeline."

"Are you saying they met by accident?" Gwen said.

Tom shook his head. "It looked to me like she'd been lying in wait. I laid into her about it, didn't I? She had no cause to be talking to the likes of him, seeing as how he'd only want one thing from her, and she didn't want to be known as that type of girl. She should have been paying attention to her future husband, shouldn't she have?"

"Roger Carter." Gwen could hardly have forgotten about him.

"And now he's dead too." Tom sighed.

"A cartwright, wasn't he?" Meilyr said.

"The best in Shrewsbury, he and his brother. Well-respected they are—were. Roger was quite a bit older than Adeline." Tom sighed again. "I should have known better than to accept his offer for her hand, but I wanted what was best for her, even if she didn't."

"Why did Roger offer for her?" Gwen said.

"He loved her, didn't he?" Tom said. "Every man did. She turned heads everywhere she went."

Gwen didn't say that what he described wasn't actually *love*, but that wasn't her place to explain either.

"Where is the cartwright's shop?" Gwen said, trying not to sound like she cared very much. Gareth had already visited the family, and she didn't want to interfere with his activities, but with Roger's murder, the more she knew about Roger the better she would be able to help. She really just wanted to see it.

"The next street over." Tom canted his head to indicate the direction. "You might be careful about how you approach Martin if you plan to talk to him. You look very much like Adeline. She and Jenny, Martin's wife, were close."

Gwen put up a hand, palm out. "I have no desire to meet him. I was just curious."

Then Tom frowned. "You know, I might have seen that other fellow, the fancy man, not two weeks ago."

"You did? Where?" It was Meilyr who leaned in this time, which was good because Gwen found her breath catching in her throat.

"Riding down the east road past the monastery, wasn't he? I was delivering cloth to the hospitaller and just coming out the main gate. Plain as day it was the same man—or at least I thought so at first," Tom said. "I almost went after him, but he was riding fast, and I had no horse."

"Did he have anyone with him?" Meilyr said.

"A man-at-arms and a servant," Tom said. "That's all. Light company for one such as he, I thought at the time."

Gwen thought, but didn't say, that he had so few men with him because he'd abandoned the rest of his men in Gwynedd.

"Did Adeline ever tell you this fancy man's name?" Gwen held her breath.

Tom shook his head. "Never mentioned a name, though it was plain he was above her station."

Gwen shared a glance with her father. Sadly, they didn't actually need Tom to tell them his name to know it: Prince Cadwaladr. Who else could it be? Like his brother, King Owain,

Cadwaladr had an eye for women, but in this case, Adeline had an eye for men too, and perhaps he hadn't needed to pursue her.

"Thank you for meeting me." The weaver was a kind, sad man. Gwen kissed him on his cheek. "I am so sorry for your loss."

He clutched her hand. "Thank you. Just seeing you here eases the pain a little, knowing you cared for her too. She was a lost lamb always." Tom smiled gently at Gwen. "Be well."

Once outside in the street, having collected Tangwen from her play, Gwen hesitated as to where they should go next.

Meilyr didn't. "Let's walk by that cartwright's shop. I want to see this place where Adeline's beloved lived."

"Whether or not they were betrothed, according to John Fletcher and Tom Weaver, the cartwright was in no way her beloved, but I suppose it can't hurt to wander by." Gwen understood her father's desire to know everything he could about Adeline, but what she didn't say was that she had begun to think that the sooner her father admitted that Adeline hadn't been his daughter, the better.

They set off down the street, turned onto an adjacent one, and then turned again, stopping in the middle of the street to inspect what was before them. Gwen had the sense that Shrewsbury had started out orderly, with each kind of merchant setting up shop in a particular quarter of the town, but in recent years, the system had been undermined by rapid growth. On this street, merchants had set up shop higgledy piggledy wherever a spot had become vacant.

The cartwright in question was located next to a glover, whose shop lay adjacent to a goldsmith. Gwen had never seen a goldsmith shop before, though she wore a gold cross around her neck that would have come from a place such as this.

"Adeline!"

A girl with a mane of dark red hair, similar in color to Roger's and coming lose from her wimple, came hurtling out of the driveway that led into the cartwright's yard and flung herself at Gwen. Gwen caught her, but only by letting go of Tangwen's hand. Fortunately, Meilyr scooped up Tangwen before she could become upset by the strange woman who was hugging her mother and alternately sobbing and laughing in her arms.

"I'm not—" Gwen tried.

"I knew you weren't dead, and they were all silly to say so. I knew you'd come back!"

Gwen knew she had to take charge of the situation before it got any more out of hand. She could feel the eyes of a dozen people in the surrounding shops and houses watching them, so she grasped the girl by the upper arms and forcibly pushed her away so that she could look into her face. "I am not Adeline. I am Gwen."

The girl stopped in mid-laugh, gaping at Gwen. The two women were of a height, and the girl's bright green eyes were filled with tears.

A man hurried out of the cartwright's shop. "Jenny! Jenny!"

Jenny put her hands up to Gwen's arms, gripping all the tighter. Tears streamed down her cheeks as she tried to get a hold of herself.

Gwen felt like crying herself just seeing Jenny's grief. "I'm so sorry."

The man came to a halt a few paces away and shook his head. "It isn't your fault. I knew that she hadn't accepted Adeline's death. And now with Roger's too—"

"We shouldn't have come," Meilyr said from beside Gwen. "We can go."

"No!" Jenny clung to Gwen still, but after a moment, she managed to take some gasping breaths, let go of Gwen, and wiped at her cheeks with the backs of her hands. "I'm all right."

Martin moved to put a hand on his wife's shoulder. "I met your husband earlier when he and John came by to tell me about Roger, but—" he shook his head, "it took seeing you for myself for me to believe that what people are saying is true."

Meilyr put out his hand to the man. "I'm Meilyr, Gwen's father."

The man grasped his forearm. "Martin Carter, John Fletcher's brother-in-law, and Roger's brother. May I invite you inside?"

Gwen hesitated. "Your house is in mourning—"

"We've seen to Roger already. You needn't concern yourself with making his death worse than it is." Martin lifted a hand to someone behind Gwen.

She turned to see what had drawn his attention. As they'd stood talking, a crowd had gathered around them, far more than she'd initially supposed. "This is so awkward," she said in Welsh in an undertone to her father.

Meilyr bowed, still looking at Martin. "We would be honored." Tangwen clung to him with her chin wrinkled up and her brow furrowed. She looked close to tears herself.

Gwen brushed one of her daughter's curls out of her face and took her back from Meilyr. "It's all right, love."

"Home," Tangwen said, transferring her arms from her grandfather's neck to her mother's.

"Soon," Gwen said.

Martin by-passed his front door and instead led the way down the driveway, which he and his wife had come down earlier to meet Gwen and Meilyr. Still wiping at her cheeks, Jenny flashed a smile at Gwen before hurrying ahead, probably to prepare food and drink. Gwen didn't have the heart to tell her that they didn't need it, since they'd just eaten and drunk at Tom's house.

In the yard, a cart had been pulled up in front of the workshop and was currently resting on only three wheels because Martin's apprentice, a well-built man in his early twenties, with bulging muscles, was in the process of removing the fourth one.

At the sight of it, Gwen stopped in her tracks. A stain marred the wood of all four wheels, and the one the apprentice was removing was missing its rim.

Leaving her father, who was saying nice things to Martin about Shrewsbury, Gwen approached cautiously, not wanting to seem too curious, but unable to keep herself away. "What are you doing?"

The man looked up to answer, went completely white, and then recovered with a visible gulp. "Oh."

Gwen would have thought his behavior suspicious if she hadn't known she looked just like Adeline. She smiled. "I'm Gwen."

"Huw." The man swallowed hard again before gesturing towards the wheel with a lift of his chin. "The wheel slipped its rim. I'm just seeing about a new one."

"For whom?" Gwen said.

"For him." The man jerked his head towards a man standing off to one side whom Gwen hadn't noticed when she'd come in. Meilyr had already recognized Flann, the talkative merchant from the monastery, and approached, both nodding their greetings to one another.

From Adeline, to Roger, to Flann, to the brothel—this was a puzzle in the making if Gwen could only get the pieces to fit.

19

Hywel

It was with a heavy heart and his most fervent prayers that Hywel saw Cadell and Gruffydd on their way, heading north the long way around the great escarpment of Eglwyseg that rose up to the east of Dinas Bran. Looking at it from the west, the range formed an impenetrable barrier, which was why they'd been forced to ride around it to the south—and why Dinas Bran had been built where it had in the first place. Most of the time, the escarpment protected Llangollen from the English. Today, it would protect Cadell from his uncle's forces.

"We need to move." Cadifor pointed with his chin towards faint specks barely visible in the distance, but which were moving towards them along the Dee River, coming from the village. "Can we get across the river before they see us?"

"If Gareth were here," Hywel said, "I'm sure he'd be able to tell us about a dozen fords between here and Chester, but I know of only two: one in Llangollen village, and a second about a mile to the south in the bend before the river turns north again."

Evan sniffed the air. "We'll see rain before long, but I think we'll stay dry at least until noon. If we can get on the high road before then, we could start to make good time."

"There is nothing I would like more than to take the high road," Hywel said, "but I don't dare do so this close to the border. Still, we can hurry. Those men aren't turning around." Within a few heartbeats, Hywel and his companions were mounted and cantering through the fields to the west of the village of Trefor.

Although they were three horsemen, obviously well mounted, nobody could tell they were fleeing Madog's men just by looking at them. Thus, Hywel had it in his mind to skirt every village in their path, rather than announce his presence by riding straight through them. Madog aside, there was still Cadwaladr to think about. Who knew how many spies between here and Shrewsbury he and Madog had between them.

A half-mile passed underneath their hooves, and then the road began to curve nearer to the river, at which point Hywel realized he wasn't going to have to search for the ford—the road was going to lead them straight to it.

Unfortunately, as they came down the last straight stretch before the ford, a young man wearing full armor and holding a sword settled himself to block their passage up the far side. The helmet didn't disguise his features entirely, and Hywel recognized him as his cousin, Llywelyn, eldest son of Madog and no more than fifteen years old. He was the very son Susanna had asked him to spare during their hasty departure from Dinas Bran.

"What's this?" Cadifor reined in.

Hywel shot a quick glance at his foster father, reminding himself that the last time Cadifor had joined King Owain's retinue had been ten years ago during the wars in Ceredigion, when Llywelyn would have been five years old. Cadifor hadn't been to court since then. Even if King Madog had brought his family to Aber or King Owain had visited Powys, Cadifor wouldn't recognize any of his sons.

"Madog's eldest and my cousin."

"Christ," Cadifor blasphemed.

"I share your sentiment." Hywel directed Glew down the bank.

As Hywel approached the water, Llywelyn's horse danced sideways, and the boy gripped his sword more tightly. "I don't want to fight you, cousin, but I cannot let you pass."

"Your father sent soldiers to kill me and my men," Hywel said.

"My father told me you'd say that. He says that was a misunderstanding."

From behind Hywel, Cadifor guffawed.

"I don't want to fight you either," Hywel said.

"My father's orders are clear." Llywelyn pushed his helmet to the back of his head, allowing Hywel to see his face more fully. "I am to return you to Dinas Bran. As he is my liege lord, I must obey."

"You can try." Hywel breathed in deeply through his nose and out through his mouth, stalling for time as he searched for a solution to what appeared at the moment to be an unresolvable problem. He had sworn to his aunt that he would spare her son if it was at all possible, but he hadn't reckoned on encountering him under these conditions. It could be, however, that she had known her husband would send Llywelyn out, and her plea had been a direct result.

"Where are your men?" Hywel said.

Llywelyn's face fell. "Close." Then he straightened his shoulders in further resolve.

It was obvious to Hywel that Llywelyn was lying. Cadifor said the same in a low voice from behind him.

"What I don't understand is how he could have become separated," Evan said. "The castle is still only a few miles from here, and Trefor closer still."

Hywel thought he knew: Madog hadn't sent out his eldest son to look for Hywel at all. Llywelyn had snuck out, thinking to capture Hywel single-handedly and prove his worth. It was a foolish thing to have done, but admirable as well, especially for a son trying to please a hard-driving father. Hywel knew that urge well himself, and he might have done the same thing when he was fifteen. "Your father doesn't know you've left the castle, does he?"

Llywelyn's spine was so straight he was almost standing in the saddle. "You shall not pass, Hywel." He was endearingly earnest.

Hywel nearly laughed, except— "Don't add to your father's mistake."

"My father doesn't make mistakes!"

Hywel groaned under his breath, reminding himself again how young Llywelyn still was, even if he'd been valued a man since the age of fourteen. He was still younger than Cadell—or even Gwalchmai, Gwen's brother, and he didn't yet see his parents as mortal. A common error, but not one Hywel had the time or energy in to rectify today.

Cadifor and Evan joined Hywel on the bank, all three of them studying Llywelyn, who gritted his teeth, resolute and stricken at the same time by what faced him. But he was steadier now too, and the determination in his eyes was no jest. Hywel was tempted to urge his horse forward and engage the boy, just to teach him a lesson. But he genuinely didn't want to hurt him, aside from keeping his promise to his aunt. And besides, Hywel's arm hurt.

"I could knock him out without killing him," Cadifor suggested. "Leave him in a bush until he wakes."

"That would be humiliating, but at least he would be alive," Hywel said.

"He must know that he cannot stand against the three of us," Evan said.

"Whatever we do, we must do it quickly," Cadifor said.

Hywel tipped his head to one side as he studied his cousin. Then he pulled out his own sword and urged his horse across the river. As the presence of the road had suggested, it was a good ford, wide and not deep, and well paved with stones so his horse had firm base to canter across.

Though Llywelyn stood his ground as Hywel reached the other side and came up the bank, his eyes widened, and he made no move to attack. If Llywelyn had been intent on killing Hywel, he would have done so before Hywel was able to leave the water. Perhaps he really had some hope that Hywel would come quietly.

"I propose a trade." Hywel pointed his sword at his cousin, but made sure at the same time to stay out of actual fighting distance.

"What kind of trade?"

"I have urgent business in Shrewsbury that cannot wait. I promised your mother to spare you if I could. If you will not let me pass, I won't be able to keep that promise."

"I don't need my mother to protect me." Llywelyn was deeply offended, as well he might be. Hywel had intended to offend him as a way to put him off his guard and start him thinking more about his mother than killing Hywel.

"I told her exactly that," Hywel said, lying outright, "but you must realize that she loves me and does not want me to come to harm at your father's hands."

"She loves me more."

Hywel bobbed his head, making sure not to laugh at the childish comment. "Of course she does, but do you really want to force her to choose between you and me? She would choose you, but it would break her heart to do so."

Llywelyn's sword wavered, his anger fading in the face of the vision of his mother's grief. When he'd come down the mountain, he'd been on fire to capture Hywel and bring him triumphantly before his father, thus gaining his father's favor. He'd had no thought for his mother at all.

"You know I'm right," Hywel said. "You have to let us pass."

"I don't!" Llywelyn's voice was full of righteousness.

"You let me go, and we both say nothing about what has transpired here. Nobody need be the wiser. Alternatively, you could tell your father that I'm alive, but I was too far away for you to stop."

"So far, I see no gain in this for me," Llywelyn said, but Hywel was only a few feet away from him now, and he thought he saw a glimmer of hope amidst the distrust in his cousin's eyes.

"The gain for you, is that I let you live, cousin." Hywel had by now come level with Llywelyn, and while both of them still held their swords, Llywelyn had dropped his guard. Careful to give no warning as to what he was about to do, Hywel switched his sword from his right to his left and continued the motion to bat Llywelyn's blade with a backhanded sweep of his arm. Llywelyn was so surprised, he released his sword, which fell to the ground.

Almost within the same heartbeat, Hywel urged Glew forward, and he caught Llywelyn's right wrist with his right hand and twisted, forcing him to slide out of his saddle if he didn't want his wrist broken.

Llywelyn fell ignominiously to earth, and Hywel went with him, dismounting in a smooth motion and dropping to the ground between Llywelyn and his sword. Llywelyn scrabbled in the dirt, trying to reach it, but by then Cadifor and Evan had crossed the river, and Cadifor dismounted in order to pick up the sword himself.

Llywelyn couldn't keep his eyes off it. "My-my sword. What are you going to do with it?"

Hywel still held Llywelyn's wrist in a tight grip, and he allowed himself a smirk, before wiping his expression clean.

Cadifor mounted his horse, Llywelyn's sword in his hand. "What is the closest village south of here?"

"Ch-ch-chirk."

"Is there a tavern there?" Cadifor said.

Llywelyn nodded.

"You may retrieve it from the tavern keeper," Hywel said. "You must give us a quarter of an hour head start. Otherwise, we won't stop at all, and you can explain to your father how you misplaced your sword."

Llywelyn's face reddened. "You tricked me."

Hywel struggled not to smile at his cousin's sulky tone. "As I said, I will never breathe a word of this if you don't either. Betray this bond, and I will come back to finish what I started. Do we have an accord?"

Llywelyn's shoulders fell, and he stopped resisting Hywel's grip. "We do. Know this, however. When you return, if you return, it will be I who will kill you."

"You can try," Hywel said. "I would expect nothing less from the son of the King of Powys."

20

Gareth

"**W**hat exactly are we doing here?" John said.

Gareth frowned, because he would have thought it was obvious, especially to someone who was gaining experience in murder as rapidly as John. "Looking for clues."

"What clues?"

"We won't know until we find them, will we?" Gareth said, and then at John's uncomprehending expression, added, "Conall had a wooden coin that would admit him to this brothel, and the girl bled out not far from here. If we kick over enough hornets' nests, we're sure to get stung eventually."

"Of course," John said, though his expression remained dubious, "but I have to tell you that I've actually never been inside a brothel before."

That fact had been made clear from the start by the twitchiness that had again overtaken John's body. Last year in Wales Gareth hadn't noticed this tendency, but then, John hadn't had to question anyone there either.

"You aren't the only one," Gareth said, deciding to make him feel better about his lack of experience.

John's head jerked up to look at him. "Really?"

Gareth made a dismissive motion with one hand. "We don't generally have establishments such as this in Gwynedd. In fact, there's no 'generally' about it. We don't have them." And then at John's continued astonished look, he added, "We have women, you understand, who might lie with a man for money or reward, but they don't gather together in one location like this. There'd be no point, since nowhere in Gwynedd is there a town even as large as Chester, much less Shrewsbury."

They were approaching the street upon which the establishment in question lay. John stopped at the corner near where Gareth and Gwen had hidden last night, stubbing his toe into the dirt between two cobbles. "I haven't worked for the sheriff long, you know."

"So I understood," Gareth said noncommittally. If John wanted to talk, he'd let him talk.

"Last year I was an undersheriff, only a short step above Luke or Cedric or any of the other watchmen. I wouldn't have been elevated to this position now if it hadn't been for you."

"How so?" Gareth said. "You told me earlier that you feared to lose your position if I didn't help you."

"That isn't quite the case." John had a disconcerting tendency to reveal information in dribbles and to withhold what might turn out to be the most important information of all simply because he didn't want to impose or tell another man his business. It was aggravating and so very English.

"What then?" Gareth said. "Speak!"

"Do you remember me telling you about how the sheriff had to attend to King Stephen with most of the men of the garrison, leaving Shrewsbury with only the dregs?"

"Of course." Gareth eyed the young man, who'd just implied yet again that he too was at the bottom of the barrel. It wasn't something Gareth hadn't thought himself, of course, but he was growing tired of having to bolster John's confidence every hour. Gareth really did think that John was better than that, and was capable of more than he was giving himself credit for. Gareth had been quite serious earlier when he'd told John as much.

"Before he left, the sheriff said that he'd elevated me to Deputy Sheriff because he didn't have any other man among those left whom he could trust or had even the minimum experience required to run an investigation. He expected me to do my best, and to keep Shrewsbury together in his absence, but I was not to go off on my own or ferret out any wrongdoing among the men I oversee."

"Such as Luke and this brothel," Gareth said.

"Yes, sir," John said.

"Why didn't he take Luke with him?" Gareth said.

"He took four of the six whom he distrusted most," John said. "The worst ones, actually."

Understanding rose in Gareth. John had hinted at this earlier but hadn't managed to state clearly what had been the sheriff's intent. "You're saying that for the sheriff to take all six men would all but have guaranteed dissent among his men where it could do even more harm—such as on the long march across England. How is it that the garrison contains so many bad apples in the first place?"

"The sheriff is the military authority in Shrewsbury, but even he doesn't have free rein over his men. He serves the king, but he also must work with Shrewsbury's town council and the Earl of Ludlow, and that requires a certain willingness to smooth ruffled feathers when he has to."

"Thus, he took on one or more men, whom he would have preferred had been given other duties, in order to maintain friendly relations. Your sheriff would see it as a minor point," Gareth said, "compared to possibly larger ones that have more significance in the long run."

"It was of less significance when he was here to manage them," John said. "My sheriff is a wise man, and this summons from King Stephen came at a bad time."

"I am coming to see that." Gareth understood those instances when duty warred with duty. A man had to choose the lesser of the evils presented to him. And nobody could disobey his king, no matter how important his duty at home seemed to be, especially not one such as the Sheriff of Shrewsbury who served entirely at the king's behest. "You should be honored he left you in charge."

"More than anything, I'm afraid to let him down." John's tone was no longer embarrassed—more matter-of-fact than anything else—as if confessing the whole of the truth of his elevation to Deputy Sheriff had relaxed him. It would have been easier if John had told Gareth all this from the start, but that wasn't the Englishman's way.

"To be honest, I know the feeling." Gareth started walking towards the brothel again.

Even before this frank conversation, Gareth and John had concluded that they needed to leave John's men behind. It seemed necessary, seeing as how Luke frequented the brothel himself, and there was no reason to think other guards wouldn't as well. Neither Gareth nor John wanted to question the manager of the brothel in the presence of someone she knew—and especially not if she had bribed that person specifically to avoid awkward questions like the ones they intended to ask her.

It was one of those ironies of commerce that, while it was a consortium of men that owned the brothel, a woman managed it. Gareth didn't know if that was because she'd once been a whore herself and had been promoted when she became too aged to sell herself, or if she'd been hired simply because the owners believed a woman would know best how to handle other women. Either way, it was a unique situation in Gareth's experience.

Unlike the night before, no guard blocked the door at this hour of the morning, which gave John no recourse but to knock. His rapping at first brought no one running, but finally a frazzled maid, wiping her hands on a food-stained apron, answered the door.

She took the appearance of two men wearing swords and stern demeanors in stride, saying, "We're not open at this hour. Come back after noon." She made to close the door again.

John put a hand on the door and his booted foot between the door and the frame. "We're not here for custom. We need to speak to the manager." Other than John's interaction with Luke, it was the most forceful Gareth had seen him. It was good to see that the younger man was capable of speaking authoritatively, and it gave Gareth hope that it was one aspect of being Deputy Sheriff that John had mastered, despite his inner misgivings. "Tell her the Deputy Sheriff is here."

"She's—" The girl stopped. "If you could wait." She tried again to shut the door in their faces, but John had left his foot where it was, and the door popped open and banged against the inner wall.

Gareth poked his head past the doorway, but he couldn't see anything beyond three curtains: one to his right, another to his left, and a third straight ahead, which the girl had ducked around without looking back.

Gareth brushed aside the curtain on the left and groaned inwardly when he saw that it enclosed a narrow space all of six feet long and three wide containing a single pallet on the floor. The curtain provided a bare minimum of privacy to watching eyes, and nothing to listening ears. The right hand curtain revealed the same arrangement. From what Gwen had said, Meilyr had disowned her mother's brother, Pawl, because of his tendency to frequent places such as this.

John pursed his lips. "What do you say to us walking straight in without waiting for an invitation?"

"I have no objection," Gareth said, "but perhaps we should wait a moment. No need to antagonize anyone unnecessarily, especially if the owners are the esteemed members of the town you say they are. We can offend them later if we need to."

That got a slight easing of tension and even a smile from John, and he removed his foot from the threshold.

Fortunately, they didn't have long to wait. Before John became impatient again, the same maid returned and beckoned them past the curtains. They walked through the central room, which bore a strong resemblance to a tavern common room—except for the curtains. Gareth counted six more enclosed areas around the perimeter of the room, presumably for the same purpose as the two he'd already noted.

The maid didn't stop but continued on into what could have been the dining area for wealthier clients, also much like a tavern might have for serving noble or high-ranking guests.

More buildings were visible through the open, rear door. As with many homes and shops in Shrewsbury, the brothel included a large yard. A quick glance out the door revealed that it contained a small storehouse; what could be a common sleeping and dressing house for the girls—like a castle barracks; a stable where a man could leave his horse during whatever interlude he spent at the brothel; and a kitchen.

Due to the danger of fire, cooking generally took place a safe distance from the other buildings. It was the same everywhere—from the largest castle to the smallest croft, in the hope that if something did catch fire, or heaven forbid, the oven exploded, the damage could be confined to a small area and the fire contained before it spread to the rest of the complex.

That did not mean, of course, that fires were never lit inside the other buildings. People had to keep warm, after all. Most, if not all, croftwives cooked porridge or stew and roasted a rabbit over the same fire pit that warmed their house. A baking oven was another matter entirely, however, burning far hotter than any open fire. Thus, the danger of the fire getting out of control was that much greater.

A goat and a flock of chickens wandered around the yard too. With at least eight girls, the maid, and the manager, and who knew how many other employees, the brothel had many people to house and mouths to feed. And seeing as how the complex abutted the palisade, it also had a gate through which the residents could gain access to the river.

Gareth turned back to the room as a black-haired woman in well-maintained middle age entered. She couldn't have been more than five feet tall. "How may I be of assistance, my lords?" She took a seat by the fire and then looked up at them, her gracious smile a flash across her mouth, signifying politeness— nothing more. Her eyes were flat, revealing nothing either.

Faced with such politeness, John fell back on his own proper manners. He put his hand to his chest. "I am John Fletcher, Deputy Sheriff of Shrewsbury, and this is Gareth ap

Rhys, of Gwynedd. I would be pleased to be informed of your name, madam."

"Agatha," she said immediately. "I understand you've recently been elevated to your position. Congratulations."

"Thank you." John's chest swelled.

Gareth could hardly believe that John had been won over so easily, but then, Gareth shouldn't have been surprised that a woman of Agatha's experience would know how to handle a young man such as John. She didn't seem to want to direct her attentions to Gareth, however, for which he was grateful. Gwen would want to know exactly what passed here this morning, and he would hate to think he would fail to maintain his dignity.

Thus, before John lost his head completely and forgot what they were here for, Gareth brought out Conall's coin. "It is our understanding that this coin allows a man entrance to this establishment?"

"It does," Agatha said.

"You are not the owner, however?" Gareth said.

"I am not." She paused for a heartbeat.

Gareth looked at her curiously, noting the hesitation in her voice and posture. "But?"

Agatha gave a slight cough. "Recently I have purchased a small stake."

"Who are the other owners?" John said.

She rattled off a half-dozen names, three he didn't know and three he did: Rob Horn, the owner of The Boar's Head Inn; Martin Carter; and Tom Weaver."

John's jaw dropped at the mention of his brother-in-law. Gareth eyed him. "You didn't know?"

"Absolutely not," he said.

Gareth turned back to Agatha, his mind churning. "You name Martin Carter but not his brother, Roger. He wasn't involved?"

"No." She frowned. "I heard he died yesterday. I'm sorry to hear that. He was a good man."

Gareth's brow furrowed. "What makes you say that?"

"He always treated me with respect. To him, money was money, and he didn't hold what I did for a living against me. Or," she amended, "if he did object, he didn't allow me to know it."

Gareth studied Agatha, knowing from her expression that she was in earnest. It seems Roger had been a contradictory man. She was the second person to say that Roger had been kind, as Martin had said the same thing in regards to Jenny. But he'd beaten his apprentice for misdeeds, real or imagined, and he'd browbeaten many others, including members of the town council.

"Did he ever come here?" John said.

"No," Agatha said.

"You are very sure," John said.

"I am," Agatha said. "It wasn't his way. I respected that."

"What about Martin Carter?" Gareth said.

Agatha narrowed her eyes slightly, but she answered willingly enough. "I'm sure that neither brother ever came here for entertainment."

Implying that Martin, at least, might have come for business reasons, which would make sense given that he was part owner.

Gareth was more glad with every moment that passed that he and John had come to the brothel. He had a brief thought that, had Agatha's profession been anything else than brothel keeper, Gwen would have liked her forthright nature.

"What exactly does this coin buy?" Gareth said.

Agatha smirked slightly before smoothing her lips into the polished smile again. "Are you interested in sampling our wares first hand? We don't get too many Welsh knights here."

Gareth kept his gaze steady on hers. "I wouldn't have thought you'd get any."

The woman's lips pinched, as if she was holding back a genuine smile this time, instead of pretending to be amused. "You'd be surprised."

"Would I?" A sudden shiver coursed down Gareth's spine, prompting him to raise one hand to indicate a point even with the top of his own head. "Did a Welshman as tall as I but in his forties, blond going gray and thickening around the waist, ever come here? You might have noticed that he judges his own worth as very great."

Agatha blinked.

Gareth couldn't even say what had prompted him to describe Prince Cadwaladr, but the impulse had been there so he'd followed it.

Then Agatha cast her eyes down so he couldn't read what was in them. "I cannot reveal the identities of my clients, or soon I wouldn't have any, would I?"

Gareth grunted his acknowledgement of that reality, frustrated because he wasn't able to tell for certain if she had seen Cadwaladr or not.

"Do you have knowledge of this man?" John thrust the image of Conall under Agatha's nose.

She reared back slightly, taking more of the light into her face, and Gareth realized that she was older than he'd first thought. Rather than in her middle forties, she was now revealed to be fifteen years older than that, and he could see more strands of gray amongst the black of her hair.

Agatha pushed away the paper. "He is unfamiliar to me."

Gareth frowned. Her response to his description of Cadwaladr aside, for the first time since she'd smiled at John, he had a clear sense that she was lying. It also occurred to him only now that it was absurd for him to describe Cadwaladr when all he had to do was draw a picture of him. The treacherous prince's supercilious smirk was burned into Gareth's memory, and he could render it with his eyes closed.

John pressed on. "Are you sure? He would be a stranger to you. Irish, with hair like fire."

She raised her eyebrows. "Irish? We don't get many more of them here in Shrewsbury than Welsh knights."

"I wouldn't have thought so," John said, "except that we've encountered our fair share in recent days."

"Why would you show his picture to me?" she said.

"We found the coin among his belongings," John said.

"But that means he didn't use it," Agatha said.

"But he bought it," John said.

Agatha shrugged. "He could have done that at any number of locations. It wouldn't have had to be at my front door."

"Where could he have bought it?" Gareth said.

Agatha reeled off a list of taverns and inns with which her brothel had a relationship. Not for the first time, Gareth was glad he'd decided to stay with Gwen and his family at the monastery. Prostitution was a fact of life, but he would just as soon keep them all well away from what they didn't need to know about. If Gwen had discovered that her innkeeper sold brothel coins, she would have wanted to know all about it.

Gareth brought out the picture of the girl. "Have you seen her?" He framed the question in such a way that Agatha would have a harder time eliding the truth than she had with Conall's image. After her initial denial, she had asked them questions instead of the other way around, which was a classic diversionary tactic.

A 'v' formed between Agatha's neatly manicured brows. "I don't believe so."

"She isn't one of yours?" John said.

"No. Definitely not," Agatha said.

That answer was definitive, surely given, and Gareth could hear truth in her voice when she spoke. But still, something about her demeanor caused him to doubt her.

John noticed the hesitation too. "A moment ago you said, *I don't believe so.* Do you think you might have seen her somewhere?"

Agatha gave the paper back to Gareth. "I thought I might have when you first showed me, but the light is dim in here. Now I know that I have never met her before in my life."

That was definitive too, except that Gareth had noticed the way she'd looked directly at him when she spoke, as if daring her own eyes to skate away and betray her. He bowed. Maybe she had never met the girl. Maybe she'd never seen her, but that didn't mean she knew nothing about her. "Thank you for your time."

Turning on his heel, he urged John out of the room, back through the common room, and out of the brothel. John didn't protest, but once they were out of earshot, he turned on Gareth. "What was that? I feel like we were getting somewhere!"

"Oh, we definitely were, up until we showed her the picture of the girl who died. Agatha definitely knows the girl—or knows of her," Gareth said.

"Do you think Agatha lied about the dead girl being one of hers?" John said.

"No," Gareth said. "That wasn't the sense I got. The girl wasn't a whore, or at least not at that brothel. Agatha's reply was so firm because she was pleased to be able to answer the direct question in the negative. It was her response before and after the denial that concerns me."

"So why did we leave?"

Gareth regarded the young deputy sheriff. "Can you really not answer that?"

John stood chewing on his lower lip. "When you first showed her the picture, she hesitated."

"Yes, and then after she declared the girl not one of hers, her resolve firmed and she was able to deny that she knew her at all—but even she couldn't think so quickly as to deny all knowledge from the start," Gareth said. "We surprised her."

"You surprised her," John said. "Is that why we left? You had unsettled her, and you wanted to give her time to think about it?"

"Essentially. I think the next step is to put a watch on her—maybe one of the young ones like Cedric or Oswin. I want to know which of the owners, if any, she contacts or comes to see her. I'm hoping that our questioning unsettled her enough to make her worried—and that worry might well give her away." He paused. "You did very well in there."

John looked disbelieving.

"I'm not just saying that. You were confident and straightforward. You asked follow-up questions with authority. I was impressed."

John flushed slightly. "Thank you. I have had good teachers."

"Sometimes it takes a while to find your feet."

"That it does." John turned back to look at the brothel. "I just hope I'm not finding them too late."

21

Gwen

Gwen bent to the wheel, which was no longer attached to the cart, her fingers reaching for the dark stain that marred its surface. The blood had dried. She glanced surreptitiously to her left. Her father, proving himself to be an able investigator in his own right, was speaking innocently to Flann about his business at the cartwright's yard.

"Too bad about the wheel," Meilyr said.

Flann shrugged. "It happens now and again. Wheels last only so long before they need repair, but I'm assured that I brought my custom to the best cartwright in Shrewsbury."

Martin's apprentice looked pleased at the compliment. Gwen stepped away from the wheel, moving towards the cart itself. She was sure that the stains on the wheels were blood, but she didn't think she could prove it, and she would love to return to Gareth with a bit of evidence that would link this cart to the girl. Unfortunately, there wasn't any obvious blood in the cart bed itself.

She glanced over at Flann, who was still speaking to her father. Meilyr distracted him with a question about his travels throughout the March. "I'm interested professionally, you see."

Seeing as how her father was the bard for King Owain of Gwynedd, he couldn't possibly be interested in whom he might sing for in the March, but he was trying to be polite, and Flann responded in kind.

Gwen still had Tangwen on her hip, and she sighed loudly, shifted the little girl in her arms, and then plopped her onto the empty bed of the cart a moment later. In an undertone, Gwen said, "Can you find something in the back to play with?"

No stranger to carts, Tangwen pushed to her feet and toddled away from Gwen, towards the driver's seat.

Gwen let Tangwen nearly reach the back before she said, "Come back here, Tangwen!"

Tangwen turned to look at her mother, a distinct frown on her face and her chin wrinkled up, not understanding what game Gwen was playing. With a muttered apology to Tangwen for using her in this way, Gwen hitched up her skirt, scrambled into the bed of the cart, and then crouched beside her daughter, her arm around her waist.

"Sorry, *cariad.*" Gwen kissed Tangwen's cheek. "Let's see what there is to find up here, eh?"

Behind her, Flann had finally noticed that Gwen and Tangwen had climbed into the back of his cart, and he started towards them. "Miss! What are you doing?"

Gwen turned to look at him, all innocence. "Retrieving my daughter. I'm sorry if I inconvenienced anyone."

She tightened her grip on Tangwen at the same moment Tangwen bent to the side of the cart and plucked a square of cloth off a slat that had splintered. Gwen could hardly believe her luck, or that Tangwen had remembered what she'd been sent to do. She didn't dare look to see what her daughter had clutched in her fist, but merely scooped her up and carried her back to the end of the cart, where her father met her to help her down.

His face was a thundercloud, but he didn't chastise her in front of Huw and Flann as he could have. Instead, he spoke in a low voice, "What are you doing?"

"Investigating," Gwen said. "This is the cart we were looking for."

Meilyr's expression instantly cleared as he turned to face Flann, his arm across Gwen's shoulder. "We'll get out of your way now." He gestured to Jenny who was hovering in the doorway to the house, a flagon in her hand. "We've been invited inside. It was nice to speak with you. Will we see you at dinner?"

"I expect so. We have one more night here before we're off." Flann's Irish brogue was particularly noticeable at the end of his sentence, making Gwen fear that he wasn't as calm about Gwen's incursion as he implied. But as long as he let her go, Gwen didn't care. And as long as he had nothing to hide—if his cart had indeed rolled through the puddle of blood in complete innocence— then he should have nothing to worry about.

"Until we meet again." Meilyr hustled Gwen and Tangwen towards the doorway where Jenny and Martin waited. Before they reached it, however, he whispered to Gwen, "What's in Tangwen's hand?"

"I don't know."

Tangwen was looking stricken, dirty tear tracks on her cheeks, though she hadn't openly cried. Thankfully, Flann appeared to have lost interest in what they were doing and was now speaking to the cartwright's apprentice.

"It's all right, love." Gwen rubbed her daughter's cheek with the back of one finger. "What did you find?"

Tangwen looked down at her fist, and Gwen gently pried her fingers open. A piece of pink cloth lay wrinkled in her palm. Gwen plucked it up and showed her father.

"It's a torn piece of fabric," Meilyr said, with something like astonishment. "Would it be too much to hope that it matches the clothing of the dead girl?"

Gwen rubbed at the fabric with her thumb, comparing it to her remembered feel of the girl's skirt. "She was wearing a dress that could have once been pink, but it's hard to be sure that it's the same, since the girl's dress was ruined by blood, mud, and water from a day spent in the river."

"I'll keep it for you until we can see if the cloth matches." Meilyr pocketed the scrap. Then he added, "It would be better if we could extricate ourselves from this quickly."

"We can be thankful Martin and Jenny aren't Welsh, or we might find ourselves encouraged to stay all day to share their grief at the loss of Roger," Gwen said.

Meilyr squeezed her arm, and then they allowed Martin to usher them into the heart of his house, consisting of a main room with a loft above, accessed by a narrow stair along the far wall. The house was larger than Tom Weaver's however, in that it also had an adjacent room, visible through an open doorway.

Jenny gestured Gwen to the table, which was entirely covered with foodstuffs: bread, cheese, onions, carrots, tarts, several pies, and two jugs of beer. "Please sit."

Gwen wanted to be polite, but she hesitated. "We really shouldn't. You've suffered a loss—"

"It would be helpful to me if you stayed," Jenny said, with a glance at her husband, who nodded. "As you can see, many of our neighbors have brought food that we can't possibly eat all of, and it would be nice to have something to think about besides Roger's death."

Having spent the last four months mourning Rhun, Gwen could understand how she felt, so she acquiesced. Tangwen was hungry again, so she was given a sliver of meat pie. Once again, Gwen and Meilyr accepted cups, though this time they were filled with beer. Martin had his own cup, which he drained and held out to Jenny, who filled it again. Gwen sipped hers tentatively, not enjoying the earthy favor. She was used to mead, which was lighter and sweeter.

Trying to find something nice to say, Gwen put a hand out to Jenny. "When is your child due?"

Jenny gaped back at her. "How did you know I was with child?"

"Those of us who've had children know the look." Gwen put a hand to her own belly.

Actual joy shone in Jenny's face. "September."

"Mine as well."

Jenny leapt to her feet, came around the table, and hugged Gwen, tight enough to make Tangwen, who was between them, squirm. "I am so happy to hear that. It will be as if a little piece of Adeline is alive again in both of us."

Gwen met her father's eyes, which had crinkled in the corners. She herself wasn't sure that she liked Jenny's sentiment. Adeline may have been Jenny's closest friend, but Gwen hadn't known the girl at all. Still, having lost loved ones herself, Gwen could understand the desire for a connection beyond the grave.

Jenny released Gwen, and returned to a seat beside Martin, who leaned forward to speak. "Your husband came by yesterday with Jenny's brother. Has he shared what he knows with you? Do you have any idea who might have murdered Roger?"

"No." Gwen's eyes skated to Jenny to see how she felt about discussing the specifics of Roger's death, but her eyes were on the table in front of her.

"What about this Irishman?" Martin said. "Have you found him?"

"No to that, also," Gwen said. "Do you have any idea why your brother might have been at Rob Horn's inn?"

"Your husband asked me that," Martin said. "It feels terrible to know that I was asleep when he died."

Gwen's eyes tracked to Jenny. "Jenny? Did Roger say anything to you?"

The girl shook her head. "I was awake for much of the night, but I didn't hear him leave. He was with us for supper, but after that, I never saw him again."

"Why were you awake?" It was Gwen's experience that, in the early stages of pregnancy, she couldn't get enough sleep.

"I had aches and pains," Jenny said. "You probably know all about that. I don't know what hour it was when I rose from my bed, but it was well before dawn. I didn't want to wake Martin with my tossing and turning."

Martin grunted his thanks. "We have a rooster who crows every morning before dawn. I need to sleep as much as I can before then."

Jenny managed a laugh. "Martin keeps threatening to make him into rooster soup."

Martin directed a gentle smile at his wife. "I slept through his call yesterday morning and woke when she returned to the room." The amusement gone, Martin stared towards the fire, which was burning low in the grate in the center of the room. Smoke wended its way half-heartedly towards the hole in the ceiling. The draft was good, with the open rear door, and the room was all but clear of smoke. "We would have lived here all together, had my brother married Adeline. Instead, he moved into a room off the carriage house, saying he didn't want to disturb us. It meant we never heard his comings and goings."

"I am so sorry." Gwen sighed inwardly, finding the losses difficult to bear too and wondering how much longer she could sit here and be polite. Ever since she'd realized that she wasn't responding to murder like she normally did, she'd found tears constantly pricking at the corners of her eyes. Reason told her she was naturally more emotional because she was pregnant—but it wasn't emotion she was feeling so much as weariness.

Martin ducked his head in thanks, but Jenny stood abruptly, looked like she was about to speak, but then burst into tears. She ran towards the doorway to the adjacent room, which Gwen guessed was the bedroom. That left Martin alone with Meilyr, Gwen, and Tangwen. They'd been asked to stay, and Gareth might have wanted Gwen to learn more from Martin about his brother's death, but circumstances made it impossible to do so—and Gwen couldn't leave quickly enough. "Thank you for your hospitality. We'll take our leave now."

"Would you mind seeing yourselves out?" Martin disappeared in the direction Jenny had gone, and as Gwen departed through the back door with Meilyr and Tangwen, she could hear his soothing words between Jenny's sobs.

Once outside, Meilyr didn't stop to chat with the apprentice, who was the only one in the yard, but strode away from the cartwright's yard at a rapid clip, as if he couldn't get them heading towards the monastery fast enough.

"When were you going to tell me you were with child again?"

"Only when I had to," Gwen said. "As with Jenny, it's early days. At first I wanted to be sure, and then I wanted us out of Aber, and then the days just seemed to pass without me saying anything."

Meilyr grunted. "I don't know what Gareth was thinking, allowing you to travel so far from home." Although his tone was grumpy, she knew by the way his mustache quivered that he was pleased, and he kept glancing at her out of the corner of his eye.

"I don't mean to worry you, Father." She shifted Tangwen to her other hip so she could hook her arm through Meilyr's. "But to tell you the truth, I'm starting to worry about me too."

22

Gareth

By the time Gwen, Meilyr, and Tangwen turned in through the gatehouse, Gareth had spent the last quarter of an hour pacing the courtyard of the monastery. At the sight of them, he hurried over, scooping up Tangwen, who had released her mother's hand and raised both arms to him. "I stopped by Tom's shop, and you weren't there." Despite Gareth's best efforts to control it, he felt his temper rising. "Where have you been?"

Gwen's face crumpled, and she blinked back tears.

Instantly, he was beside her, and he wrapped his free arm around her shoulders. *"Cariad!* What's wrong?" He swallowed down any further admonitions, not wanting to make whatever was bothering Gwen worse. She'd been with her father, who had nearly as much interest in protecting her and Tangwen as Gareth did.

"Nothing. I'll tell you later." Gwen pressed at her eyes with her fingers.

Meilyr held up a square of cloth. "She was doing her job, Gareth."

Gareth frowned, distracted by the cloth, but at the same time not willing to dismiss Gwen's unhappiness that easily. "What is that?"

"It's a piece of cloth Tangwen found in a cart that could be the one that ran through the puddle of blood in the alley," Meilyr said. "It's owned by Flann, the merchant who's staying here."

Gareth forced himself to take a deep breath. "Why don't you start at the beginning?"

"After our meeting with Tom Weaver, we stopped by the cartwright's yard," Gwen said.

"It was my idea, Gareth," Meilyr interjected. "I just wanted to see it."

Gwen nodded. "We didn't mean anything by it, but while we were still in the street, Jenny ran out to greet us."

"That's John Fletcher's sister," Meilyr said.

Gareth had known that, but he didn't say so. Instead, his eyebrows went up. "What did she say?"

"She mistook me for Adeline." Gwen's voice turned gravelly again for a moment, but then she continued, "And then Martin came out too and invited us inside. I felt so bad for Jenny, I couldn't refuse."

"Just as we arrived in the yard, his apprentice, Huw, was removing one of the cart's wheels to repair it," Meilyr said, his eyes on Gwen. "It had slipped its rim."

Gareth raised his eyebrows. "How did you find the cloth?"

"Tangwen found it when she climbed into the cart bed." Gwen glanced away, flushing slightly. "I might have accidently set her in it while I was talking to the apprentice."

Gareth barked a laugh. "Accidently on purpose you mean."

"I have no doubt that Prince Hywel would have approved," Meilyr said.

"How did you know it was Flann's cart?" Gareth said.

"He was there," Gwen said, "and told us."

It was as if Gareth had swallowed a stone that then dropped with a plop into his belly. "He saw you find the cloth? You talked to him?"

Meilyr put out a hand to appease his son-in-law. "Flann knows nothing. We came into the yard at Martin's invitation, and Tangwen ran around in the bed of the cart before Gwen plucked her out and apologized for getting in the way. She said nothing else to him or to Huw that might give Flann cause for concern. She certainly didn't mention the blood on the wheels or the missing rim."

Gareth couldn't help but be skeptical, but since he had no evidence to counter their assertions, and they had done genuinely good work, he couldn't really criticize. "I should track down Flann. Was he still there when you left?"

"No," Meilyr said, "and it seemed too nosy to ask the apprentice if he knew where he'd gone."

"He hasn't been back here either." Gareth gazed past his father-in-law to the gatehouse, as if Flann might appear under it at any moment.

"We should compare the square of cloth to the girl's dress," Gwen said.

"Go on, you two." Meilyr reached out to take Tangwen from Gwen. "My granddaughter and I will practice our music."

"Thank you." Gwen kissed first Tangwen's cheek and then her father's, and Tangwen went to her grandfather willingly.

Gareth was glad to see that they all seemed to be getting along better than ever, despite Gwen's unstable emotions. So, somewhat bemused, Gareth took Gwen's arm to escort her to the room where Gareth and John had examined Roger and the girl earlier. While it was tradition—not only in England but in Wales too—that a family should lay out the body of a relative in their own house, sometimes that wasn't possible. This room was kept available in the case of a death where it was needed.

Now that Meilyr had spoken to Tom Weaver and Gwen had met him, it was a relief to know that half of the purpose of this journey was accomplished. The second half, the issue with Cadwaladr, remained to be pursued. That Cadwaladr had been sighted was a huge step forward, but it didn't necessarily mean that Gareth had a plan as to where he needed to go from here. And while King Owain had given Meilyr leave to travel, that license had just expired. In truth, Gareth was lucky to have the murder investigation to pursue because of the obligation it gave him to stay in Shrewsbury a little longer.

Once they reached the little room, both he and Gwen hesitated on the threshold. Gareth needed to wait for his eyes to adjust to the dim light inside, and he hoped that was the reason

Gwen had paused too. He didn't think the smell in the room was terribly bad. The door had been left open, and incense burned in a dish on a side table. Gwen hadn't mentioned the baby or how her stomach was behaving—or misbehaving—very often in the last few days, but he could tell from the way her hand passed over her belly every now and then that she was thinking about it.

The only light came from a single candle, which flickered in its sconce on the wall, illuminating the two shrouded forms on the tables that took up the majority of the room. In one corner, a monk at prayer occupied a low stool.

Gareth hesitated again, not wanting to disturb him, but he looked up as they entered. "May I help you? Was there something more you needed to see?"

"No." Gareth hastened to reassure him, not wanting the monk to fear that Gareth had brought Gwen to examine the bodies. "We were looking for the garments these two were wearing when they died."

"They are no longer here," the monk said, which Gareth already had seen and was the reason he was asking. "You should speak to the hospitaller about what happened to them. He was in the kitchen last I saw."

"Thank you," Gareth said. "When is the funeral to be?"

The monk blinked. "Didn't someone tell you? It will begin within the hour. And then after the service at the graveside, the abbot will say mass in the church."

Gareth nodded. It was better that the bodies didn't wait another day for burial.

"It seems the church will be full this night." The monk smiled gently. "I regret that the mourners will be coming more for Roger Carter, since he was important in the town, than for the girl."

"But the girl will be buried alongside him?" Gwen said.

"We care for every soul here, madam, whether or not anyone is here to witness it."

"We understand. Thank you again." Gareth guided Gwen back out of the room, into the courtyard, and across it to the complex of buildings that comprised the kitchen and washing house for the monks.

As a woman, Gwen wasn't usually allowed in this portion of the monastery, but Gareth decided to ignore the stricture since she was with him, and it was she who'd acquired the cloth. He didn't want to offend the monks' sensibilities, but he could hardly see how Gwen spending a few moments in the kitchen might cause a novice to rethink his vocation.

In the hours since noon, the sky had become overcast and now threatened rain. The sun wouldn't set for another two hours, but it already seemed like it had. The wind whipped across the courtyard, scattering leaves and urging loose pebbles to bounce among the cobbled stones. It also pushed Gwen and Gareth along a passageway between several buildings and around to the back of the monastery towards the kitchen door, lashing them at the last second with an extra gust that made them arrive on the threshold in something of a fluster.

With a laugh, Gwen pushed back her hood in the warmth of the kitchen. She was utterly beautiful, and Gareth had a pang of conscience about what he'd thought earlier, because he couldn't see how any man could choose to be a monk when there was even one woman like Gwen in the world.

Before them, monks and laymen were hard at work: chopping, kneading, roasting, or stirring. Several others scrubbed out pots and trays. Everyone looked up at their entrance, and Gareth saw the flash of a smile on the faces of several before they went back to preparing the evening meal.

Gareth did not see the hospitaller immediately, and he took another step into the kitchen. The cook, a thickset man, as befitting his profession, hurried over, wiping his hands on a cloth. He wore a large apron over his habit, and had a swath of flour above his right eye where he must have swiped it.

"Is there something you needed—for the little girl perhaps?"

Gareth couldn't help smiling himself at the man's earnestness. With her bright eyes and curious mind, Tangwen made an impression, even on stalwart monks, wherever she went. Much like her mother, in fact. "She awaits supper with anticipation. But no, we were looking for the hospitaller."

"He is in the cellar." The cook snapped his fingers at a novice, sending him to retrieve the hospitaller from whatever far reaches of the building he'd got to. A few moments later, the man in question, a monk even more rotund than the cook, puffed into the kitchen. "How may I help you?"

Gareth stepped back towards the doorway, encouraging the hospitaller to follow so that his words wouldn't carry to the other inhabitants of the kitchen. Undoubtedly, their ears were perked to every nuance, but Gareth would rather not broadcast his request to all and sundry. "We were wondering if we could examine the clothing worn by the two awaiting burial."

The hospitaller had leaned in to hear Gareth better, but now he straightened, frowning. "I'm sorry, but you can't."

"What do you mean?" Gareth said. "Why not?"

"I don't have them. I offered to return Roger Carter's clothes to his brother, Martin, but he didn't want them. And since the girl has no kin that we know of—" The monk's broke off, his expression regretful.

Gareth found a growl forming in his throat. Sensing his impatience, even though he had been trying to hide it from the hospitaller, Gwen put a calming hand on Gareth's arm. "It's all right. We'd just like to know what you did with them."

The monk raised his hands and dropped them, conveying helplessness. "They're gone. I sent them to the leper sanctuary at St. Giles."

23

Gareth

"Martin Carter suggested it. After consulting the prior and seeing that the clothes were washed and mended, I did as he wanted. Roger's clothing was particularly fine, and it seemed a shame to waste it for even a day if it could be of use to someone less fortunate," the monk concluded, apologetically.

"We understand," Gareth said, though he couldn't entirely keep the disappointment out of his voice.

St. Giles was the sanctuary for lepers on the outskirts of Shrewsbury, maintained and funded by the Abbey of St. Peter and St. Paul.

"I didn't know you still needed them," the hospitaller said.

Gareth raised a hand, in half forgiveness, half apology. "It is my fault for not requesting that you keep everything here for at least another day or two. We haven't identified the girl as yet, and I wanted to take another look at her garments in case they contained some clue I missed the first time. Ah well."

The monk nodded, and they all turned away—the hospitaller to return to his duties, and Gwen and Gareth to shelter in the overhang of the roof outside the kitchen door. While they had been consulting with the hospitaller, the first patterings of rain had sounded in the courtyard and on the slate roof of the monastery buildings.

Gareth put a hand at the small of Gwen's back and canted his head in the direction of the archway that would take them back into the courtyard of the monastery. As they ran through it, the cool rain felt good to Gareth after the warmth of the kitchen, but it was coming down so hard that by the time they reached the shelter of the gatehouse, they were wet all over.

Gwen sighed. "I suppose you should ride to St. Giles, but is it uncharitable to say that I don't want you anywhere near a leper?"

"I confess I'm not looking forward to going there either, but I don't know if I can avoid it."

"Still," Gwen said, "we just need to see the dress. You wouldn't have to take it off the back of a needy indigent."

Gareth smirked. "You know, I really think this task might be one to leave to John Fletcher."

"It is important to include him in every aspect of the investigation. It would be wrong to keep something as important as this to yourself." She laughed.

Hiding a smile, Gareth shook his head. "I would have to think about how guilty I'd feel if I suggested it."

Gwen made a rueful face. "If you said it was important, he would go, you know he would."

Gareth pocketed the cloth. "Which is why I won't ask it of him. I will either go myself, or we'll figure out some other way to get the information we need." Then, the bell in the tower began to toll, calling the mourners to the funeral.

The townspeople clearly had been waiting for it to ring, because several dozen immediately entered the courtyard through the gatehouse. They were joined by a host of monks, all of whom were hunched against the weather, with their hoods up and their hands tucked into their wide sleeves.

With the wind and rain coming from the south, and his back to the east-facing curtain wall, Gareth was warm enough. He rested his shoulder next to Gwen's, gazing out at the falling rain as they waited for everyone to line up. "Are you going to tell me what's going on with you?"

Gwen clenched her hands tightly in front of her.

He reached out and grasped both her hands in one of his. "*Cariad,* whatever it is, just tell me."

Gwen gave a little cry and tipped back her head. "I don't know if I can do this anymore, Gareth."

"Do what?"

"This." She waved a hand. "Investigate murder."

"My love, you've never been obligated—"

"Yes, I have! How much worse is it to let you go into danger on your own when I know that at times my presence can help? And—" she shook her head, and the tears she'd refused to let fall earlier trickled down her cheeks, "—I used—we used—Tangwen twice in the last two days to distract a possibly dangerous man so we could further our investigation. Our own daughter."

Heedless of propriety, Gareth wrapped both arms around Gwen and pulled her to him. She sobbed into his chest, and he just held her, finding his own eyes filling with tears at her sorrow.

Finally, she quieted, and he said, "I too have been questioning, Gwen. I can talk to Prince Hywel. We can stop doing this. We can say no to John Fletcher."

She said something into his cloak he didn't catch, and then she pulled back to look into his face. "It isn't that I want to stop. I simply want to feel, and I want to do what is right. I just don't know what that is or how to do both."

Gareth hugged her close again. "We can figure this out—together, as we always do." Then he tipped up his chin to point across the courtyard. "The funeral procession."

The rain didn't care about death or Gwen's regrets, and the monks didn't stop for it either. The line of mourners that had formed up near the church parted so the dozen monks carrying the two bodies in wooden caskets could get into position behind the abbot and the prior, who would lead the procession. It seemed like half the town had come to the monastery for the funeral and, if what he could see on the other side of the gatehouse was any indication, the other half was waiting in the road or at the gravesite on the Abbey Foregate side of the church.

Gareth wouldn't know until the two were buried, but if the custom here was the same as in Wales, the body would be carried to the funeral in wooden boxes, and then removed and placed into the ground for burial. Not to reuse the casket would be a disturbing waste of good wood, and it was only the wealthy who might insist on being buried in a box—though usually they were laid to rest in stone mausoleums, tombs, or in the church itself, and thus would be carried to the funeral ground in the same wooden box as these poor souls.

Meilyr appeared from the guest hall. Beside him, Gwalchmai was holding Tangwen's hand. Meilyr nodded at Gareth from across the courtyard, whispered a few words to Gwalchmai, who nodded too but stayed where he was, and then Meilyr strode out into the rain to join the procession. Gareth and Gwen met him at the end of the train of monks.

"I thought the younger folk could stay behind," Meilyr said, by way of greeting.

"I'm glad you thought of it," Gwen said. "I don't need Tangwen soaked to the skin, and she will attend enough funerals in her life without going to one of a man and woman she never met."

Sadly, that was no understatement. Their young daughter had already attended a dozen funerals. Hardly a week passed in Gwynedd without the loss of someone Gareth knew, though not all deaths brought heartache. Just a few days before they left for Shrewsbury, one of the old matrons of Aber village had finally passed at the ancient age of eighty-six. Most of Gwynedd turned out that day, and her daughter—herself very elderly at nearly seventy—lamented the fact that her mother would have loved it if everyone had come to see her *before* she died and to have celebrated her life while she was still living it.

That funeral was particularly notable, but King Owain or Prince Hywel almost always sent a representative from Aber to any funeral if at all possible. Death was a part of life and the acknowledgement of it shouldn't be avoided, simply for the emotion it brought forth.

"You have your finery on." Gwen looked her father up and down. Her tears had passed, and she was back to being her clear-eyed self. Gareth wasn't fooled—and it wasn't as if she was trying to fool him. He meant what he'd said about figuring this out together. "Do you have a role in the service?"

"I told the abbot that I knew several funeral prayers in English and offered to sing one for the benefit of the common folk," Meilyr said. "He would have had Gwalchmai, of course, but I persuaded him that I would do a serviceable job."

His father-in-law's tone was mocking without rising to anger, though at one time he would have felt justified in expressing it. Meilyr had mellowed since Gareth's marriage to Gwen but, at least in regard to his music, he knew his worth. An unfortunate consequence of King Owain's grief was that he'd banned all music at Aber, even mournful tunes. That lack had left Meilyr cooling his heels in the hall with nothing to do. He'd composed a lengthy elegy to Rhun, which he'd sung in private to Hywel, Gareth, and Gwen, but he hadn't been able to play it in the hall for the king. It was out of that frustration that he'd asked permission to leave.

When they'd first arrived, Meilyr had been introduced to the monks as Gwynedd's official court bard, but the abbot clearly hadn't realized what that meant. He soon would. The abbot had been impressed with Gwalchmai, but everything the young man knew he'd learned from his father.

The three of them fell into place at the end of the procession. Although they could have reached the cemetery by way of the abbey's gardens, it was more ceremonial to leave by the front gate, walk a few yards along the road through the Abbey Foregate, and then turn into the cemetery in front of the church.

"Let's take a moment to think about what we know," Gwen said, speaking evenly and as if they weren't walking at the rear of a funeral procession in the pouring rain.

Gareth looked down at her. "Really?"

"The sooner we discover what happened here, the sooner we can go home."

"All right," Gareth said, willing to play along because Gwen wasn't wrong. "Well ... yesterday morning, a girl died in that alley, spending her life's blood in a puddle, having been stabbed with a jagged stick from a crate. We didn't find her body because someone carried her away and threw her in the river. Given the square of cloth, likely she was moved in the back of Flann's cart, though with the dress gone and the cart wheel mended, we might never be able to confront him with it."

"We know what he might have done," Gwen said, "and that tells us where to keep looking for answers."

"Next, with Conall and Flann, we have an Irish connection," Meilyr said, joining in. "One wonders if the girl could have been Irish too."

"We have no evidence to indicate it, so we shouldn't speculate more than we already have, Father," Gwen said, but her smile was gentle as she spoke, so he would know her words weren't meant as chastisement.

Gareth cleared his throat. "Next, we have the murder of Roger Carter in Conall's room and Conall's subsequent disappearance, albeit without his possessions, including his horse."

"Didn't John mean to spend the afternoon inquiring of Conall's business associates?" Gwen said. "Would it be too much of a stretch to wonder if Flann was one of them, or if maybe he was *the* connection, which is why nobody has come forward to say that he knew him?"

"Flann claimed not to recognize Conall's picture, but neither of us liked his manner," Gareth said.

"So we have Roger dead in Conall's room. A brothel coin found among Conall's possessions. Flann and Will going to the same brothel. Conall and Flann as Irishmen. Flann and Will as owners of the cart, which was mended in Roger's shop, the cart having been used to transport the dead girl." Gwen almost laughed as she came to the end of her litany. "Perhaps it's time that John had a talk with Flann and Will."

Gareth had a finger to his lips, tapping thoughtfully. "Definitely, though I'm sorry to say that without a witness, we have only coincidence to connect him to either murder. Does Flann strike you as the type of man who is going to break under pressure?"

"No, unfortunately. He might bend, but you couldn't believe a word he said." Gwen pursed her lips. "His partner, though? Maybe Will would tell us something if we got him alone."

"Flann said he was returning to the monastery tonight. Maybe we ought to invite John to dinner, so they all could meet," Meilyr said.

"That is a good idea," Gareth said, and then he lifted his chin to point to the west. As they passed through the front gate back onto the road, John Fletcher himself hurried towards them from the east bridge across the Severn. "And there is the man in question."

Meilyr continued on, since he was part of the service, but Gwen and Gareth slowed to wait for John to reach them. His hood covered his face to the point Gareth could barely make out his features in the depths. He'd recognized him from his walk alone.

"Any luck?" Gareth said.

John gave a quick shake of his head. "Conall was a ghost, it seems. And if he has any sense in him, he's long gone by now."

He gazed past them to the townspeople who were crowding into the graveyard. When Gareth and Gwen had stepped to one side after noticing John, everyone who'd gathered on the road for the procession had passed them. Now, Gareth wasn't sure there'd be space to breathe inside the graveyard wall, much less for the three of them to stand.

Gareth gestured towards the crowd. "As you can see, the whole town is here. I was hoping for a smaller turnout so that the murderer, were he to put in an appearance, might stand out somehow."

"Faint hope of that in this rain," Gwen said. "Everyone's hoods are up and their coats and cloaks are tucked tightly around them. We'll be lucky if we recognize anyone at all."

That wasn't entirely true. From where they stood on a slight rise in the road, Gareth could see the coffin and the lead mourners. Martin walked bareheaded beside Jenny, who was well-wrapped in her cloak—appropriate since she was with child, and it would be more than unfortunate if she fell ill as a result of attending her brother-in-law's funeral. Martin had his arm around her and was being nothing but solicitous, but Gareth couldn't help remembering how little grief had showed in his voice when he'd been told of his brother's death—and how angry at John he'd been last night.

Clearly, that side was one Martin kept hidden, and Gareth wondered what else might be lurking beneath the surface and the friendly face he showed the world.

The three of them started forward again, and John sighed glumly as he slouched along through the puddles. Shrewsbury had two murders and a missing man and, even with Gwen's discoveries, which Gareth related to John as they walked, they were no closer to concluding their investigation than they'd been yesterday morning when all they had to go on was a puddle of blood in an alley.

They turned through the cemetery gate and came to a halt next to Meilyr, who was standing on the outskirts of the crowd at the northern side of the cemetery, near the wall that separated the graveyard from the road. The graves had been dug fifty feet away at the far eastern side of the yard, and the monks had begun the ritual of placing the bodies in the ground, wrapped only in their linen shrouds.

"That's my cue." Meilyr left them for the gravesite.

"Perhaps we should stand over there." Gareth led Gwen and John to a willow tree, grown so large that it overhung the cemetery on one side and the road on the other. He hoped that they'd be less noticeable over here, and the vantage point would give them a good view of the overall crowd. From this location, Gareth could see the faces of two-thirds of the people who'd come to send Roger Carter on his way. The burgeoning foliage above their heads also lessened the number of raindrops that were able to reach the ground and soak them.

Abbot Radulfus nodded at Meilyr's approach. In response, the bard bowed in the abbot's direction, turned towards the crowd, and began to sing.

Gareth wasn't a musician, but even he could tell that Meilyr was in fine form today, spurred on, perhaps, by the abbot's initial skepticism. Sometimes songs sung in a foreign language left Gareth struggling to understand the words, but Meilyr enunciated so clearly that he had no trouble this time:

I pray it may be

When my soul departs
This mortal form
That to death I gladly go
As to a feast

It was a far cry from the more flowery Welsh death poetry, or anything written by Prince Hywel—or Meilyr himself, for that matter, but the delivery was exquisite. The silence among the listeners was absolute, except for the rat-a-tat of the rain on the leaves above their heads and on the slate roof of the church.

Meilyr finished his song, and the abbot gave his performance the respect it deserved, pausing through ten heartbeats for the mourners to settle and shift their attitude from awe to reverence, though it could hardly be said in this instance that there was much difference to find between the two. Then Radulfus began the Latin service.

For his part, Meilyr remained standing with bowed head beside the open grave. That was wise of him. Gareth had been around Gwen's family enough to realize that after a performance like that, Meilyr would be exultant, eyes glittering with an extremely inappropriate pride—given the setting—at a job well done.

Gwen shifted from foot to foot, indicating that she'd lost interest in the service now that her father had finished his work. And then, proving he'd read her right, she leaned into Gareth and spoke under the cover of the rain and the monks' chanting, "I haven't told you all that we learned from Adeline's father."

Gareth looked down at his wife. "You learned something about these deaths?"

"No—this is about Cadwaladr."

Unbelievably, in the last few moments, Gareth had entirely forgotten about the treacherous prince. And that realization recalled to mind the wise words of Taran, King Owain's steward, who had comforted Prince Hywel when he'd gone to him with a grief for Rhun too great to bear.

The steward had said, "At first, you will think of Rhun with every breath. Then you will think of him every hour, and then twenty times a day. He will be the first thing you think of when you wake and the last when you go to sleep.

"And then, one day, you will fall asleep too quickly to have thought of him.

"That day will be a good one, and not because you've somehow betrayed your brother's memory by forgetting him. On that day, you will be honoring his memory by learning to live without him."

The thought of Cadwaladr's betrayal coupled with Gareth's desire for revenge had existed alongside Gareth's grief for Rhun— as it had also in Prince Hywel. It stunned Gareth to realize that finally, after four months, in the middle of a quest, the entire purpose of which had been to uncover the whereabouts of Cadwaladr, Gareth had forgotten him, even for a moment.

And, as Taran had promised, it was suddenly a good day. He looked up into the tree branches above his head, allowing his hood to fall back and the raindrops to plop into his face. It was as if a weight had been lifted from his shoulders: he could mourn Rhun; he could hate Cadwaladr. But he didn't have to be consumed by the thought of either anymore.

Gwen had been watching him curiously, since he hadn't responded yet to her statement. Looking around to make sure that they couldn't be overheard, Gareth tugged her farther down the cemetery wall, towards the rear of the crowd of mourners. John stood a few feet away with his back to them, his shoulders hunched against the rain.

"Tell me quickly," Gareth said.

So Gwen related Tom's story about witnessing Cadwaladr's departure east from Shrewsbury, accompanied only by a man-at-arms and one servant. Instinctively, Gareth stared east too, as if willing to Rhun's killer to ride out of the rain.

But he wasn't there, and Gareth knew in his heart that the trail, if it had once led to Shrewsbury, now only led from it.

24

Gareth

"Where are you going?" Gwen said.

Gareth swung his cloak around his shoulders and tightened down the toggles that held it closed at his chest without answering. He knew she wasn't going to like what he had to say.

The rain continued to fall, and everything was cold and damp. The funeral service had been followed by a mass for Roger Carter, paid for by his brother Martin, which in turn had been followed by dinner. Gareth and Gwen had invited John Fletcher to join them, in hopes that the two merchants, Flann and Will, would put in an appearance, but they had not.

Afterwards, Gareth had stopped the hospitaller to ask after them and had been told that Will had collected their things that afternoon—during the funeral, in fact.

"Did he say where they were going?" Gwen had asked.

The hospitaller had shaken his head regretfully. "Not to me. He left a generous donation to the abbey, however."

As he might have.

Now, Gareth said to Gwen, "I need to have a look at that brothel again. If the cart is mended, that's the only other place we know Flann and Will to have gone, and it's the only piece of this puzzle that connects all the rest."

"Is John going with you?"

"He had duties to attend to as Deputy Sheriff."

"Let me come with you. Please. You should not be going alone."

Gareth stopped in the act of pulling the hood of his cloak up over his head. "You cried in my arms not four hours ago about your involvement in this investigation. I'm not taking you with me."

"Gareth," Gwen said in her most reasonable voice, "I've been a part of this from the beginning, and you yourself said that we would see this through together." She poked his chest with one finger. "That includes now."

Gareth rubbed at the spot she'd poked as if it hurt. "What about Tangwen?"

"She's asleep and need have no part of this."

Gwen's tears had gone, but even if they'd been a momentary aberration caused by her pregnancy, they still deserved respect. When he'd first stood over the pool of blood, he'd acknowledged within himself the extent to which investigating murders affected him. Gwen was right that they needed to reassess this particular service for Hywel—and with a second child on the way, what it did to them as parents.

Gareth studied his wife for a few more heartbeats and then nodded, if reluctantly. "I suppose, if I'm truthful, it wasn't my intent to enter the brothel. I simply had a thought to look around the outside of the town wall, where the gate opened onto the river."

"What are you going to see in the rain and the dark that can't wait until tomorrow?" Gwen said.

"I won't know until I find it, but if I wait until tomorrow, there will be nothing to see, not with this rain," Gareth said.

"I will tell my father and Gwalchmai that I'm off with you." Gwen snatched up her cloak and hurried from the room before Gareth could protest that he hadn't given his permission for her to come.

But then, having run only a few yards, Gwen pulled up short and spun around, such that Gareth, who had started down the corridor after her, almost ran her over. "What if the girl wasn't at the brothel by her own will?"

Gareth caught her by the arms. "We discussed that. She could have run away from the brothel, but John Fletcher has been showing her picture all over town to no avail. If any man visited her there, he won't admit to it, and the proprietor isn't talking."

"No, I mean—" Gwen took in a deep breath. "Conall was Irish, right? And Flann is Irish."

Gareth felt himself on the verge of laughter. "I don't believe being Irish is a crime, Gwen."

Gwen shook her head vehemently. "No, I didn't mean that. What if the girl came from Ireland too, or even farther afield, and not by her own will?"

"You mean someone stole her from Ireland to be a whore here?" Gareth scratched at his forehead. "It's possible, I suppose. Though, if she was working at the brothel, it would have been a simple matter for her to tell one of her clients who she was and what had happened to her. It isn't as if Shrewsbury has a slave market."

"You and I both know that doesn't mean all trade stopped. There were still slaves in Dublin when we were there four years ago, even if the slave market was closed. I know it's a stretch, but I can't stop thinking about that girl bleeding to death in the alley, and the fact that nobody will admit to knowing her. She was running away, and someone killed her."

"There are far more reasonable explanations," Gareth said.

"We just can't think of any," Gwen said tartly.

Gareth pursed his lips and stared at the wall above Gwen's head. "She could simply be an unhappy English girl from somewhere else who ran away from a husband."

"But what if she isn't." Gwen stepped closer. "Just think if she isn't the only one, just like that brothel isn't the only one. There could be other girls here against their will."

"Well, there are other brothels—" Gareth dropped his eyes to fix them on Gwen's face. "John said that the owners of the brothel to which the coin gained entry had opened a second establishment outside Shrewsbury. It's to the east of here, just beyond St. Giles."

"We haven't even looked at it," Gwen said, "and with the departure of Flann and Will, I don't think looking at it can wait until morning."

Gareth wavered. Gwen had wanted him to discover whether or not the girls at the brothel were there by their own volition, and he'd refused her. Now, however, he didn't know if he could walk away from her fears again. That girl had to have come from somewhere, and someone had killed her. Others might see her as no different from a hundred other girls, but she was Gareth's responsibility now. She'd been buried without a name. She might as well have been faceless. She certainly had been afraid.

Still thinking, Gareth nudged Gwen to walk down the corridor towards the stairs. "I'm not taking you to the brothel. We have to respect John's sensibilities in that regard, but you can come with me most of the way, maybe to that abandoned mill at the edge of abbey land, and wait for me there."

Gwen wrinkled her nose, indicating she didn't like it, but she didn't argue. "Even if I'm wrong, and she was here by her own free will, girls that age don't wander the countryside by themselves. She had to have come to Shrewsbury with someone, stayed with someone, seen someone."

Gareth froze in the act of taking a step. "Maybe she did. In addition to Flann and Will, she's one of two people in this investigation who are complete strangers to Shrewsbury, Gwen.

Maybe the reason nobody has come forward to identify her is because the one person she knew was Conall."

25

Gwen

Since Tangwen was asleep, all that was required was to tell Meilyr and Gwalchmai where they were going. And once Gareth assured them that he wasn't actually taking Gwen to the brothel, neither objected to her accompanying him as far as the mill. It wasn't that late even—not even eight in the evening—and even with the rain, people were still out and about. There shouldn't be any danger. Whether in England or Wales, if people didn't go out because it was raining, chances were they never went out at all.

The brothel they were going to investigate lay on the main road from the southeast into Shrewsbury, just past St. Giles along the road to Atchem, where there was another bridge across the Dee. According to John Fletcher, the brothel doubled as an actual inn. Travelers seeking to avoid the higher rates in Shrewsbury—or wishing to avoid the town altogether—might choose to stay there instead.

"I don't mean for us to be long," Gareth said. "Two hours at most, which means we should return shortly after compline."

Compline was the late evening prayer before the monks retired for three hours of sleep.

"And if you're not back by matins?" Meilyr said. Matins was the midnight prayer. Monks said prayers every three hours throughout the day and night.

"We'll be back. Don't worry." Gareth said.

"But if you aren't," Gwalchmai insisted.

Gareth rolled his eyes at his brother-in-law's worried look. "Tell John Fletcher I went to the brothel. *Don't* come searching yourself. If we really do find ourselves in trouble, that wouldn't be the way to help."

Meilyr and Gwalchmai seemed satisfied with that response, so Gareth and Gwen collected their horses from the stable and led them out the back of the abbey. The path they took paralleled the main road that ran to the east and took them through the abbey gardens and fields to the abandoned mill the abbey laborer had mentioned when he'd told Gwen and Brother Julian about seeing Conall.

Settlements of varying sizes lay to the east of Shrewsbury. First was the Abbey Foregate, really another village in and of itself, which even had its own priest. A hundred yards on, these homes gave way to fields on both sides of the road. If it had been daylight, Gwen could have made out crofts and barns belonging to people who might worship in the Foregate, but who didn't live in Shrewsbury proper. After another half-mile, they passed the back entrance to St. Giles, which was closed up for the evening, or they might have returned to the road and the front entrance in order to ask about the dead girl's dress.

As it was, their current mission was more urgent. "The mill is just up ahead," Gareth said, "and then the brothel is a matter of a few hundred yards to the east, to the right of the main road.

"I thought you said you hadn't been here before?" Gwen's eyes narrowed suspiciously.

"I haven't! Before we left, I asked the layman working in the stable where it was." Gareth's expression turned sheepish. "It didn't feel right speaking to one of the monks about the location of a brothel."

"I can see why it wouldn't." Amusement bubbled up in Gwen, surprising her. It was raining and cold, but she was out with Gareth. Yes, they were investigating a murder, but in this moment, she had to admit that there was no place she'd rather be.

She took in a deep breath, probing in her mind around the edges of what she was feeling. She was starting to think that perhaps the problem wasn't with *her* at all, and her detachment from this investigation wasn't wrong. Maybe what was wrong was murder itself. To feel numb to it after a while was a natural reaction to something so unnatural that nobody could keep doing what they did—feeling what she'd always felt—and stay whole.

That didn't mean she and Gareth should keep on as they had, however. They would have to make a pact, for starters, that from now on Tangwen and this baby would always come first, and that they would try harder to keep Gwalchmai and her father out of their cases. And maybe not answer when John Fletcher called.

Gareth directed his horse into the trees, and Gwen followed, ducking her head as branches, heavy with rain, dumped water on her head as she brushed past them. Within three paces, she couldn't see anything at all, and all of a sudden, the illicit nature of this endeavor had her breath catching in her throat. She wouldn't have said she was afraid, necessarily, but she didn't like how dark it was, and not being able to see made her heart beat a little faster.

As always seemed to be the case, Gareth was unerring in his ability to find a track that would take them through the woods, though at one point he dismounted and helped Gwen down before grasping the bridle of his horse and leading it forward. By then, they didn't have far to go, and soon they came to a halt on the edge of a clearing beneath the sheltering branch of an overhanging oak.

The mill lay in front of them on the far side of a large clearing. A torch on a long pole jammed into the ground shone near the front door.

"I thought you said it was abandoned," Gareth said.

"Who told you that?"

Gwen turned at the voice a moment before a hand clapped over her mouth and pulled her away from Gareth. Before she could bite down on it, the hand was removed to be replaced by a gag, and then her hands were wrenched behind her back to be tied at the wrists, and a bag thrown over her head. All she had was the impression that her captor was a large man with a fierce expression.

She tried to scream, but she choked on the gag instead. She heard shouting and the clash of swords, which she assumed meant Gareth was trying to fight off the attackers, but from inside the bag she couldn't make out what was happening.

Then the fighting stopped, and the only sound she heard was a thud and heavy breathing. "Put them with the others," the same voice said.

Gwen experienced a moment of weightlessness before she was thrown over a man's shoulder. She jounced along upside down, hardly able to breathe through the gag and with all the blood rushing to her head. She was thankful she was only a few months pregnant and the baby so small, since she barely showed and her womb hadn't grown to the point that being upside down on a man's shoulder would have been utterly unbearable.

They went a hundred steps, though they felt like a thousand. Then a door creaked, and her captor walked across a wooden floor with clunking steps, made louder and heavier by the weight of her on his shoulder. Then another door creaked, and it actually hit the top of her head as it closed behind them. More footfalls, this time descending wooden steps, and then the footfalls became more muffled. The man dropped her to the ground and pulled the bag from her head.

Gwen blinked her eyes, adjusting them to the light, though it wasn't a difficult transition since the room was hardly more illumined than the absolute blackness of the bag. What light there was came from the glow of a lantern in the hand of a second man. She took in a breath, and now that she felt a tiny bit more in control, she realized that she recognized him as Flann's partner, Will.

They'd come down a narrow set of stairs, with only six steps, to a damp dirt floor to end up in a room approximately fifteen feet long and twenty wide. An L-shaped bend hid the far corner. Wooden beams supported the ceiling above her head, and the walls themselves were made of wood, plastered to keep out the wind, though as she leaned back against the wall, she could feel the force of the weather, rattling something loose. A strangely narrow door—closed, of course—was centered in the wall opposite the stairs.

It was an exit, though Gwen didn't know to where until she noted the rhythmic creaking and sound of splashing water coming from beyond the narrow door. She'd briefly been in a room just like this in Aberystwyth. It made up the lower level of the mill, necessary to give access to the water of the mill race and to maintain the waterwheel, but where nothing could be stored because of the dampness.

These men, however, were storing women here. Crowded together against the rear wall were a dozen women of varying ages, though none looked older than thirty. They were dirty and obviously cold, since they huddled against one another, some sleeping, others merely staring vacantly at the newcomers.

Her initial captor, a man with a scruffy brown beard, stuck his face into Gwen's. "We have one rule here: if you scream, you die. Do you understand? There's nobody out there to hear you anyway."

Gwen nodded, not because she planned to obey, but because she needed him to remove the gag, and she would have promised him anything if only he would do so.

He did.

"What do we do with him?" A third man with a neatly trimmed black beard, who was younger than either Will or the man who carried her, appeared at the bottom of the steps with Gareth on his shoulder. Blood dripped down Gareth's left arm, and he had blood on his face from a wound at his hairline. If Gwen's hands had been free, she would have put them to her mouth.

"Is he dead?" Will said.

Blackbeard laid Gareth on the ground ten feet from Gwen. "No. Just knocked out. It seemed a waste to kill him when someone will pay a pretty penny for a warrior like him."

"If he can control him," Will said.

Blackbeard jerked his chin to point at Gwen. "Isn't that his wife?"

Will nodded.

The man smirked. "It won't be hard then, will it?"

"We'll leave it to fate. If he lives, we'll sell him." Will stood with his hands on his hips, looking down at Gwen, though he didn't speak to her but to Blackbeard. "How long until we're ready to move?"

"Flann hasn't returned from town," Blackbeard said.

Will pressed his lips together. "We can wait another hour. Then we have to leave in case someone comes looking for these two."

Scruffy beard scoffed. "Who is going to care about a couple of Welsh dogs?"

"I saw Gareth with the Deputy Sheriff," Will said. "Fletcher might care. The girl did see the wheel we fixed."

"They don't know anything," Blackbeard said.

Will shot Blackbeard an unreadable glance. "They know everything now."

"Fat lot of good it will do them." That was scruffy beard again.

Gareth's head lolled to one side, but now that Gwen had managed to blink back her tears, she could see his chest rising and falling. It might even be that the blood on his arm was from a surface wound and not grievous—though if it suppurated, any wound could be mortal.

Gwen supposed it wasn't surprising that her captors hadn't questioned her, since she was a woman, and her value was only in what they could sell her for. She certainly wasn't going to volunteer the information that her father knew where she was. Even if the whole lot of them were leaving this place within the hour, they could hardly travel far undetected, not with this many people to transport. A cart could only move so fast, and she doubted that these women were going to be in any condition to ride horses. Besides, they would have had to be tied onto them, which would be even more noticeable, whether or not it was dark.

All that passed through Gwen's head as a way to reassure herself. Rhun's death had shaken her confidence that everything would always turn out all right in the end, because that time it hadn't. Despair threatened to overwhelm her, but she hadn't spent nearly ten years as Hywel's spy for nothing. For Tangwen's sake, and the sake of her unborn child, she was going to get them out of here—or die trying.

Her hands itched to touch her husband, and she prayed that these men wouldn't hurt either of them anymore, and that they might even leave. *Leave us alone leave us alone* cycled through her mind in a litany, as if somehow her thoughts could be conveyed to them and influence their behavior. She presumed that the exterior door, which she made sure not even to look at in case one of them noticed, was locked or even nailed shut, or else they wouldn't have left the women here without a guard in the first place. If someone watched the door, there would be no reason for any of them to remain inside the room.

As the men obeyed her unvoiced command and moved towards the steps, Gwen gave a huge sigh of relief and turned her attention to her fellow captives. A few of the women gazed back at her, blinking sleepily, but none seemed very awake, and none had said a word throughout the entire exchange among the men. One of the women curled up into a ball on the floor, and it was then that Gwen realized that not only were the woman's hands free, but none of her companions were constrained at all.

Sadly, Will took the lantern with them, but after the door closed behind him, it looked as if he then set the lantern on a table near the door because it continued to shine faintly into the room through the many gaps between the slats of the walls and around the doorframe. Thus, even in its absence, Gwen was able to see how rickety her prison really was. Maybe they assumed, because they were leaving within the hour, that she didn't have time to escape. With Gareth unconscious, she had to admit she was at a disadvantage.

But she wasn't helpless.

Gwen propped her shoulder against the wall of the cellar, using it to brace herself until she could get her feet under her. Even though her hands were tied behind her back, she was able to feel for the knife in her boot that Gareth always insisted she carry. He would be missing all his weapons, of course, but the men hadn't bothered to search her.

Gwen edged towards the woman closest to her. She was about Gwen's age, with lighter color hair, dark eyes, and a ragged dress. "Can you untie me?" Gwen said in English, holding out the knife. She was willing to do it herself if she had to, but slicing through the ropes with the knife at such an awkward angle might well end up with blood everywhere.

The woman looked at her blankly, so Gwen tried again in Welsh.

The woman's eyes widened. "I can't," she replied in the same language. "He'll beat me."

Hell.

Gwen didn't often resort to profanity, but the situation seemed to call for it. She gazed around at the faces turned towards her, and even as she looked at them, she saw many lose interest, or perhaps even forget that she was there. Gwen puzzled over their odd behavior for a moment before concluding that they must have been given some kind of potion that muddled their minds. She had to get out of here before it was given to her too.

Gritting her teeth, acknowledging that she was on her own and her and Gareth's best hope for survival was herself, she gripped the hilt of the blade, turning it on end in her palm, and sawed through her bonds.

It was only as the bonds fell away, having nicked the fat part of one thumb but freed herself nonetheless, that Gwen noticed the man lying in the far corner of the room. His arms were tied behind his back at the wrists and his legs at the ankles. Thinking that he could be an ally, once she cut his bonds and provided she could wake him, Gwen hastened through the women, who didn't even move aside to let her pass. It was as if they didn't even see her.

She dropped to one knee to turn the man so she could see his face, and then recoiled when she realized she was looking at Conall, the missing merchant. He wasn't looking so renegade anymore—nor, seeing as how he was as much a captive as they, much like a murderer.

26

Hywel

"What do you mean they aren't here?" Hywel swept a hand across his brow, pushing the wet hair from his face and glaring at Meilyr.

Meilyr tried to defend his son-in-law. "My lord, the Deputy Sheriff asked for Gareth's help with a murder—"

Hywel made a slashing gesture with one hand, cutting him off, "You don't say."

To suggest that it had been a long day would be an understatement. Hywel had been looking forward to a warm fire and a meal at the behest of the monks, but instead he'd been met in the stable by Meilyr with his bad news. It wasn't Meilyr's fault, of course. If Gareth thought he had difficulty controlling Hywel at times, Hywel had nothing on Gareth himself. The man could find himself in trouble just pulling on his boots in the morning.

Or Gwen could.

Neither would have turned their back on John Fletcher if he'd asked for their help.

"Have you told John Fletcher that they're missing?" Hywel said, his eyes going to the rain pounding on the cobbles of the monastery's courtyard.

"I was about to go myself, since Gwalchmai and Tangwen are finally asleep," Meilyr said. "Gareth said not to worry about them until at least an hour after compline."

"We're there now," Hywel said.

"Where are your men, my lord?" Meilyr said, looking past Hywel for his *teulu*, which, of course, wasn't with him.

"It's a long story." Hywel growled under his breath. "Never you mind John Fletcher. I will send Evan to find him."

"John is here, my lord," Evan said from behind Hywel.

Hywel turned to see Evan and John Fletcher entering through the wide stable doorway, both shaking rain off their cloaks as they did so.

John bowed. "My lord, it is a pleasure to see you again. Why did you need me?"

"Gareth and Gwen have gone missing," Hywel said. "What brings you to the abbey if not that?"

"I detained a merchant, Flann MacNeill, as he was leaving the town," John said. "I came here to ask Gareth if he'd like to be present when I questioned him."

"I thought you didn't have enough information to hold Flann?" Meilyr glared at the young sheriff, as if it was his fault that Gareth and Gwen were missing.

"I didn't, but at Gareth's suggestion, I put the manager of a local brothel under watch, and she met with Flann not an hour ago. Young Oswin reported the meeting to me, and I decided that Flann had become enough of a person of interest in regards to these murders to justify questioning him."

"I'm sure Gareth would want to be part of that, were he here." Hywel shook his head, trying to dismiss the buzzing in his ears that came from knowing nothing about anything that was going on. He wasn't even going to ask who Flann MacNeill was, how a brothel came into it, or how either were connected to murder. It was bound to be a long story, which he didn't have time for. Hywel turned back to Meilyr. "Where did Gareth and Gwen go?"

"They wanted to spy out another brothel beyond St. Giles," Meilyr said, and then at Hywel's derisive laugh, put up both hands, "though there was something about leaving Gwen at the abandoned abbey mill."

"Why a brothel?" Hywel said.

"It is owned by the same group of men as the one in town that Gareth suspected of being linked to the murders he's investigating."

"And what is that link?" But before anyone could answer, Hywel waved his hands in frustration, feeling like he was going in circles. "Never mind. Fletcher, lead the way to the brothel." Then Hywel pointed at Meilyr. "You stay here in case Gareth and Gwen return."

"Yes, my lord."

Hywel found that he was no longer interested in a warm fire, and though his horse had been ridden far today, another mile wasn't going to harm him. In short order, John roused a dozen watchmen from the Abbey Foregate and the Eastgate region of Shrewsbury, to give him a good complement of men, and with Hywel, Cadifor, and Evan, rode onto the main road.

Never talkative to begin with, Evan's face had settled into grim lines of determination—as well as exhaustion, Hywel surmised—a match to Hywel's own expression. Cadifor looked impassive, as always, and he rode close to Hywel's side as if the Englishmen with whom they rode might turn on him at any moment. Cadifor didn't speak English, and that had to be making him uncomfortable. Hywel's English was only passable, but since John himself spoke both Welsh and French, they found themselves getting by.

Fortunately, the ride to the brothel, which they took at a gallop, took no time at all, though John pulled up when they still had a hundred yards to go. Hywel and the others stopped too, in response to John's raised fist giving a silent command.

Four months ago, John had attacked Gareth in the courtyard of the abandoned monastery in Clwyd, but that overt confidence had been sheer bravado, overlaying an insecurity that had colored his actions.

This John was a different man, one who'd grown accustomed to giving orders and having them obeyed. Hywel didn't begrudge him his authority. He didn't know the area at all and still didn't understand what they were doing here or why Gareth and Gwen had thought to investigate the brothel on their own. He did understand that they could be in trouble—and that was all the information Hywel needed to act.

A door banged somewhere up ahead, and a man shouted in English. With the rain and the distance, Hywel couldn't make out the words, but John nodded. "My lord, perhaps the two of us could move closer to the brothel itself to spy out the situation, while the others fan out into the woods around it. If Gareth and Gwen have been captured, I don't want their throats slit because we're seen coming."

Hywel nodded, signaling that Evan and Cadifor should go with the others. He and John rode openly into the clearing in front of the brothel. The main building had a sign out front with the picture of a dancing girl, which was certainly appropriate. Other buildings lay behind the main one in the yard, which had a fence around it, more to delineate that property, Hywel thought, than to keep anyone out. Or in.

The brothel was a large building, two stories high, nearly forty feet wide at the front, and seemed to extend at least that far at the back. Torches shone brightly from stands on either side of the doorway. They had to have been fueled by oil since the rain was pelting freely down.

As they approached the front door, it opened, and laughter echoed through the night towards them. A man came out and circled around to the back of the property. The whole scene would have been inviting if Hywel wasn't fearing for the lives of his friends.

"It sounds like they're doing a brisk trade tonight despite the rain," John said. "Do we go straight in the front?"

"No—let's follow where that man went first and see what's there," Hywel said. "The complex appears to include more than just the inn and extends far back from the road."

In addition to the main building, three other structures were associated with the brothel: a kitchen; a two-story, house-like structure; and a long low building, from which the man who'd left the brothel led his horse, indicating it was the stable. He mounted and rode away without ever looking in Hywel's and John's direction.

John headed towards the stable, lifting a hand as he approached the boy, who stood in the entrance to take his bridle.

Hywel dismounted and led Glew under the eaves himself, shaking out his cloak before entering because the rain had become torrential. Once inside, without waiting for permission, Hywel strode down the center aisle, past a dozen occupied stalls, looking from one side to the other until he reached the second to the last stall on the left. It was without shock or even surprise that he recognized Gareth's horse, Braith. Gwen's horse was housed in a nearby stall.

Braith whickered gently at him, recognizing him, and even as Hywel's mind galloped down pathways he would rather not think about, he patted the horse's neck reassuringly. Hywel himself was far from reassured. Gareth and Gwen had to be here, but from what Meilyr had said, Gareth had not planned to take Gwen inside the brothel.

Then John approached, having given up his horse to the stable boy. "Are we really staying? Gareth and Gwen must have entered the brothel, else why leave their horses?"

"No, we are not staying." Hywel pointed with his chin to his friends' horses. "Braith still wears her saddle, which means Gareth didn't care for her before he left her here. That is unlike him and would have aroused my suspicions if they weren't already as high as they could go."

"Where could he have gone?"

Hywel pictured the yard outside the stable. "We'll search every corner of this property. Get your men. Gareth and Gwen have to be here somewhere." He shivered, less from the rain dripping from his hair onto his neck than at the thought of his friends in trouble. Then his brow furrowed. "Meilyr mentioned an old mill where Gwen was supposed to wait for Gareth. Do you know it?"

"I-I don't know exactly—"

Hywel didn't wait for John to finish stuttering his uncertainty but strode back towards the stable boy. "Did you see the owners of those horses come in?" He indicated Gareth's and Gwen's horses.

"No, sir. They were here when I arrived."

"And when was that?"

"Less than an hour ago."

Hywel stepped closer. "Someone mentioned an old mill nearby. Where is it?"

"I don't know of any mill—" he broke off, his expression belying his words.

"Where?"

"Out the back is a track that goes west to the old mill race—"

But Hywel was already heading for the door.

27

Gareth

Gareth woke with a moan and a splitting headache. He tried to sit up, but Gwen was beside him in an instant, her hands on his shoulders and her face close to his.

"Hush. I don't want them to know you're awake."

Even as Gareth blinked his eyes clear, he nodded his understanding. He didn't need the bandage around his head to spur his recollection of being ambushed as they left the woods in front of the mill, and with that memory, a searing pain shot through his left shoulder and back. "How long was I out?"

"Not long. It's been a quarter of an hour or so since the men left."

Gareth's eyes cleared some more, and with a few controlled breaths, the pain in his shoulder and in his head lessened to manageable levels. The room was dimly lit by light seeping through the cracks in a nearby wall. He could see well enough to note the general shape of it, and that they weren't alone. "What do we have here?"

"Slaves," a man's voice spoke without inflection from somewhere to Gareth's left. "Us too, if we don't get out of here."

Gareth turned his head in the direction of the sound to find the spitting image of the drawing in his pocket staring back at him. Conall was leaned up against the wall, his legs sprawled out before him and an expression on his face not far off from how Gareth was feeling.

"You're Conall." Gareth could hardly believe it.

"He didn't murder Roger Carter, if that's what you're wondering," Gwen said. "In fact, he doesn't know anything about any murders, not even the girl, though he can make a good guess about who she was."

Conall flopped a hand towards the dozen women who sat on the floor together a few paces away. "She was one of them, brought into Shrewsbury to display to a client. She escaped. Your wife says one of these men murdered her, though I can't see the point in that. They didn't kill me because they can sell any person for some amount of money." He looked Gareth up and down. "Admittedly, they got closer with you, but you're not dead either."

"They plan to sell us?" Gareth was unable to keep the incredulity out of his voice.

Conall snorted. "They can sell every one of us to a master, who will never believe, nor care if he did believe, what our lives were before."

"Which was what, in your case?" Gareth said.

"I serve Diarmait mac Murchada, King of Leinster, sent by him to discover who has been taking women from his lands to sell to foreigners." Conall bent infinitesimally from the waist, though even that small movement seemed to pain him.

Gareth could sympathize with the pain—and the reason for him being here. Although Conall's Irish forbears had enslaved their enemies with the same enthusiasm as Gareth's had, in recent years, both nations had come to see that the practice created more problems than it solved, and kings had thought better of enriching the traders in the Dublin slave market with the blood of their own people. Here in England, the Norman kings, at the behest of the Church in Rome, had sought to stamp out the slave trade wherever their writ stretched. King Stephen was not going to be pleased to learn that slavery had been alive and well in one of his market towns.

Still, Gareth wasn't prepared to take Conall entirely at his word. "Leinster has traded in slaves and captives for generations beyond count. Why would Diarmait care?"

Conall stared hard at Gareth, though because he was in so much pain, Conall's eyes were the only part of him that moved. Then his lips twisted. "Whatever our past history, Diarmait no longer countenances slave-taking."

"How did you end up here?" Gareth said.

That prompted a mocking laugh. "I posed as a trader—as a possible source of women. Unfortunately, I must have given myself away—" he broke off as sound of a door banging came from the other side of the wall.

They all looked at each other, a little wide-eyed, afraid that their captors were returning already.

"We have to get out of here," Gwen said.

"You have a plan for doing that?" Gareth said.

"I have a plan now that you're awake." Gwen tipped her head in the direction of the wall behind her, in which a door was set. The orientation of the room indicated that the door led to the outside.

"One would presume that it's locked," Gareth said.

"Yes, but the floor is dirt, isn't it?" Gwen said. "And if I'm not very much mistaken, the bottom panel is rotting from contact with the damp earth."

Gareth's eyes narrowed, trying to see what she was talking about, but the room was too dimly lit. He shifted to rise to his feet, having momentarily forgotten about his wounds, and nearly screamed from pain. He tasted bile and fought to control both it and the pain.

"You were stabbed in the back and hit on the head," Gwen said, "but you were very lucky too. The man's aim wasn't true. As it is, the knife split the links of your armor but stopped on your shoulder blade. I bandaged both wounds before you woke, but the shoulder wound is in an awkward place. If not for Conall, I don't think I could have wrestled your mail off you at all."

"How much blood did I lose?" Gareth said.

Gwen closed her eyes for a heartbeat, which he took to be a bad sign without her having to say anything more. "Both wounds bled freely, but that's good because it cleaned them in a way I could not."

As a last measure, while Gareth sat patiently, Gwen took a length of cloth, ripped from the bottom of her petticoat, and wrapped it around his body so that his upper arm was affixed to his side. She tied it, so he couldn't move his left arm except below the elbow.

"Is this really necessary?" he said, looking down at his arm.

"You move that arm, you open the wound, my friend," Conall said. "I've seen it before. Be thankful you can still bend your arm at the elbow and use your left hand if you have to."

"You may have to," Gwen said. "Can you stand?"

Gareth put his right arm around Gwen's shoulder and allowed her to help him to his feet. His shoulder screamed at him, and a staccato beat pounded behind his eyes. He breathed evenly and deeply, trying to master the pain, but he knew even as he struggled against it, that it was his master for now.

With a low groan, Conall proved himself more agile than Gareth, and rose to his feet all on his own. He teetered back and forth for a moment, prompting Gwen to put out her free hand to steady him, but then he straightened.

"What of these women?" All Gareth could manage was to move one finger, but he used it to gesture to the women in the room, who seemed to be taking little interest in what they were doing.

"I don't know what's wrong with them," Gwen said, "but whatever it is, it prevents them from being able to help us."

"At least they're not a hindrance," Gareth said.

"They've taken a potion that derives from a variety of hemp," Conall said. "It isn't the same plant as is grown here that we use for rope or cloth but a pungent herb that traders bring to Europe from the east. It dulls the senses when smoked or eaten. Devil's Weed, they call it."

Gareth had never heard of it and wished he'd remained ignorant.

"I want you both by the door," Gwen said, "ready to leave the moment I've dug underneath it."

"Do you actually think either of us will be able to crawl?" Gareth said.

"Do you want to live?" Conall said.

That shut Gareth up. He allowed Gwen to rest him against the wall by the door. She handed him her knife, for what purpose wasn't immediately clear, since he wouldn't be able to defend himself in his current state. But he didn't protest further as she went to the nearest girl, removed her boot without asking, and began to work with the heel at the dirt underneath the door.

The girl to whom the shoe belonged watched with uncurious eyes. Meanwhile, it was as if the weather knew that they were trying to escape and was doing its best to help. Raindrops and wind pounded at the wall at his back and shook the whole building with its force. The noise was such that he could hardly hear Gwen's efforts, and he was sitting right next to her. The water also soaked the ground below the door, making the soil easy to move.

He watched Gwen work for a few moments and then focused instead on the door opposite, through which their captors would come if they came.

In short order, Gwen had created a gap six inches deep into the soil under the door. She dropped the boot and started working with both hands at the wooden panel above it. Gareth gave her back the knife, and she began to pry out the nails that held it.

"Gwen! Gwen!" A hoarse whisper and scuttling sounds came from the other side of the door.

Gwen exchanged a wide-eyed look with Gareth before bending to look through the hole she'd made. "Cedric?"

"Yes!" Cedric's voice came clearly from the other side of the door. "And Tom Weaver, Adeline's father. We've come to rescue you."

Those were the most beautiful words Gareth had ever heard—not that he hadn't had faith in his wife. But if they were going to get out of here alive and hold off their abductors when they inevitably discovered that their captives were escaping, five was better than three, especially when the two newcomers were men and could actually stand.

The shriek of an iron nail separating from wood came loudly—so loudly that Gareth feared one of their captors would return—but no one did. That far away, the sound blended in with the general cacophony of the rain and the creaking of the water wheel, which seemed to have picked up its pace in the storm.

A moment later, Cedric was ducking through the doorway, followed by Tom.

"I'm so sorry. I'm so sorry," Tom repeated as he crouched by Gareth. "I didn't know it would be like this. I swear it."

"Why are you sorry?" Gareth said. "You're saving our lives."

Tom shook his head again as he helped Gareth to his feet. "I knew it was wrong, but Martin said we could make so much money, and I thought that if Adeline had more money, she would marry Roger and stay."

Gareth's mind was stuck on the name *Martin*, but he nonetheless allowed the weaver to take nearly all of his weight and practically carry him out of the mill while Gwen held the door open for them.

Cedric helped Conall out but then turned back for the women, who were making no move to escape. "What do we do about them?"

"We'll send John Fletcher back for them." Gwen returned the boot to the girl who owned it, but the girl made no move to put it back on.

Meanwhile, Tom Weaver was still saying over and over again, "I knew it wasn't right."

"What wasn't right again?" Gareth said, exasperated with the man's inability to articulate what he meant, and perhaps his own inability to understand through the fog in his head.

Tom brushed his sodden hair back from his face. "Taking these women. I went to Martin to say I wanted out, that I didn't trust Flann or Will. He tried to reassure me, but then Roger came, and he overheard us talking. They fought."

"Are you saying that Martin killed Roger because Roger had found out he was involved in the slave trade?" Gareth was shaking with pain and cold, which made him uncertain that he'd heard correctly. "And you didn't stop him?"

"I didn't actually see the murder." The big man's shoulders hunched. "At the shop, all they did was hit each other. I tried to separate them, but Roger clubbed me with a fist on my forehead, and I went down. Gwen saw the cut when she met me, but I passed it off as a result of being clumsy. By the time I could stand again, Roger was gone, and Martin was helping me to my feet. I never saw Roger alive again."

While Tom had been talking, they'd been hugging the side of the mill as they followed the path around it, forced to go single file by the flow of the mill race. Gareth was so focused on what Tom was saying—and on staying upright—that he didn't notice the others pulling up short until he nearly ran into Conall's back.

Martin Carter was just dismounting in front of the main door to the mill. He seemed as surprised to see them as Gareth and the others were to see him. He gaped at them for a moment, and then threw back his head and laughed, heedless of the rain and the wind that buffeted them all. "I see I'm just in time."

From behind Gareth, Tom let out a squeaking grunt that was unmistakably fear. "Martin."

Now that the true villain was revealed, Gareth found himself quite calm. He'd been beaten and stabbed at the behest of this man, but Gareth still found himself able to study this version of Martin Carter with an objective eye. Martin's brother, Roger, had been difficult—respected but unloved—and all the while it was Martin who had been the true villain.

Gareth had unveiled the wrongdoings of two-faced men before, but rarely had he encountered a man who could maintain such a complete façade, behind which his true self remained hidden. Gareth had a sudden pang of sadness for Jenny, Martin's wife, and he wondered how much she knew. She lived with the man, but that wasn't to say she knew him. It seemed she might have lied for him, however, since according to Tom's testimony, it was Martin who'd killed Roger and then stashed the body in Conall's room, which he knew would be empty since he'd already imprisoned Conall.

Martin hadn't yet pulled the blade from the sheath at his waist, but weapons suddenly appeared in the hands of the men with him, and they stood as if they were prepared to use them.

"I'm so sorry, Gareth," Cedric said from beside Conall. "We must not have been as secretive as we hoped."

Gareth was in no shape to fight, without armor or sword, though Gwen had given him back her knife after she'd used it to pry out the nails. Cedric pulled out his sword, which he had a right to wear as a watchman, but Gareth didn't know how much he could count on the youth. He was nineteen, inexperienced, and couldn't fight off a dozen men all by himself.

For his part, Tom dithered. Gareth supposed he was very fortunate that the big man had found Cedric and chosen to free them when he did. He'd acted when it mattered most. Just because a man had the body of a fighter didn't mean he had the character of one.

When they'd arrived, only one torch had lit the yard in front of the mill, but it had been joined by three more—along with three carts, two enclosed by fabric. They were parked in various stages of readiness, presumably for their imminent departure. A cart path headed into the woods to the east, the same one Gareth had planned to take to the brothel before he'd been set upon from behind by Martin's men.

Martin jerked his head towards the front door of the mill. "Let those fools inside know that several of their charges have escaped." One of his men obeyed, loping to the door and going through it. Curses came from inside the mill, distinguishable even over the sound of the rain, which continued to pour down.

"Martin has too many men," Cedric said in an undertone. "We are outnumbered."

"I am sorry to say, I am nearly useless," Gareth said by way of a response, "but I will fight beside you."

"Martin Carter! Put up your blade!"

Martin spun around as John Fletcher and a host of men surged into the clearing. Rather than simply running their opponents through, however, they reined in, which wouldn't have been Gareth's choice. John had surprised Martin, and Gareth was more glad to see him than he could say, but Martin and his men were prepared for a fight, and John would have been better off attacking first and asking questions later. Of course, as a man of the law, he might not have felt that he would be justified in doing so.

As it was, Martin's men had no such qualms and reacted immediately—not by running, which would have been so much easier, but by launching themselves at their foes. Running away wouldn't have solved anything for them. They had to leave no trace of John and his men—or Gwen and Gareth—in order to survive themselves.

Tom Weaver had no intention of letting Gareth fight, and he dragged him towards the trees, despite Gareth's objections. While Conall and Gwen came with them, Cedric, bold young man that he was, charged straight for Martin Carter.

Martin had swung around to face John, naturally viewing him as the greater threat, but at Cedric's roar of rage, he turned back to meet Cedric's blade. Their weapons clashed, and Gareth strained through the dark and the rain—and Tom's protests—to see what was happening.

Then Evan appeared beside him. "Come with me."

Gareth gasped to see his friend. "What—?"

"The prince is here, and he told me to get you away before I return to help finish them off. If we don't hurry, Fletcher's men will have won before I can do that."

"I'm not leaving—"

"That is a direct order from Prince Hywel." Evan urged Gareth to mount Evan's own horse, which he'd brought, and boosted Gwen up behind him.

"What about—?"

"Go!" Evan slapped the horse's rump, and the creature leapt away through the trees. Conall and Tom ran behind them, stumbling a bit in the dark, though Evan's horse found his way with no trouble through the brush.

"I've never run away from a fight in my life," Gareth said.

"Hywel came all this way." Gwen had her arms around Gareth's waist, holding on. "He wasn't able to save his brother. Let him have the satisfaction of saving you."

28

Hywel

Hywel hadn't had time to count his opponents, but at first glance the two sides appeared evenly matched—even with sending Evan to help Gareth and Gwen. Hywel had let John Fletcher lead the assault, but now he cursed himself for doing so because John had opted to give the men a chance to surrender instead of simply killing them all. Hywel didn't know what they'd done, exactly, but they'd harmed Gareth and Gwen, and that was good enough reason for Hywel to attack first and ask questions later.

Before Rhun had died, he'd told himself that he could go through life with a kind of amused detachment. It seemed to him that with his mother's death at the very hour of his birth, the worst thing that could happen to him had happened before he'd lived a single day. He'd been wrong, however. Rhun's death had proven that.

As he'd grown to accept the mantle of grief and anger as a permanent part of himself, that detached cynicism had been renewed—possibly even more so than before. He had thought, on the whole, that he didn't care whether or not he lived or died, as long as Cadwaladr died before he did.

But tonight, the sight of Gareth and Gwen stumbling around the side of the mill, Gareth with a bloody bandage around his head, had sent a fire surging through him. *By God, he did care.* He wasn't detached, and he was overcome by a rage like he'd never experienced in battle before.

Since Hywel and Cadifor had hung back, they had more room to maneuver than John did. When the lead conspirator, whom John had called Martin, raised his blade against the young watchman who'd accompanied Gareth and Gwen from around the corner of the old mill, Hywel and Cadifor spurred their horses forward. They didn't have quite the same advantage as if they'd descended a hill or if they'd had more space to pick up speed, but Glew was swift and well-trained, worthy of his name, which meant *valiant.* In battle, he obeyed Hywel's every wish almost before Hywel commanded it.

He cut through the first opponent like he was chopping wheat, slicing through his midsection with one swing of his arm and hardly noticing where he fell because he had already turned his attention to the next man to stand against him. That Englishman also fell in one blow, the side of his face sliced clean off by the downsweep of Hywel sword.

Blood spattered Hywel, but again, he hardly noticed. A red haze colored his vision, and his whole attention was directed at the leader, who was fighting the young man who'd come in with Gareth and who was completely outmatched. John Fletcher was struggling to reach him too, but he had several men and a cart between him and Cedric.

Then one of Martin's minions put his axe through John's horse's forelock, and the horse crashed to the ground. Before he was crushed beneath the animal, John cleared his feet from the stirrups and rolled free. Unfortunately, that meant Cedric was even more on in own than he had been before.

But not for long. With a roar, Hywel spurred Glew at Martin while Cadifor got between John Fletcher and the man who'd killed his horse. It was all Martin could do to parry the first blow Hywel directed at him, which left him completely unprepared for the second.

Hywel had sharpened the blade of his sword such that just touching it could make a finger bleed. He'd done it with the vision of Cadwaladr's neck bared before the sword, and even as he undercut Martin's arm, slicing through it and then through the man's neck in one complete blow, it was Cadwaladr's face that he saw on Martin's head, which hit the ground with a thud and rolled away from the body.

With a gleeful shout, Hywel checked his horse in front of the mill and turned, looking for more men to fight. At some point while Hywel wasn't looking, Evan had returned to the clearing. He stood ten yards away, breathing hard, his sword bloody and a dead man at his feet. With such an assist from Gwynedd, the remainder of Martin's men had been dispatched by John's soldiers or were even now fleeing into the woods.

Hywel made to spur his horse after one of these escapees, but Cadifor caught his bridle before Glew could charge. Rain pattered on Cadifor's upturned face, and he shouted something at Hywel, but Hywel couldn't hear him through the thundering in his ears. He still held his sword high, and he was anxious to continue the battle, but then Evan was there too. He took Glew's nose in his hands and talked to him.

"My lord, it is over." Cadifor's words finally penetrated through the haze in Hywel's mind.

He blinked and looked around as if seeing the scene for the first time. He realized he had no memory of how many men he'd killed or how he'd done it. Hesitatingly, he lowered his bloody sword. He had never lost himself like this, not in all his years of fighting. He still felt the anger at Rhun's loss, but he was almost more angry at himself for losing control just when he needed it most.

"Get down, son," Cadifor said, his voice no longer urgent.

Hywel obeyed, landing unsteadily on his feet beside his foster father. He rested his cheek against Glew's neck, so exhausted he didn't even know if he could walk. "What about the others?"

"We can leave them to John." Cadifor tipped his head to indicate the mill and spoke to Evan. "Would you find out if there are more prisoners in there?"

"Consider it done." Evan bent to clean the blood from his sword on the cloak of one the downed men and then walked towards the door to the mill, which was open.

"Are you hurt at all, my lord?" Cadifor said.

"No." The short response was all he could manage. "You?"

Cadifor shook his head. "They weren't soldiers. They should have known it was over before it started."

John had been walking among the dead men, looking into their faces, his own pale in the torchlight and glistening with sweat and rain, but now he came over to where Hywel and Cadifor waited. "You and your men saved the day, my lord."

Hywel nodded.

"It would have been less necessary if you'd simply run Martin through at the start." Cadifor said, as willing to instruct John as he was Hywel. "You were too noble for your own good,"

Hywel glanced to where Martin Carter's head lolled several feet from where his body had fallen. He wished it was Cadwaladr's head, understanding now that in the heat of the fight, he'd wanted it to be so badly that he'd made himself see it. Now that the rage had cooled, it left him shocked at how hot he'd burned.

John was called away by one of his men, and once again, Hywel was alone with Cadifor.

"Can you tell me what happened out there, my lord?"

"You know what happened."

"You lost yourself."

Hywel tipped back his head, so the drops of rain could cool his face. If it hadn't been for how slick his sword hilt had been in his hand when he was fighting, he wouldn't have even noticed that it was still raining. "It shouldn't have happened. I shouldn't have let it happen. Rhun wouldn't have let it happen."

Cadifor moved closer so his face was only a foot away from Hywel's. "Look at me, son."

Hywel didn't want to, but he had never been able to disobey that voice.

"I have loved you from the moment I first held you in my arms after the death of your mother. We don't share blood, but you are my son as much as any of the others. Your name is Hywel ap Owain. You are a warrior-poet and the *edling* of Gwynedd. You are not Rhun."

"My father—"

Cadifor gave him a small smile and placed a hand on his shoulder. "Your father needs you to be you. He's already lost Rhun. Don't deprive him of Hywel too."

Hywel stared at Cadifor. He had never thought about his role that way, and as they looked at each other, something broke loose in the back of Hywel's mind—not his sanity, not his control—but the relentless fear of failure that had been fueling his anger all this time.

Then Evan returned, even as Hywel was still reeling from Cadifor's words. "There are a dozen women in there, my lord, Welsh and Irish."

Cadifor made a guttural sound.

"What is the purpose of keeping them?" Hywel took a step to follow Evan. "Were they to work in the brothel?"

"They were to be sold as slaves." Gareth's voice rang out from behind Hywel, and he turned to see him and Gwen halting a few feet away. They'd ridden in on Evan's horse. Gareth's eyes were bright, and even as Hywel watched, he dropped to the ground in an easy motion.

"A moment ago, you were at death's door," Hywel said as his friend approached, after helping Gwen to dismount too. "Why didn't you return to the monastery like I ordered?"

"Answers weren't to be found at the monastery." Gareth tipped his head to indicate his left shoulder. "Gwen patched me up enough to be going on with."

"What answers are you talking about?" Hywel said. "Are you saying these men were slavers?"

Gareth gestured to a man who'd accompanied them down the track but whom Hywel didn't know. "This is Conall, who serves Diarmait mac Murchada, King of Leinster."

"My lord prince." Conall stepped closer and bowed. "King Diarmait has grown concerned about the stealing of women from his lands. I tracked the raiders to Shrewsbury and attempted to insinuate myself into their operation. My hope was to lure them to Ireland so that my king could arrest them." He spread his hands wide. "I don't know what gave me away, but Martin there—" he jerked his head to indicate the body on the ground, "—discovered something about me that made him mistrustful. I have spent the last two days in that mill with the captive women."

Gwen took up the explanation. "Most of the women are not Irish, however, but Welsh."

Hywel's eyes narrowed. "How is that possible? We've heard of no war in Wales that involved slave-taking."

Gwen made a murmur of assent. "Which means either these women were abducted like those from Leinster—"

"—or their lord sold them himself," Gareth said. "It has happened in the past, though not for a long time."

Conall took in a breath. "As it turns out, the answer is both."

Gareth gestured forward two more men, watchmen of John's who held the arms of a woman between them. "She runs the brothel here." He waved a hand at the two men. "You don't have to hold her. She's done nothing wrong as far as we know."

As far as we know covered a lot of ground, but Hywel simply nodded at Gareth that he should continue.

"Jane, here, can describe the man she believes provided the funds for this undertaking, and who derives the most wealth from its success." Gareth tipped his head to the woman. "Go on."

The woman was quivering before Hywel: cold, wet, and scared. The yard had turned into one great puddle, and soon even well-oiled boots would be filling with water. Hywel hadn't put up his hood, since he was still steaming from the fight, and if his cloak hadn't been nearly soaked through, he would have offered it to the woman.

"The man was richly dressed—as much so as any nobleman—even Lord Ludlow," Jane said. "Those snooty merchants in Shrewsbury who pretend to be above what we do, even as they patronize us and reap our profits, have nothing on him." Jane made a motion as if to spit on the ground, but then caught herself at the last moment, remembering where she was and whose company she was keeping. "He wore a sword, and spoke no English."

"What did he look like?" Gareth said.

Jane scoffed at that, as if what Gareth was interested in hearing was the least interesting part about the man. "Tall, fair hair going gray, a paunch he tries to hide. I never heard his real name. He only went by *Gwynedd.*" The woman canted her head. "Flann referred to him as *the prince*, though I never learned what he was supposed to be the prince of, seeing as how he was here and not in Wales."

Gareth turned to John. "Too bad we didn't take any of Martin's men alive."

John had been staring at the ground while the woman was talking, having pulled up his hood to protect his head from the rain, but now he looked up. "But we did."

"Who?"

"The man you suspected: Flann. We took him into custody not two hours ago. It was to invite you to question him with me that I arrived at the monastery when I did, in time to ride here with Prince Hywel."

Hywel allowed himself a mocking laugh. He had many of his own questions answered now. That Cadwaladr knew Martin Carter went a long way towards explaining how he'd come upon Adeline, Gwen's lookalike. "Perhaps it's time to tell me what this is all about."

29

Gareth

Gareth had a moment's fear as they rode back through the dark to Shrewsbury that John's guardsmen might have let Flann go, once John himself didn't return in a timely fashion to question him. Fortunately, John's men were better trained than that. For Gareth's part, he felt no anger at Martin, just impatience that killing had been necessary. There was enough death in the world as it was without adding to it.

Gareth had spent the ride back into Shrewsbury relating to Hywel, Conall, and the others everything that had happened in the last few days, after which the prince had explained how it was that he'd come to Shrewsbury with only Evan and Cadifor as companions. Imminent war with Powys didn't make slavery in Shrewsbury a paltry matter—but it did mean that they needed to finish up their business here quickly so the prince could return to Aber and his father. Tomorrow, however, would have to be soon enough, and they took a moment to stop at the monastery infirmary to augment the work Gwen had done on his head and shoulder.

The infirmarer had been horrified to learn that Gareth planned to go out again, but after Abbot Radulfus himself appeared to hear the story of what had happened at the old mill, Gareth convinced them both that questioning Flann could not wait even another hour. Leaving Gwen in the care of her father, Evan, and Hywel, Gareth made his way to the castle, accompanied by Conall, who'd also been seen to by the infirmarer.

"Are you, by chance, acquainted with Godfrid, Prince of Dublin?" Gareth had been debating whether to ask Conall the question ever since he met him, wondering if it was politic since Dublin and Leinster were often at odds, but he decided he had nothing to lose by asking. And he was curious.

Conall was still obviously in pain, but he managed an eye roll at Gareth's question. The infirmarer had mentioned cracked ribs and had looked askance at the bruises along the entire length of Conall's body. Still, he was managing to sit on a horse. "He is renowned throughout Ireland, though I have never met him. I have seen him from a distance, but since I don't speak Danish, I am of little use as a spy in Ottar's court." He paused. "I gather you know him?"

"He is a friend," Gareth said. "I had a thought to ask if he'd approached your king for aid."

"In overthrowing Ottar?" Conall said. "I wouldn't know. The man's a pig—Ottar not Godfrid—" Conall hastily put out a hand to reassure Gareth about whom he was speaking, "but he rules with an iron fist now that Torcall is dead."

"Godfrid's older brother would have things be different."

Conall barked a laugh. "Wouldn't we all."

John greeted them as they arrived at the castle, and he led them immediately to Flann's cell. The merchant had been pacing in front of the back wall of his prison. Shrewsbury Castle had cells in the basements of its towers, but Flann hadn't been stored there. This was just an empty guardroom at the castle's east gatehouse. At the time when John had arrested him, Flann had been only under suspicion.

As Gareth opened the door, Flann swung around. "It's about time." But then Flann's expression of outrage faltered and his face paled as he saw Conall following Gareth into the room. With a grin, John Fletcher came last, taking up a position with his back to the door.

John had asked Gareth to begin the questioning with the idea that they would take turns with Flann until he told the truth. Flann's first response would be to stonewall them or feign ignorance. They needed to get to the bottom of the intrigue here. Unlike Tom, Flann held a position of authority in Martin's organization, and they needed him to talk.

"What's this?" Flann said.

"This—" Gareth pulled out one of the stools at the table and sat, "is where you start talking."

"I've done nothing wrong."

"We know that's not true," Gareth said. "The question before us is the extent of your wrongdoing. Is it just slave trading, or does it extend to murder too?"

Flann gaped at Gareth, and then his eyes tracked to Conall, who had set himself up against the side wall of the room, his arms folded across his chest and his legs crossed at the ankles.

"I didn't kill anyone!" Flann said. "I'm a merchant!"

Gareth slapped his hand on the table. "If that's true, then tell us everything—about Martin and Roger Carter, about Conall here, about the girl who died, about who is involved in the trading of the Irish and Welsh women we found at the mill."

Flann licked his lips, his eyes tracking again to Conall.

"Yes, we know about them because we rescued Conall," Gareth said. "Tom Weaver named you and Will de Bernard as the London connection to the slave ring. Tom told us that Roger Carter confronted his brother, Martin, about his involvement in the slave trade. How many times did you steal women from Wales and Ireland? And how many did you take in all?"

Tom had returned to town as well, after having been questioned at length by John, and then sent home. The weaver had been foolish and was now remorseful. With Martin dead, nobody saw any reason to punish him further. John had then sent out a warrant for the arrest of Will de Bernard, Flann's companion, who'd disappeared after leaving Gwen and Gareth in the mill and hadn't participated in the subsequent battle.

Flann swallowed. "I really don't know what you're talking about."

Gareth rose to his feet and took a step towards John. "What do you think about charging him with the murder of the girl in the alley? We know it was his cart that hauled her body to the river, which means it was he who killed her and threw her in. That should be enough for the sheriff when he returns. Meanwhile, he can rot in a cell."

John played along, "It will be Will's and Tom's testimony against Flann's, and since Flann has Irish blood, it will be easy to convince the sheriff that it is they who are telling the truth, not Flann."

Flann's face had drained of color. "I didn't kill anybody! Did Will say I did to save his own skin? That traitor!"

John sneered. "If you didn't, then who did? Do you accuse Will?"

"No! Nobody killed her. The girl ran away from us, and by the time we caught up with her, she'd bled to death in that alley. Fell on a broken crate, the stupid chit."

While it wasn't the scenario they'd envisioned, Gareth believed him. "Who was she?"

Flann waved a hand dismissively. "Some girl from Powys. I didn't know her name."

Gareth found himself grinding his teeth, and he was very close to punching the man. He needed to know where in Powys the girls were from, but he had a few more questions to ask first. "It was you and Will, who hauled the body away and threw it in the river?"

"We thought it would sink to the bottom. It was supposed to sink to the bottom and be carried away by the current." Flann sounded annoyed that, even in death, the girl hadn't done as she'd been told.

"She was dead when she went in the water," Conall said, somewhat absently, "that's why she floated."

The longer Gareth spent in Conall's company, the more he became convinced that the Irishman played a similar role for his king as Gareth played for Prince Hywel—though Gareth would not have been the man to impersonate a slave trader. If Hywel ever needed a liegeman to do that, he would have to find someone else.

Flann tsked through his teeth. "As I have since realized."

"I need the name of the man from whom you buy slaves in Ireland," Conall said.

"He died," Flann said. "That's why we had to switch to Wales."

"And who was it that found you the Welshwomen?" John moved forward from the doorway.

Flann leaned back from the table. "Oh. So that's it."

Gareth didn't know what he meant, but he wasn't going to give Flann satisfaction by inquiring.

Flann gave another little tsk. "What do I get if I tell you?"

"We don't need you to say anything more," John said. "One of the others will tell us what we need to know."

"Maybe that's true, but you want to know now." He pointed with his chin to Gareth. "He's practically quivering with the need for it. Why?"

"Give. Me. A name." John's fists came down on the table, and he leaned on them, looming over Flann.

Flann shook his head. "I didn't kill anybody. Trading in slaves is a crime in England, but not a hanging offense. If I tell you who our contact was, I need you to put in a good word for me with your sheriff."

John's face was a thundercloud.

"Done," Gareth said without asking for John's permission. If John didn't like it, he could take it up with Hywel later.

"We got them from the King of Powys himself."

"From Madog," Gareth said, without inflection. "Really. Why should I believe you?"

Flann shrugged. "You don't have to believe me, but I tell you that he pledged to turn a blind eye to our raids as long as he got his cut of the profits."

John stepped back from the table and glanced at Gareth, his expression clearly saying, *what more should I ask him?*

John might not know what to ask next, but Gareth certainly did. "Did you go to Dinas Bran to negotiate this deal?"

"What? No, of course not. We worked through his intermediary, his wife's brother."

"I need you to say his name," Gareth said.

Flann was growing impatient with the questions, the answers to which he thought should be obvious, and he waved his hand dismissively. "Cadwaladr, Prince of Gwynedd." Flann rocked on the back legs of the stool, pleased by the reaction he was receiving for his tale. "Exiled, wasn't he? And short of gold? What better way than slaving to make a great deal of money quickly."

John's brow was heavily furrowed. "Who do you sell to?"

Flann laughed. "Who don't we sell to? English thanes, Norman lords, and then farther afield. Who wouldn't want a Welsh woman to warm his bed?"

"One who isn't afraid of having his throat slit in his sleep." Gareth was disgusted with Flann's complacency and unforgiving that his men had planned the same for Gwen.

Flann laughed again with what seemed like real amusement. He either wasn't taking his situation seriously, or he thought he had genuine leverage. "There's always that, though we keep them pretty quiet most of the time."

Gareth shook his head in puzzlement. "Conall mentioned the name of the herb you gave them. Devil's Weed, wasn't it?"

"That's right," Flann said. "We put it in cakes, they eat it, and all the fight goes out of them. We'd run out of weed, which was another reason why we needed to get moving before the effect wore off."

Gareth was going to have to dunk himself in the monastery brook when this was done just to wash off the stench of Flann's iniquity. "When were you to meet Cadwaladr next?"

"Two weeks' time, in London," Flann said. "We'd have a payment for him then."

Instantly, a vision formed in Gareth's mind of riding to London and setting a trap for Cadwaladr there, but Flann's next words forestalled that idea before it could fully form.

"If you're thinking of using me as bait, it's no good. Cadwaladr had friends among my men, and more in Shrewsbury.

He'll know, long before the two weeks are up, that things did not go well here, and he'll scarper."

John had been standing with his hands folded on the top of his head, as if he was trying to force his mind to accept the enormity of the plot that had been implemented right under his nose. Now he said, "We're done here."

Taking that as a command to leave, Conall and Gareth turned towards the door.

Flann put out a hand. "Wait! What about me?"

Gareth turned back. "John will speak to the sheriff, as he promised."

"When will that be?" Flann said.

John shrugged. "In about a month."

Gareth was unable to keep the grin of satisfaction off his face as he closed the door on Flann's horrified expression.

30

Gwen

"We've come full circle, Gwen," Hywel said. "And I am no closer to calling Cadwaladr to account than I was the day Rhun died."

They had just left Sunday mass, at which Gwalchmai had sung beautifully as promised. The church had been packed to the rafters with residents of the Abbey Foregate and the town. To a man, they were horrified at the events of the past few days. The brothels were one thing—to the minds of many, they were a necessary evil, and while, to Gwen, a woman who'd been allowed to live freer than most, the girls involved were effectively enslaved, that didn't seem to be an opinion shared by anyone else.

Regardless, actual slavery was another matter entirely, and nobody was happy with the fact that it had been going on right under their noses.

"I am so sorry, my lord," Gwen said.

"We'll find him, my lord," Gareth said. "He can't run forever."

"No, I suppose he can't, not if he ever hopes to see his children again. And when he returns, I will make him answer for what he's done."

They stood in the courtyard of the monastery, off to one side so as not to impede the passage of the churchgoers. The rain had stopped, finally, in the early hours of the morning. Gwen hadn't managed much sleep, but she'd had more than Gareth.

"Do we know yet the name of the girl who died?" Gwen said to Gareth.

"No," Gareth said shortly. "I can't see a way of finding out either. I have her picture, but—"

Hywel broke in. "Uncle Madog might know."

Gwen was still having trouble wrapping her head around the conspiracy which had Hywel's uncle turning a blind eye to English raiding parties stealing girls from their homes, as long as he got his portion of their subsequent sale. But then, she was having trouble with the fact that he'd tried to murder Hywel too.

"What of Jenny, Martin's wife?" Gwen said.

"She appears to have known nothing of her husband's activities," Gareth said.

"I believe her," Gwen said. "Either she didn't know, or she didn't want to know, which to some degree amounts to the same thing."

"John has spoken with her at length," Gareth said, "but none of the survivors, including Tom, have named her as a participant in either the brothel or in the slave ring."

"I'm glad, for her and John's sake," Gwen said. "She's lost everything."

"She owns a cartwright's workshop," Gareth said. "That's something."

Hywel had been gazing off into the distance, but now he shook himself. "Are you ready to go home? With Martin dead and Conall alive, you know everything now, don't you?"

"What about Will de Bernard?" Gwen said.

"Nobody has seen him," Gareth said. "John can send word to London that he's wanted in connection with these deaths, but—"

"He might not have gone to London," Gwen said, "and why would he when he can lose himself in territories controlled by Robert of Gloucester?"

"John might not be able to send word of what has transpired here to Robert, but I can." A thoughtful expression came over Hywel's face. "My father remains on good terms with Earl Robert."

All of a sudden, Gwen's heart felt lighter. If England had been ruled by Welsh law, Robert would have been king—and a more able king could not have been found in all of Christendom. Once he learned of it, Robert would be offended by what had happened here and would not want to harbor a slaver, even if he'd sinned in Stephen's lands. Robert's hold on the reins of his fiefdom was loosening due to illness and age, but Gwen knew as surely as the sun would rise tomorrow that the man would do what he could.

"Gwen, I need to talk to you." Jenny Carter, John's sister and Martin Carter's widow, hurried towards them, having come from the service at the church. She was well wrapped in a shawl that she'd pulled up over her head and held tightly under her chin, and she was chewing on her lower lip as if she was nervous. It wasn't a posture that Gwen would have said came naturally to her. Jenny was as vibrant and alive as any girl Gwen had ever met—and she elbowed Gareth in the ribs so he would look at her too.

Gareth's expression softened at the girl's approach. Jenny was not only newly widowed, but had been forced to accept that her husband had been a villain. The next few days and weeks were not going to be easy.

"I came as soon as I could get away." Jenny embraced Gwen.

"I am so sorry for everything that has happened," Gwen said.

"None of it is your fault," she said. "I was the one who was deceived—by Martin, by Adeline. It turns out I knew nobody as well as I thought I did."

"You know your brother," Gwen said.

That got a nod, but Jenny brushed any other comfort away. "You need to know that whatever bad things he did and harm he caused, Martin didn't kill his own brother."

Gareth expression showed skepticism, though his voice remained gentle. "You sound very certain. How can you be?"

Jenny looked him full in the face. "I know you think that I was mistaken about Martin spending the night in bed—or maybe you think that I lied—"

Gareth opened his mouth to protest, even if Gwen knew that had been exactly what he'd thought, but Jenny didn't let him speak.

"—but I didn't lie. Martin did spend the night at home. I admit now that I didn't know Martin as a wife should, but I do know that he would never have set foot in Rob Horn's inn, not for money, not for hatred. Never."

"Why would that be?" Gwen said.

"He found the smell of tanning leather unbearable," Jenny said. "I've seen him lose his dinner on the ground at the slightest whiff of that smell, which is why his and Roger's business was located to the northwest of the castle, as far from the tanning works as possible. At Martin's urging, the Council passed restrictions as to where leatherworking could take place and ruled that no more tanning businesses could be established within the town of Shrewsbury. It was Martin's hope that the council could eventually force the entire industry to move outside the town, beyond the river. Believe me, he would not have murdered Roger in that inn for any amount of gold."

"Fear can be a powerful motivator," Gareth said. "The fact that you knew of his antipathy to the smell could make his crime one he thought he could get away with, because nobody would believe the murderer could be him."

Jenny was shaking her head even as Gareth was speaking. "Not Martin. No. But I know who did."

Gwen put a hand on her shoulder. "Whoever it is, just tell us."

Jenny took in a breath. "Huw, Roger's and Martin's apprentice. What's more," she added in the face of their disbelief, "he's been missing since this morning, since word came to us about Martin's death."

"Why would Huw murder Roger?" Gareth said.

"Roger treated him badly. You've heard that, I'm sure. But what you don't know is that I overheard Huw telling Martin that he blamed Roger for Adeline's death. What you don't know is that Huw was in love with her."

31

Gareth

The manhunt for Huw was, according to John, one of the largest in the history of Shrewsbury. Once Jenny had convinced John that she was telling the truth—or that it was at least worth finding out if she was right—John sent out every one of his men to find Huw. Even Luke took to the effort with a will. In the fighting at the brothel, he'd lost his friend, Alfred, one of the few casualties for the victors, and was on fire for revenge against someone who was still alive.

Privately, Gareth was concerned that the apprentice would never make it to the castle to be questioned—and not because the killing of Roger Carter needed to be avenged. With the primary organizers of the slave ring missing or dead, the watchmen and the townspeople who helped in the search felt, as Luke did, the need to punish *someone* even if it was only a hapless apprentice. John had set a three-man watch on Flann for the same reason—just to make sure he lived to speak to the sheriff.

Fortunately, it was Oswin and Cedric together who found him. Huw had tried to flee the town through one of the gates that led to the river—this one belonging to a stable, where Huw had apparently hidden for the bulk of the day.

The two young watchmen had been among the men John had sent to patrol the river side of the palisade, and they happened to be walking past as Huw opened the gate, just as darkness was falling. The apprentice was strong, but it was two against one, and Cedric was able to call in a few of his fellow watchmen who were within hailing distance. He also managed to convince them not to kill the apprentice outright, and they brought him to the castle.

After looking him up and down, John decided that, as with Flann, it should be Gareth, as a fellow Welshman, who would be the first to question him. So, with John looking on through the barred window of the door to Huw's cell, Gareth brought in a straight back chair, turned it around so he could rest his arms across the rail, and sat.

He held the pose for a count of thirty, hoping the silence would unnerve Huw. Most people who weren't criminals by nature struggled not to fill a silence, especially when they were guilty of what they'd been accused of doing. It seemed to Gareth that Martin had been a natural villain, but Huw wasn't cast from the same mold.

Huw started fidgeting right away. He was sitting on a stool opposite Gareth, with his hands tied behind his back and each ankle tied to one of the stool's legs.

Finally, Gareth decided he could afford to break the silence. "You killed Roger Carter. There's no point in denying it. One of the maids at Rob Horn's inn was on her way to the latrine when she saw you leaving the yard. She thought you'd been with a girl, which is why she hadn't mentioned it before."

Huw brought his head up at Gareth's initial statement, but unlike some accused murderers Gareth had questioned, he didn't color or pale. He simply looked at Gareth with a neutral expression on his face. "I was so careful to leave nothing of me behind. It seems it would have been better to leave something of Martin's in the room, but I didn't think of it at the time."

Gareth narrowed his eyes. The supposed apprentice had spoken to him in the Welsh of an educated man, not that of an illiterate peasant. "Who are you, really?"

"I am who everyone thinks I am," Huw said, "a cartwright's apprentice."

"But what more?" Gareth pressed.

"I was born in Morgannwg, to a mother who loved me, and to a father, a steward for a minor lord, who saw to my education," Huw said. "It wasn't until my mother's dying breath that she told me about my sister, born a year before I, whom she'd given away to a man named Tom Weaver."

Gareth was generally good at controlling his reactions, but this was not the interview he'd expected to be conducting. "You're telling me that Adeline was your sister?" It seemed Jenny had got it wrong too, though she'd been far closer to the mark than anyone else.

"By the time I found her, after nearly nine months of searching, she was engaged to Roger Carter and had no idea that Tom Weaver was not her real father—none at all. I didn't want to spring my identity on her without warning, so I decided that if I was happy with her circumstances, I would let her be and return to Wales. I had some experience working in wood, so I apprenticed myself to Roger to get close to them both."

"But you weren't happy," Gareth said, not as a question.

"Roger Carter was a hard man. He was very kind to Jenny, but less so to others, and certainly not me. He didn't love Adeline, and Adeline had nothing but disdain for him, which she proved by getting herself involved with that Welsh nobleman and running away."

"If what you say is true, and you were Adeline's brother, why did you stay once she died?"

Huw bobbed his head, as if agreeing that, to an outsider, his behavior appeared strange. "I wanted revenge—on Roger Carter, on Tom Weaver, and on that Welsh prince, though I never saw him again after Adeline died, more's the pity. He was really the one for whom I was waiting." Huw made a motion with his head. "Then I found out about what Martin Carter was up to, and that he was up to it with that same prince, and I stayed in hopes of killing two birds with one stone."

"Roger Carter beat you," Gareth said.

Huw smirked. "No worse than my own father did. I can take a few beatings if it means lulling a man into a false sense of security. I could have killed Roger at any time. I was merely waiting for the right moment."

Gareth had a thought that he might have liked Huw if they'd met under different circumstances—and if Huw's character hadn't been twisted so far to one side. He spoke of murder as if it were nothing. Gareth, who'd killed far more men than Huw, had never done so with the cool demeanor that Huw was displaying now.

"Walk me through what happened that day," Gareth said. "We know from Tom Weaver that he, Roger, and Martin had a fight. Did you witness it?"

"Oh yes," Huw said. "Nobody ever treats an apprentice like he's a person, with ears. Tom came to Martin to say that he wanted out, that owning part of the brothel was one thing, but enslaving— and killing girls—was something else entirely. Martin told him to shut up.

"Unfortunately, Roger was home, and he overheard. It seems he'd been suspicious of his brother for a while—following him around and such—and now that he knew the truth, he demanded to know who else was involved. Names were mentioned, including Conall, that red-headed Irishman you were looking for. They got into a shouting match that ended in fisticuffs and with Tom getting walloped by Roger.

"I stayed in my bunk in the workshop until late that evening, just watching to see what else would come of it. Martin returned from wherever he'd gone off to, but the two brothers didn't speak again in my presence. Martin went to bed with his wife as if nothing had happened but, after midnight, Roger left his bed. On a whim, I followed him. I thought he was going to free the slave girls, quite honestly, but he went instead to Rob Horn's inn, to Conall's room, though I didn't know who it belonged to at the time.

"I waited outside to see what would happen, and when nothing did, saw my opportunity. With the sheriff gone, and only Jenny's brother left to run things, it seemed the perfect moment." Huw grimaced. "I didn't count on you coming into it."

Gareth ignored the last comment, though it was, in a way, a compliment to him. "You confronted Roger?"

"I did, and there's irony for you. Roger went to Conall's room to accuse him of slaving, but he wasn't the slaver, and you spent all this time looking for his killer in the wrong places." Huw seemed very pleased with himself and the way he'd almost pulled one over on Gareth. "It was for Adeline that I killed him. I'd brought a length of rope from the shop. All I had to do was knock on the door. He must have thought it was Conall returning. He allowed me to get close, I kicked out at one of his knees to lay him low, and then got behind him and strangled him." Huw spoke matter-of-factly, neither proud of what he'd done, nor sorry.

"The wounds on his hands and face, then, were from the earlier fight with Martin and Tom?" Gareth said.

"I suppose." Huw shrugged. "He tried to fight me, but I was the stronger, and it was over quickly."

"And you went back to the cartwright's yard as if nothing had happened?" Gareth said.

"It would hardly look good for me if Roger was found murdered and the next day his apprentice went missing, would it? I figured I could leave after a day or two, say that with Roger gone,

I wanted a different life. Or maybe not say anything at all. Wales is only a few miles away, after all, and the sheriff's writ runs only to the border."

"You're going to hang, you know," Gareth said.

Huw shrugged. "That may be."

"You're not sorry, are you?" Gareth said.

"That Roger's dead?" Huw said. "Not in the slightest."

Gareth glanced towards the door. John had turned to speak to someone behind him, so Gareth took the opportunity to lean in and question the man about something that had nothing to do with the case. "Do you know the name of Adeline's father?"

Huw really had no idea how important the answer to that question was to Gareth or he might not have answered so readily. "Pawl. My mother loved him, but he died right after Adeline was born. My mother had no father to protect her, and with Pawl's and her family gone, she couldn't keep her."

Gareth straightened in his chair, a chill crawling up and down his spine. "Pawl had no family?"

Huw lifted one shoulder in a half-shrug. "He had a sister who married a bard. My mother never learned their names, and since Pawl said the husband was a good-for-nothing, my mother never saw the point in trying to find him."

Gareth looked down at his feet. Meilyr was going to hate this news, and it would bring him anguish. He had been both shamed and guilt-ridden at the thought that he'd had another daughter, and that the mother had kept the news of Adeline's birth from him. If he had known that Pawl had fathered a child, he would have moved heaven and earth to find her and raise her as his own. None of this was Meilyr's fault, but he would feel as if it was.

Gareth stood up and left the room. He had no more to say to Huw. The casual way he'd murdered Roger made Gareth sick to his stomach. He felt the same way about Martin, who'd ruined life after life without thought to anyone but himself and the weight of his own purse.

The investigation was over. It was time to go home.

32

Hywel

"There you are, you truant!" King Owain bounded out the front door of Aber's main hall, cloaked and booted as if for a ride. "You're just in time." He caught Hywel up in an enormous hug, lifting him off his feet.

Truly unable to believe the transformation in his father, Hywel took a moment to return the embrace. "In time for what, Father?"

The king set Hywel back on his feet. "We are off in a moment to the marshalling of men at Denbigh. An attack on my sons, even if unsuccessful, cannot go answered."

That had Hywel gaping at his father even more. Rhun's death had gone unanswered for four months, but an attack on Hywel and Cadell couldn't wait even a week to be countered with an army? Part of Hywel was gratified at his father's obvious concern, but part was distrustful too, and he suspected that something more than love was behind his father's rush to war.

King Owain frowned as he took in the demeanor of his obviously weary son. "We expected you two days ago. What is the disposition of Madog's men?"

"He isn't coming, or if he is, the men of Powys don't know about it." Hywel gestured towards Conall, who'd ridden with them from Shrewsbury, intending to introduce him, but King Owain's eyes strayed beyond him to where Meilyr and Gwalchmai had dismounted behind the others.

"Meilyr!" King Owain strode towards the bard. "Don't tell me you've been all the way to Shrewsbury too? My hall has been empty of music. We've had to prepare for war without the inspiration of the brave deeds of our ancestors."

Meilyr stared at the king, as uncomprehending as Hywel had been, and then uncharacteristically stuttered, "I apologize, sire. I went to—" That was as far as he got before he gave up, realizing that the only sensible reply was simply to bow before the king.

"Never mind." King Owain waved a hand in the air. "Did you find what you were looking for?"

"Yes, my lord," Meilyr said.

"Good, good. You will come with us to Denbigh, of course."

"Of course." Though Meilyr shot a worried glance at Hywel as he spoke.

Hywel didn't know that he had ever helped Meilyr with a single thing in his life, but he obliged his old teacher by drawing his father's attention away from the bard. "Meilyr might have found what he was looking for in Shrewsbury, Father, but I didn't."

The king's brow furrowed as he gazed at his son.

The open courtyard wasn't the place to have this discussion, but Hywel stepped closer and told the truth anyway. "I sent Gareth to Shrewsbury in hopes of discovering the whereabouts of Cadwaladr. He had definitely been there, and even now is in league with Madog in more ways than one—"

"Tell me on the way!" King Owain spun away from Hywel, striding towards his horse, whose head was being held by Gruffydd.

Their eyes met, and they both shrugged. Gruffydd had done exactly what he'd said he'd do, and Hywel had no cause to complain about the outcome. Gareth and Gwen were looking at the king with the similar stunned expressions, islands of inactivity in the midst of the marshalling men. Conall looked merely amused, which seemed to be his natural state.

For Hywel's part, he was having trouble absorbing the fact that not only was the king better, but he was leaving Aber, and he expected Hywel and his companions to come with him. Hywel could hardly have hoped for a better scene to return to than this, with the possible exception of the complete absence of Cristina, his stepmother.

She stood on the top step of the hall, and he didn't have to see her glare to feel it boring into him. Cristina didn't like him. She was supremely jealous of the standing of her own sons, who were well down the line of heirs to the throne of Gwynedd. Still, Hywel gave her a nod, though if he'd been a good stepson he would have bowed.

Gwen brushed her shoulder against his arm. "If looks could kill, my lord."

Hywel just managed to stop himself from glancing at his stepmother again. "I can't see how she had anything to do with Rhun's death or with the attack on Cadell and me at Dinas Bran, but I have no doubt that she would not have grieved my loss."

"Nor Cynan's, Madoc's, Cadell's, Iorwerth's, or the loss of any other son who stands in the way of Dafydd's patrimony," Gwen said. "We must be very careful from now on."

Nodding agreement, because he'd known it already, even if he'd never articulated the fear, Hywel boosted Gwen back onto her horse and mounted his own. Only then did he turn to look back at the door to the hall.

Cristina had already disappeared inside, without so much as a raised hand to the company, much less a kiss goodbye for his father. In the past, she'd been very careful to treat the king with constant affection, in between their screaming bouts, of course. At those times, Cristina's ill humor would have roused his father's temper, but that didn't seem to be happening today either. Hywel had never wanted his father to marry Cristina in the first place, so he could only cheer the king's determination to leave.

Gareth frowned and said in an undertone. "Could your father truly be putting her aside?"

Hywel watched the king. "I would never have dared think it, but that's what it looks like to me too."

For a heartbeat, Hywel's father eyed the spot Cristina had vacated. Then he turned his gaze on Hywel himself and motioned that he should come to him. Hywel obeyed, and his heart lifted at his father's genuine smile at his approach.

"Come, son," King Owain said when Hywel reached him, "It's long past time to go."

The End

Historical Note

In the end of that year died Rhun, son of Owain, being the most praiseworthy young man of the British nation, whom his noble parents had honourably reared. For he was fair of form and aspect, kind in conversation, and affable to all; seen foremost in gifts; courteous among his family; high bearing among strangers, and fierce towards his enemies; entertaining to his friends; tall of stature, and fair of complexion, with curly yellow hair, long countenance; with eyes somewhat blue, full and playful; he had a long and thick neck, broad breast, long waist, large thighs, long legs, which were slender above his feet; his feet were long, and his toes were straight.

When the report of his lamentable death came to his father Owain, he was afflicted and dejected so much, that, nothing could cheer him, neither the splendour of a kingdom, nor amusement, nor the sprightly converse of good men, nor the exhibition of valuable things; but God, Who foreseeth all things in His accustomed manner, commiserated the British nation, lest it should perish like a ship without a pilot, and preserved Owain as a prince over it. For before insufferable sorrow had affected the mind of the prince, he was restored to sudden joy, through the providence of God.

There was a certain castle called Gwyddgrug (Mold), which had been frequently attacked, without its falling; and when the liege men of Owain and his family came to fight against it, neither the nature of the place nor its strength could resist them, till the castle was burned and destroyed, after killing some of the garrison, and taking others, and putting them in prison. And when Owain, our prince, heard of that, he became relieved from all pain, and from every sorrowing thought, and recovered his accustomed energy.

-- *Brut y Tywysogion*
(The Chronicle of the Princes of Wales)

In addition to the above quote from the *Brut y Tywysogion,* this book is full of bits of historical information I didn't know anything about before a few years ago when I started writing the *Gareth & Gwen Medieval Mysteries.* I didn't even know that the Danes ruled Dublin for hundreds of years, and I especially did not know that they ran an extensive slave trade out of the Dublin slave markets.

Slavery predated the Danes, of course. Slaves were taken in raids through history, and the Romans were huge practitioners of slavery. Before the Danes took Dublin, the Irish raided their neighbors and the Welsh coast for slaves as a means of subduing their enemy. Often these slaves would be ransomed for gold or land. The Danes transformed slavery into an actual trade after they established Dublin. Essentially, the framework of slavery and slave-taking changed from having mostly to do with power relations between lords to being about money.

In *The Renegade Merchant,* I mention that King Owain's father, Gruffydd, in the late 11th century, partially paid for the retaking of Wales with slaves, and he was hardly the only one. But by the 12th century, slavery was on the wane. Slave-taking became far less common, and since the Normans had made slavery illegal—in large part thanks to the influence of the Church—the Dublin slave market went into decline and then closed altogether.

Another subject about which I knew nothing before delving heavily into the twelfth century was the history of prostitution. It is, of course, said to be the oldest profession, and has taken many forms over the millennia. Again, the Romans were proud proponents of it, and the existence of brothels was legal in England (albeit frowned upon by the Church), even to the point that the Bishop of Winchester in 1162 was granted the right to license prostitutes and brothels in London.

Finally, there is Shrewsbury, a border town in the March of Wales. Much of what I knew about Shrewsbury before starting to do my own research came from Ellis Peters and her wonderful and beautifully written *Brother Cadfael* books. The *Gareth & Gwen Medieval Mysteries* have now moved beyond the time in which her books are set, but many elements remain the same, including the Abbey of St. Peter and St. Paul and its Abbot Radulfus, and the town of Shrewsbury itself.

I would like to take particular note of the wall which surrounds the town in the *Brother Cadfael* books and in *The Renegade Merchant*. My research indicates that the town wasn't given a *right to murage* (which means to charge a tax to build a town wall) until 1218 when King Henry ordered the town to make itself defensible. That isn't to say that it didn't have a town wall earlier—just that there is no mention of it. I chose to harmonize the specifics of the town of Shrewsbury in my book with what Ellis Peter's described in hers.

Also—a note on the use of the word *villain*. Nobody was more surprised than I to discover that the word used in the context of *The Renegade Merchant*, has its origin in *villainy* from Anglo-French *vilanie* and Old French *vilenie,* meaning to be of low character, unworthy act, disgrace, or degradation. This definition dates to a hundred years before its use as *villein*, meaning a feudal class of half-free peasants (c. 1200 v. c. 1300). I'd always thought the origin was the other way around.

About the Author

With two historian parents, Sarah couldn't help but develop an interest in the past. She went on to get more than enough education herself (in anthropology) and began writing fiction when the stories in her head overflowed and demanded she let them out. While her ancestry is Welsh, she only visited Wales for the first time while in college. She has been in love with the country, language, and people ever since. She even convinced her husband to give all four of their children Welsh names.

She makes her home in Oregon.

www.sarahwoodbury.com

24091124R00190

Made in the USA
Middletown, DE
14 September 2015